Tycoon's One-Night Revenge

by Bronwyn Jameson

"Convince me that this marriage is what you really want, Susannah."

His gaze dropped to her lips. The taste of his kiss slid through her veins. This was what she'd expected last night and she'd armed herself against the assault. Now he'd caught her unprepared. She needed to breathe, to ease the swell of emotion in her chest. "I can't stay, Donovan."

"I'm afraid you have no choice."

"How long are you holding me hostage?" she asked.

"As long as it takes," he said, then stepped closer.

Available in May 2009 from Mills & Boon® Desire™

Bedded by the Billionaire
by Leanne Banks
&
Tycoon's One-Night Revenge
by Bronwyn Jameson

Baby Bonanza
by Maureen Child
&
For Blackmail…or Pleasure
by Robyn Grady

The Desert Lord's Baby
by Olivia Gates
&
Seduced for the Inheritance
by Jennifer Lewis

Bedded by the Billioanire

by Leanne Banks

"You may have seduced one DeLuca, but I'm not as easily impressed as my brother."

"I haven't been trying to impress you," she told him. "And what makes you think I would want to go round two with anyone with the last name DeLuca?" She stood and whirled away.

He snagged her wrist, pulling her against him. Her hand fell against his chest and she felt his heart against her palm.

"Hold on to that thought," he said. "You're going to need it. But just so you know, if you ever went to bed with me, you would never think of it as round two."

Bedded by the Billionaire
LEANNE BANKS

Tycoon's One-Night Revenge
BRONWYN JAMESON

All the characters in this book have no existence outside the imagination of the author, and have no relation whatsoever to anyone bearing the same name or names. They are not even distantly inspired by any individual known or unknown to the author, and all the incidents are pure invention.

First published in Great Britain 2009
by Harlequin Mills & Boon Limited,
Eton House, 18-24 Paradise Road, Richmond, Surrey TW9 1SR

ISBN: 978 0 263 87098 5

51-0509

Printed and bound in Spain
by Litografia Rosés S.A., Barcelona

BEDDED BY THE BILLIONAIRE

by

Leanne Banks

Dear Reader,

Have you ever made a doozy of a mistake? One that impacted you and perhaps others for months, maybe years to come? Most of us make mistakes every now and then – if not every day. But I wanted to write about a heroine who had made a huge mistake by getting involved with and becoming pregnant by the wrong kind of guy. What I love about my heroine Lilli is that she decides to make the very best of the situation, and be the best mother possible.

What kind of man would be a match for her? I was inspired by the idea of writing about a man of steel with a deep sense of responsibility, but no heart. A billionaire who does not believe in romantic love, who guards his heart because the men in his family have a history of being ruined by scheming women who use them. Max DeLuca is determined never to be played the fool by a woman. So what happens when it looks like his worst nightmare has come true? Is it possible that the man of steel could actually have a heart of gold?

Enjoy the ride of this passionate story and stay tuned for more billionaires coming your way in the near future.

I wish you love…

Leanne Banks

LEANNE BANKS

is a *New York Times* bestselling author who is surprised every time she realises how many books she has written. Leanne loves chocolate, the beach and new adventures. To name a few, Leanne has ridden on an elephant, stood on an ostrich egg (no, it didn't break), gone parasailing and indoor skydiving. Leanne loves writing romance because she believes in the power and magic of love. She lives in Virginia with her family and her four-and-a-half-pound Pomeranian named Bijou.

Special thanks to Cindy Gerard, Rhonda Pollero and all my wonderful, supportive writing friends and the great Melissa Jeglinski, who continues to make my work better!

This book is dedicated to the comeback kid in all of us.

One

"I understand you're pregnant with my brother's child."

Lilli McCall instinctively put her hand over her swollen belly and studied Maximillian De Luca. She'd reluctantly allowed him and his associate into her small suburban Las Vegas apartment. Heaven knew, she'd had several unwelcome visitors since Tony De Luca had died two weeks ago.

She'd spotted the family resemblance between Tony and Max through the peephole of her door—the natural tanned complexion, similar bone structure. Only this man wasn't as pretty as Tony. Tony had been full of easy smiles and charm, and ultimately lies. This man's face was so hard she wondered if it would break into pieces if he smiled.

Tony had told her about his brother, Max. He'd frequently complained that his brother was cutthroat, even with his own family. He'd called him the man of steel, a steel mind and a steel heart.

Lilli had detached herself from Tony for good reasons. She wanted nothing to do with him, his friends or his family.

"Miss McCall?" Max prompted.

Taking a quick breath, she gave a slow nod, willing herself not to be intimidated by the tall man. "Yes, we got involved after my mother died, but things didn't work out between us," she said in a voice she knew was stilted, but she couldn't smooth it for the life of her.

"The details aren't necessary. As you know, my brother died in an automobile accident. He had no will and no provision for children, so—"

"I didn't expect anything from him," she interjected.

He paused, his gaze flickering over her in a considering way again. "Really," he said in a doubtful voice.

His tone jabbed at her. "Really," she said. "Tony was kind to me after my mother died, but it became clear to me that I didn't belong in his world."

"Why is that?"

"I—" She hesitated, her chest tightening as she remembered the fateful night that had made her break up with him for good. "We had different values. I wanted the baby brought up in a different environment."

His gaze fell to her pregnant belly. "You came to that decision a little late, didn't you?"

In more ways than he could know, she thought. "Yes, but I can focus on the baby or on my failures. Focusing on my failures isn't going to help me. So," she said, more than ready for him to leave, "since I wasn't expecting anything from Tony, you don't need to—"

"That's where we disagree," he said and nodded toward the man standing behind him. "Jim, could you give me the paperwork? Lilli, this is Jim Gregory. You may recognize him as someone who has knocked on your door a few times recently."

Lilli tore her gaze away from Max long enough to look at the older man and recognized him. "I apologize," she said. "I live by myself, so I'm not really comfortable opening the door to men I don't know."

"I understand," Jim said and she thought she saw a hint of compassion in the older man's eyes. "Here it is, Max," he said, producing some papers from a manila envelope, along with a pen.

Max took the papers and pen and handed them to Lilli. "It's a simple document. In exchange for one million dollars now and another million dollars if and when the child reaches the age of twenty-five, you agree to give up any rights to my brother's inheritance. If you should die or fail to raise the child in a responsible manner, you agree to relinquish custody of the child to a suitable guardian of my choice."

Lilli felt her jaw drop to the floor.

"It's all there," Max said. "Let me know if you have any questions."

Lilli stared blankly at the paper and felt her hands begin to shake with anger. Shoving the papers back at him, she stepped backward. "Are you nuts?"

"Should have known," Max said to Jim. "I told you she would want more money."

Stunned, Lilli continued to stare at him. "So you *are*

nuts," she said. "You didn't hear me earlier, did you? I didn't expect anything from Tony. I don't now. And I certainly don't expect anything from you. And if you think for one second that I would let someone I've never met choose who raises my child, you're totally crazy."

"That clause is just to protect the child in the event of your death or in case you develop any dangerous habits." He placed the agreement on top of her mother's marble-top table. "Read it. Sleep on it. I'll negotiate the amount within reason."

She snatched it up to give it back to him again.

He shook his head and held up his hand. "The drama is unnecessary. It costs a lot to raise a child. It will be difficult since you're doing it alone. Think about your child's needs. Do you really want to give up everything this money can buy for your child?" He paused while her heart pounded in her chest five beats. "I'll be in touch."

As soon as the two men left her apartment, Lilli flipped the dead bolt in place. Incensed and insulted, she paced into the den. Her pulse was racing in her ears, her nails digging into her palms as she clenched her hands together. Who in hell did he think he was, coming into her home and talking to her that way?

Granted, there were a few things that didn't put her in the best light, such as the fact that she'd even gotten involved with Tony in the first place, and the fact that she was unwed and pregnant. But everyone made mistakes. The solution was owning up to them and making the best of whatever choices have been made.

Although she hadn't intended to get pregnant by Tony, Lilli was determined to be the best mother she could be. Even with all the uncertainty and responsibility she was facing, from the moment she'd learned she was carrying a life inside her, she'd felt a little less lonely.

Lilli walked into the nursery she had begun to decorate and took a deep calming breath. She'd given the walls a fresh coat of paint and hung a puffy Noah's Ark wall hanging with removable animals. The crib was solid maple, and she'd already attached a mobile with friendly colorful butterflies and birds. With her next paycheck, she planned to buy soft crib sheets and blankets in blue for her little guy.

Pressing her hand to her belly again, she thought of Max De Luca. She'd never met a man like him. Arrogant, insulting, charm-free. At least to her. She couldn't deny, though, that in different circumstances he would have fascinated her. But lions had always fascinated her, too, and she knew better than to get into a den with one of them.

"That went well," Jim said in a wry voice as Max led the way to the black Ferrari.

Loosening his tie a fraction of an inch, Max unlocked the car and slid behind the steering wheel. Max preferred being in the driver's seat. It gave him the illusion of control. He slid into the leather seat. "Damn Tony for this," he said, even though his grief was still fresh. "He was going to be a father, for God's sake. You would think he could have at least provided for his child."

"You've been cleaning up his messes a long time," Jim said as Max sped out of the apartment complex. "Just curious. Did you have to be a total ass to her?"

Max had known Jim since he was a child and that was the only reason he allowed the older man to talk to him so bluntly. "She surprised me," he said, shifting into fourth as he turned onto the interstate. "I was expecting one of those showgirls he went through like cheap wine."

"I told you she's a pediatric dental hygienist."

"I figured that was her day job. She had to have another angle." He shook his head. "She looked almost wholesome. I mean, aside from the bump, she had a nice body as far as I could tell. Did you notice she was wearing bunny slippers?"

Jim laughed. "Hard to miss them."

"She wasn't wearing a speck of makeup. Her hair color didn't look like it came out of a bottle. She looked soft," he said, still trying to come to grips with his impression of Lilli McCall. "Real. Not Tony's type at all."

"She must have been his type for a while."

Max felt his chest tighten in a strange way. How had Tony lucked into her? A woman like that shouldn't have been abandoned. Not if his first instincts about her were correct. "Yeah. He got lucky."

Lilli was that irresistible combination of soft and sexy that every man craved. It was all too easy to wonder how that mouth of hers would feel all over a man's body.

He felt himself grow warm at the thought and shook his head. He'd never been attracted to one of his brother's women. Turning the AC on high, he directed the vent at his face.

"I really ticked her off with my offer," he said, his lips twitching in amusement. She'd looked as if she would have gladly ripped out his vocal cords. He'd found her reaction surprising and oddly attractive.

That didn't change the fact that everyone had their

price. Even a blond woman with pink cheeks, bee-stung lips and blue eyes that lit up like sparklers when she was angry. "She'll take the money," he said to Jim, shifting gear. "They all eventually do."

Max would clean up this mess. He had a lot of practice. Left to deal with his father's disastrous personal and financial choices, Max had worked nonstop during the past ten years to rebuild the family name and wealth.

His investments had delivered triple returns. The merger of Megalos Resorts with De Luca Inc. to form Megalos-De Luca Enterprises had sent the shares of his stock in the company skyrocketing. Determined to keep talent in the merged company, the new board paid the top performers eight-figure salaries.

Max's father may have been kicked off the board of the family company, but Max was determined that the next CEO would be a De Luca. Nothing would stop him. Especially not a feisty little blonde who happened to be carrying a De Luca baby in her belly.

The following evening, as she left the dental practice where she worked, Lilli winced as she flexed her fingers. Three-year-old Timmy Johnson just couldn't resist chewing on her index finger. Although she wore rubber gloves, they didn't always protect her from a chewing child.

She worked late three nights a week for two reasons. One, she earned a little more money working after five and two, she didn't really have anything else to do in the evenings. It wasn't as if she were a party animal. She'd left that brief period of her life way in the past.

Pulling her keys from her purse, she walked toward

her trusty four-year-old blue Toyota Corolla. Just as she neared her car, two men stepped in front of her. They both appeared to be in their twenties and they looked so much alike they could have been brothers.

"Lilli McCall?" one of them said.

The one man looked vaguely familiar, although she couldn't recall his name. One of Tony's friends? She tensed. "Why do you ask?" She backed away.

Both men took a step toward her. "We're hoping you can help us."

She bit her lip and took another step back. "I—uh." She cleared her throat. "How could I possibly help you?"

"We're here about Tony," one of the men said with a shrug. "He left some unpaid debts. We knew you two were close and we were hoping you could help us."

She shook her head. "I broke up with Tony a long time ago."

"Not before he knocked you up," the other guy cracked. "That baby's gotta be worth something to the De Luca family. Tony must have left you something."

"He didn't," she said, even though her throat was squeezing tight with fear. "Look at my car. It's four years old. I'm working as a dental hygienist. Do I look like someone who is loaded?"

The men frowned.

"Maybe you're hiding it."

Frustrated and afraid, she shook her head. "I'm not. Just leave me alone."

"It would be a lot easier to leave you alone if we got our money." One of the men pulled a card out of his pocket and walked toward her.

She wanted to run, but her feet seemed to grow roots into the pavement. The man pressed his card into her hand. "Call me if you find something. We'll check back in case you forget."

Her heart racing, she watched the two men leave and felt sick to her stomach. How much longer would they harass her? And how many more of Tony's so-called business acquaintances were going to show up at her door?

Taking a deep breath, she walked quickly to her car and got inside. Maybe she should move out of town. That could be expensive, though, and she'd like to keep the few friends she'd made over the last couple of months. The idea of being surrounded by strangers after she had her baby unsettled her.

She mulled over a dozen different options as she drove through a fast-food restaurant and ordered a milk shake. After she got home, she sipped on it and changed into a tank top that covered her pregnant belly and a pair of terry cloth shorts. Then to drown out her disturbing thoughts, she turned on the television to watch a rerun of her favorite medical drama.

Five minutes later, her doorbell sounded. She sighed, hoping it was her best friend Dee, off early from her second job as an aerobics instructor. The doorbell rang again before she could reach it. She looked through the peephole, but her porch light wasn't on. She could only make out the shadow of a man.

Fed up, she pounded on her side of the door. "Go away! I don't have Tony's money. I—"

"Miss McCall," a male voice cut in.

Lilli immediately recognized that voice. Mr. Steel, she'd named him. She bit her lip.

"Lilli," Max De Luca said again. "Can I come in?"

She glanced down at her outfit. It was far from swimsuit bare, but she knew she'd feel more comfortable wearing something else. Armor would work. "I'm not really dressed for visitors."

"This won't take long," he insisted.

Swallowing a groan, she opened the door. "I don't think we have anything else to—"

Max walked past her. He was dressed in a black suit that probably cost more than her car. Meeting him again, she could see why Tony had resented his older brother. Max was taller, his shoulders were broader, and he oozed enough confidence for a dozen men. Lilli suspected he was the type who would command any situation no matter how he was dressed. Despite the hard edges of his face, there was something sensual about the shape of his mouth. His thick black eyelashes gave his dark eyes a sexual cast.

If he were inclined, she would bet he could reduce a woman to melted butter with just a look. There was nothing boyish about him. He was all man and he would want a woman as tough and confident as he, a raving beauty. Lilli knew she would never make the cut.

Max stared at her, his dark eyes flashing. "Why do you keep talking about my brother and his money?"

She met his hot, hard gaze. "Since Tony died, some of his business acquaintances have been asking me to pay off his loans."

He frowned. "You? Why you?" His expression turned cynical. "Were you involved in some of his business dealings?"

"Absolutely not. I told you I stopped seeing Tony

over six months ago because I realized we didn't share the same values." She remembered that terrible last night and closed her eyes, trying to push it from her mind. "We were only together for about four months."

"Long enough for you to get pregnant," he said.

Offended by his tone, she glared at him. "Just in case you weren't paying attention in your high school biology class, it doesn't take four months to get pregnant. It takes one time. One slip." She shook her head. "Listen, I didn't ask you to show up at my home, insult me, offer me a big check and threaten to take my baby away if you don't approve of how I'm raising him."

"Him," he said. "So it's a boy."

"Yes," she said and felt her baby move inside her. Cradling her belly, she watched as Max's gaze raked over her from head to toe. After lingering on her breasts and legs, his eyes moved back up to her mouth. The intensity in his eyes made her feel as if she'd stayed out in the sun too long.

He finally lifted his gaze to hers. "How many men have come asking for money?"

"Five or six," she said. "They usually come in pairs. I stopped answering if I don't recognize who's ringing the doorbell."

"So this has happened, what three, four times?"

She bit her lip. "More like seven or eight," she admitted. "And two men showed up in the parking lot of my office after work tonight."

He paused one moment then nodded. "You shouldn't stay here by yourself any longer. You can come and stay at my house. I have ten bedrooms with staff and security."

Stunned, she stared at him. "Whoa, that's kind of

fast. Don't you think they'll stop coming around when they realize I really don't have anything to give them?"

"But you do," Max said. "You have a De Luca growing in your belly. Did any of them give you contact information?"

"One of the guys tonight gave me his card."

"Please get it for me," he said in a voice that was so polite and so calm it made her uneasy.

"Okay," she said and went into her bedroom to retrieve the card from her purse. She gave it to Max.

"I'll have Jim find out about this guy by morning." Max looked at her intently. "You got involved with a De Luca. We're a powerful family and there are people who resent us. There are people who want to hurt us. If you really care about the safety of your baby, then you need to come home with me."

She immediately shook her head. "I just met you. Why in the world would I leave my apartment to go to your home?"

"Because you'll be safe there," he said, impatience threading his voice. "Do you really trust that door against someone determined to get inside?"

Her mouth went dry at the image of an intruder, but she refused to be intimidated. "You're deliberately trying to scare me."

"No, I'm not," he said. "I'm merely protecting you and my nephew."

His words rocked her. He seemed to take the responsibility for granted, where Tony had been just the opposite. She shook her head. Could two brothers be so different? "How do I know you're not like him?" she had to ask.

His eyebrow creased in displeasure. "Like who? Tony?" He gave a harsh laugh. "I'm nothing like my brother. Or my father, for that matter."

She wondered what that meant, but from his expression, she suspected there was a world of history in his statement. A world she wasn't sure she wanted to know. She felt his shimmering impatience, but she resisted the pressure. "The only thing I know about you is what Tony told me."

Max gave a slow nod. "And that was?"

She bit her lip, reluctant to repeat the insults. "I'm not sure it's a good idea for me to—"

"Okay, then let me guess. Tony said I was heartless and unforgiving, straitlaced, boring, power-hungry and greedy."

She winced at his accuracy. "I'm not sure he used those words. He did refer to you as a man with a steel heart and steel mind. And he said you were ruthless."

"Ruthless," he said with a nod. "That was the other word I forgot. Not that far off the mark. I can be ruthless and I guard my heart and mind. I'm not distracted and I won't be tricked or deceived. But tell me, if I were completely cold and ruthless, why would I give a damn about you and your baby's safety?"

Good point, she thought, but the man still made her nervous.

"What do your instincts tell you about me?" he demanded.

She bit her lip again, and felt a flash of disappointment in herself. "My instincts got a little off-kilter after my mother died. I'm not sure how much I can trust them."

His expression was enigmatic. "Then you have a choice to make. You can either trust your door to those thugs who have been showing up and who aren't going away. Or you can trust me."

Two

"Dee," Lilli said. "This situation is crazy."

Max paused just inside the open sliding-glass door that led out to the patio, and watched Lilli as she paced and talked on her cell phone. After just one night in his home, she looked rattled and nervous. He couldn't remember a time when he'd had to work so hard to get a woman to stay overnight at his place, and this one hadn't even slept in his bed.

"Oh, it has to be temporary," she said. "It has to be."

He turned to walk away.

"It's clear that I don't belong here and I'm sure Max De Luca would be thrilled if I could disappear from the earth."

He stopped at the mention of his name, curious despite himself. Turning around, he watched her wavy hair bounce against her shoulders and her silver hoop earrings reflect the late-afternoon sunlight. She was wearing shorts that revealed her long, shapely legs, and he noticed her toenails were painted a vibrant pink. A silver chain wrapped around her ankle. She was an odd mix of feminine and practical. He didn't know why, but he'd liked the combination of strength and vulnerability he'd witnessed in her last night. She'd been determined not to be a pushover, but she'd also revealed her regret over her involvement with Tony. Although Max could name a million reasons, he wondered what had made Lilli decide to break up with his brother.

"How would I describe Max? Tony always called him a man of steel, but he didn't mean it as a compliment." She laughed. "Yes, he's disgustingly good-looking and completely lacking in charm." She sighed. "Maybe I just bring that out in him. Anyway, I can't imagine staying here. I can't imagine a baby living here, spitting up on carpets that probably cost twice what my car does. And speaking of my car, you would get a good laugh at how ridiculous it looks in the garage next to a Ferrari."

Max felt a twitch of humor at her colorful descriptions. Crossing his arms over his chest, he decided to listen to the rest of the conversation. She was providing him with more amusement than he'd had in a while.

"His wife? I don't even know if he has one. This house is huge. Maybe she hides in a different wing. Or maybe he keeps her chained to his bed to take care of his every *need and pleasure,*" she said in an exaggerated voice. "Come to think of it, he's not wearing a ring and he doesn't really strike me as the kind to pin himself down to just one woman. Not that it's any of my business," she added. "I would move to the other side of the world except I hate the idea of going to a new place with a baby and not knowing anyone."

The honest desperation in her voice slid past his cynicism.

"I know I should be more brave about this. Maybe it's just hormones. And what happened when I was with Tony doesn't help."

Besides the obvious, what exactly had happened between Lilli and his brother? Max wondered, and he decided to make his presence known. Clearing his throat, he pushed the sliding-glass door farther open.

Giving a jerk of surprise, Lilli turned to look at him. "Uh, yeah I should go now. Dinner next Tuesday with the girls. I wouldn't miss it. Bye, Dee." She turned off the phone and lifted her chin defensively. "I, uh, didn't see you."

He nodded. "Was your room okay last night?"

"It's beautiful, of course," she said. "Your entire house is beautiful."

"The parts of it you've seen," he said, recalling what she'd said about his bedroom. He could practically see her mind whirling, wondering how much he'd heard. "It was too late for me to give you the complete tour last night. I should do that tonight."

"Oh, you don't have to—"

"I insist. The rumors about the dungeon are all false," he joked and watched her eyes widen. Swallowing a chuckle, he continued to meet her gaze. "And your bed? Did it work for you? Too soft? Too hard?" Last night the image of her in bed had bothered him. He'd wondered what kind of nightclothes she wore, if she ever slept naked.

"Oh, no. It was very nice, thank you." She cleared her throat. "I've been thinking about my living arrangements and—"

"So have I," he interjected. "If you're free for dinner, we can discuss it then."

She worked her mouth in surprise then shrugged. "I'm free."

"Okay, then we can eat on the terrace." He glanced at his watch. "Will you be hungry in an hour?"

"Sure," she said. "How do you dress for dinner?"

He allowed himself a leisurely gaze down her body. He wondered why she made something inside him itch. "Casual is fine. It will be just you and me."

Despite Max's insistence that dinner would be casual, Lilli changed from shorts into a periwinkle cotton baby-doll dress she hadn't worn in a while.

To bolster her confidence, she stepped into a pair of sandals with heels. She suspected she would need every bit of confidence she could muster when she told Max that she was returning to her apartment.

She walked downstairs through a hallway of marble and a living area that looked as if it had been taken out of a high-end decorator magazine. The sliding-glass door was open and Max stood, holding a glass of red wine, in front of a warming stove. With his back to her, she couldn't miss the V-shape of his broad shoulders and his narrow waist.

She felt a strange dip in her stomach at the sight of him and grabbed an extra breath. He must have heard her because he turned to face her. He was dressed in slacks and a white open-neck shirt that contrasted with his tanned skin. Moving beside a small table already set with plates and platters with sterling covers, he pulled out a chair for her.

"The chef prepared orange juice and seltzer for you. Is that okay?"

"Very nice," she said, surprised he'd known about the no-alcohol-during-pregnancy rule because he didn't seem to have any children of his own.

"My chef has prepared one of his specialties. He's excellent, so you should enjoy it."

A woman dressed in a uniform appeared from the sliding-glass doors. "May I serve you now, Mr. De Luca?" she asked.

"Yes, thank you, Ada," he said. "Lilli, this is my assistant housekeeper. She assists my chief housekeeper, Myrtle. Ada usually covers the 6:00 p.m. to 6:00 a.m. shift, so if you need anything after hours, feel free to ring her."

He had an assistant housekeeper? Lilli took another gulp of her drink, feeling more out of place than ever. "It's nice to meet you, Ada."

"My pleasure," Ada said with a smile and proceeded to serve the meal.

As soon as Ada left, Max turned to her and lifted his glass. "To a good meal and a meeting of the minds."

His gaze dipped to her décolletage and she felt a shocking awareness of him as a man. A strong, sexual man. Pushing the feeling aside, she took a deep breath and gave a determined smile. "It was very generous of you to invite me to stay here last night and tonight. I've given it some thought and I believe it will be best for me to move back to my apartment."

He shook his head. "I'm sorry. I can't allow that."

She blinked. "Allow?"

"I have some information that makes the choice clear, but I intended to tell you after our meal. I suspect you're concerned about staying here. You're probably afraid this setup isn't conducive for a baby."

She nodded. "Yes."

"Please go ahead and eat."

Lilli wanted to protest, but politeness compelled her to force down a forkful of the beef dish. The delicious taste momentarily distracted her and she took another bite. "Oh, you were right about your chef. This is amazing."

"You'll find I'm often right," he said. "I learned at an early age not to allow emotion to determine my choices."

"Why?" she asked, taking another bite.

"I watched my father spend half his fortune trying to keep his mistress happy."

She heard cynicism creep into his tone again, and for the first time understood why. "I'm assuming his mistress wasn't your mother," she ventured.

"She wasn't. She was Tony's mother."

"Oh," she said again, remembering something Tony had told her. "But I thought Tony's parents were dead."

"They are both dead. Died in a boating accident."

She set down her fork. "I'm so sorry."

He shrugged. "It was ironic because the boat was called Franco's Folly. My father's name was Franco. He spent a good part of his life chasing after things that eventually ruined him. Something I refuse to do. But that's a different subject." He took a sip of wine. "Jim did some research on the man who gave you his card yesterday. Trust me, he's bad news. You may as well be a sitting duck if you move back to your apartment without protection."

"Protection?" she echoed, appalled. "That's got to be an exaggeration. The man was a little pushy, but he backed off when I told him to. I'll just have to be very firm—"

"Lilli," Max interjected in a quiet, ultracalm voice that immediately got her attention. "It turns out he's involved with the local mafia. They're not above kidnapping or murder to collect on a debt."

Lilli froze, her appetite fleeing. "Oh, my God."

Nausea rose inside her and she turned from the table, automatically turning away. Terror coursed through her. How could she protect her child?

She felt Max just behind her. His body heat warmed her back. "You won't need to worry if you stay here. No one would dare hurt you as long as everyone knows you're in my care."

"Maybe I should go ahead and move out of town. I didn't want to do that, but—"

"You're too vulnerable for that right now," he said.

She turned to look at him. "What do you mean, too vulnerable?"

"Physically, for one thing. It's not like you'd be able to beat off an attacker."

"But if I moved away, I wouldn't have to beat off anyone."

He shook his head. "They're watching you too closely. Maybe later, but not now."

"Oh, God, I feel so stupid," she said, fighting back tears. "How did I let this get so out of control?"

"It could be worse," he said. "You can set up a nursery here. I'll cover the cost. We'll make the necessary adjustments in the house. Your life will be just like it was before, with a few perks."

"Just like before," she said, laughing with gallows humor. *As if anything could ever be like before.* "There's no way I could allow you to cover the cost of the nursery. It wouldn't be right. And I can't imagine living here. It's just so—"

"So what?"

"Perfect. This isn't at all what I pictured for my child."

"Why wouldn't my home be appropriate? I'm a blood relative. How is it right for your child not to know his uncle?"

Oh, Lord. She hadn't even thought of it that way. Her heart splintered. Her father had left before her third birthday and since her mother's relatives had lived on the other coast, she'd never had an opportunity to meet them, let alone enjoy any sort of family bond.

She shook her head. "I'd never considered any of this. Once I broke off with Tony, I knew it would be just me and the baby. I didn't think Tony's family would want to be involved, and frankly I didn't want anything to do with anyone bearing the name De Luca."

Max narrowed his eyes. "Tony and I are not the same man."

"I'm beginning to see that," she said. "I need to think about this."

"Finish your dinner," he said, cupping her arm with his strong hand. "We can discuss this more later."

Lilli's stomach jumped. She wasn't sure if it was a result of Max's hand on her bare arm or the terrible news he'd just delivered. She looked into his eyes and had the sense that this man could turn her world upside down in ways she'd never imagined. She stepped backward, needing air, needing to think. "I'm sorry, but I can't eat right now. Please excuse me. I need to go upstairs."

Max watched Lilli as she fled the patio through the door. With each passing moment, he felt more drawn to her, but for the life of him, he couldn't explain why.

Her immediate rejection of his offer to pay to furnish the nursery had caught him off guard. He was so accustomed to covering expenses for a multitude of people that he rarely gave it a second thought.

Women had always been more than happy to accept his generosity. In fact, on a couple of occasions, his companions had tried to take advantage of him. One woman had even gotten herself pregnant by another man and tried to make Max take responsibility for the child.

Lilli was the exact opposite. Unless it was all an act, which it could be, he thought, his natural cynicism rising inside him. Still, Lilli didn't strike him as a woman adept at hiding her emotions or motives.

He suspected she didn't want him to know that she was attracted to him, but he had seen it in her eyes. The attraction was reluctant, but strong, the same as it was for him.

In other circumstances, he would want her for himself. And he wouldn't just *want* her. He would take her.

Lilli paced her bedroom for two hours. With her head feeling as if it were going to split into a million pieces, she lay down and surprised herself by falling asleep. When she awakened at eleven-thirty, her stomach was growling like a mountain lion.

"Sorry, sweetie," she murmured, rubbing her stomach. The idea of that dinner going to waste nearly made her sob. Max had told her to call Ada, the housekeeper, if she needed anything, including a snack, but Lilli couldn't imagine imposing at this hour.

Dressed in a tank top and shorts, she quietly crept downstairs to the kitchen. She opened the refrigerator and peered inside. She found the leftovers and turned around.

"I'm glad you got back your appetite," Max said, startling her so much she almost dropped the container she was holding. Swearing under her breath, she managed to save the dish. Her heart racing, she backed away and closed the refrigerator door.

"I didn't think you would be down—" She broke off when she saw that he was shirtless, his pajama pants riding low on his waist. His chest was a work of art. Her mouth went dry.

"I heard a noise," he said casually, as if he didn't know that seeing him half-naked took her breath away.

She needed to keep it that way, she told herself and locked her gaze on his forehead. "I was hungry. I can just grab an apple and go back upstairs."

He moved closer to her and pulled the dish from her hands. "Why would you eat an apple when you can have this?" He put the dish in the microwave and started to warm it up.

Lilli tried very hard not to allow her gaze to dip across his naked shoulders, but she didn't quite succeed.

When the plate was hot, he directed her to a seat at the table.

Twenty minutes later, she'd polished off a reasonable portion of beef, bread and a brownie he'd insisted she eat.

She leaned back in her chair and stretched her legs. "That was delicious. Thanks."

His gaze enigmatic, he gave a slight smile. "You're welcome. Not bad for Mr. Steel."

Lilli blinked, then realized there was only one way he could have known she'd called him that. Her cheeks heated with embarrassment. "How long were you listening to my phone conversation?" she accused.

"It wasn't premeditated," he said. "I was going to tell you about the report I got from Jim, but you were so absorbed in your conversation that you didn't notice me."

Lilli closed her eyes, wishing she could hide. "Great."

"And no, I don't have a wife or mistress tied to my bed. I haven't found it necessary to tie women up to keep them in my bed."

She opened her eyes. "I didn't mean it the way—"

He waved his hand. "We may as well get this on the table. I know you're attracted to me," he said without a millimeter of arrogance.

She opened her mouth to deny it, but her throat closed around the lie.

"I'm flattered that you think I'm hot," he said. "But it's probably a good idea that you also think I'm cold because, for some reason, I find you attractive."

Lilli gaped at him, sure he was mocking her. "No."

"Yes," he said.

"But I'm pregnant," she blurted out. "And not with your baby."

"Your pregnancy doesn't conceal your other assets. It doesn't conceal your fire." His gaze traveled to her breasts and lower to her legs, then all the way back up to her mouth, making her feel as if a hot wind had blown over her. He gave a short laugh as if the joke was on him. "Don't worry. I'll get over it. You may have seduced one De Luca, but I'm not as easily impressed as my brother."

She felt as if he'd slapped her. "I haven't been trying to impress you," she told him. "Besides, your brother did the seducing, not me."

"It doesn't sound like you fought him."

"I didn't," she told him, but there'd been a time he'd taken advantage of her. "My mother died one week before I met Tony and I freely admit I was a mess." She met and held his gaze for a long, fierce moment. "And besides the fact that you're hot, what makes you think I would want to go round two with anyone with the last name De Luca?" She stood and whirled away.

He snagged her wrist, pulling her against him when she stumbled. Her hand fell against his chest and she felt his heart against her palm, his heat all over her.

"Hold on to that thought," he said. "You're going to need it. But just so you know, if you ever went to bed with me, you would never think of it as round two."

Looking into his hard, sensual gaze, Lilli felt a shiver run through her. Somehow, deep inside her, deeper than her bones, she knew that again he wasn't bragging. He was just telling the truth.

Three

Lilli awakened to the sound of the Bose alarm clock on the elegant bedside table. The strains of classical music lulled her into consciousness. Rolling to her side, she pulled the pillow over her head.

Just a couple more minutes. This bed was divine. It felt so wonderful she hated to leave it. Much better than her lumpy mattress back at her apartment.

She stiffened at the thought and immediately sat up in bed. Frowning, she told herself not to get used to this level of luxury. Sometime, more likely sooner than later, she would be living in a place where she was both the chief housekeeper and assistant housekeeper. There would be no Bose stereo systems and the closest she would get to a gourmet meal prepared by a chef would be a frozen dinner.

Rising from the bed, she padded across the luxury carpet to the large shower in the connecting bathroom. She would need to get up earlier since her commute to work was longer from Max's home. The very thought of him made something inside flutter and flip.

Hunger, she told herself. It had to be hunger or the baby. After she donned her colorful scrubs, she headed downstairs and was surprised to see Max pacing and speaking into a cell phone via a Bluetooth in his ear. He wore running shorts and a tank top that showed off his muscular legs and arms. Everything about him oozed strength. "Tell Alex we're limiting our domestic expansion until we see what happens with the dollar."

He saw her and lifted a hand. "Yes, I know Alex still resents that I was promoted over him. We each serve an important purpose. I provide the balance. He provides the fireworks. Tell him I said to think global. I'm working from home this morning. I'll be in the office this afternoon and will get an update then. Thanks. Bye."

He immediately turned to Lilli. "Good morning. Did you rest well?"

She nodded. "Yes, thank you."

"We have fresh-squeezed orange juice and the cook will be happy to prepare anything you like."

She shook her head. "I need to get on the road if I'm going to make it to work in time."

He frowned. "You can't skip breakfast. What about the baby?"

"I'll grab something at work. We always have fruit and bagels in the workroom," she said.

He shot her a disapproving glance. "That's not good nutrition."

"I don't think my baby is suffering. I'm taking my prenatal vitamins." He moved toward her and she struggled with the urge to flee. She was doing her best to keep her gaze fixed on his eyebrows. She refused to look into his eyes, or at his mouth, or at that stubborn chin or at those shoulders. Or lower. Feeling a flush of heat, she stepped backward. "Better go. See you la—"

"Your things from your apartment should be here by the time you return," he said.

Lilli stopped abruptly and blinked. "Excuse me?"

"I arranged for someone to pack your belongings and bring them here. Duplications like most of your furniture, dishes and linens will be put in storage. All the baby items will be moved into the nursery."

Trying to catch up with him, she shook her head in confusion. "Where is the nursery?"

"Across the hall from your bedroom," he said. "A decorator will be calling you later today so you can tell her what you would like done to it."

She shook her head again. "Did I ever actually say that I was going to stay here?"

He lifted a dark eyebrow. "There was another choice?"

She sighed, hating him for being right. "Well, you could have given me a little time to adjust to the idea. There's no reason I couldn't pack my own stuff and—"

His eyes widened in horror. "Moving in your condition?"

She sighed. "I'm very healthy. Women have been getting pregnant and delivering babies for years. In ancient times, it wasn't unusual for a woman to be working in the fields one minute, having her baby the next, then back at work immediately."

"I won't have you in the fields, period," he said in a dry tone. "In terms of the speed of the movers, there was no need to wait. We both agree, even if you don't want to admit it, that you belong here until we figure out a safe place for you and the baby. And that will be months from now."

She made a face at his imperious tone. Lord help her, he sounded like an emperor.

"In the meantime, I've asked my personal attorney to draw up some documents regarding custody of the child in case something should happen to you."

Lilli felt a chill. "I already told you I'm not signing those papers. If signing those papers is part of the bargain for me staying here, then I'm leaving."

"I never said that."

"No, but even you admitted that you could be ruthless. I'm not signing my child over to Ruthless Mr. Steel," she said, mentally drawing a line and daring him to cross over it.

"Yet," he said.

"I won't be manipulated over this," she warned him.

"Manipulation is for sissies," he said with a scoff.

"Then what do you call what you do?" she asked. "Bullying?"

"Reason and logic prevail among rational human beings."

Lilli knew she wasn't totally rational about this subject. It was too close to her heart. She took a shallow breath and met his gaze. "I don't want you to intimidate me about this," she said in a quiet voice.

He studied her for a moment, his gaze more curious than threatening. "Okay. Are you open to gentle persuasion?"

"Not if it involves any power plays," she said.

He nodded, stepping closer. "Deal. By the way, I'm hosting a casual business gathering Friday night. It's just a barbecue. Feel free to drop in and fill up a plate."

His closeness made her feel as if he'd set off a dozen mini electrical charges inside her. He lifted his hand to a stray strand of her hair. "Your hair reminds me of your personality."

He looped the strand around one of his fingers and she felt her heart accelerate. "How is that?"

His mouth stretched into a sexy grin. "It's the color of an angel's hair, but the curl shows it's rebellious."

Looking into his eyes, she felt as if she were sinking into a place where she was aware of only him. He was the most dynamic man she'd ever met in her life. She felt totally fascinated and totally out of her league.

Grasping on to that thought, she took a shallow breath and stepped back. It was a move totally motivated by survival. Max De Luca was a powerful force, too powerful for her.

The strand of her hair stretched taut between them. Max hadn't released her. She lifted her hand to unravel her hair from his finger, brushing his skin. "I should go. I don't want to be late," she said and fled out the door, feeling as if she'd been burned.

Max arrived home after going several rounds with Alex Megalos, Director of Domestic Operation and Expansion for Megalos-De Luca Enterprises. Alex had been Max's rival for his current position as Director of Worldwide Operation and Expansion.

Talented and aggressive, Alex was always trying to focus resources and energy in his area. Max, however, was forced to continually remind Alex that he had to consider the big picture.

Alex provided a lot of energy, but he also caused more than his share of heartburn. Suffering from a burning sensation in his gut even now, Max just wanted a quiet peaceful evening and an opportunity to wind down. He headed for the bar downstairs and poured himself a glass of red wine.

Sitting in the darkness of the den, he took a sip and savored the stillness of the moment.

A crashing sound followed by a scream shattered the quiet. Alarm shot through him. Immediately jumping to his feet, he raced upstairs. That had been Lilli's scream. What had happened?

Rounding the corner, he found her on the floor of the nursery surrounded by scattered pieces of a crib and tools.

"What in hell are you doing?"

Dressed in shorts that revealed her long legs, her hair straying from the ponytail in back, she glanced up at him with a scowl. "Trying to put this crib back together. Your moving guys took it apart."

He frowned, entering the room. "They should have put it back together." He reached into his pocket for his cell phone. "I'll get my driver up here immediately. He's excellent, extremely mechanical. He'll put it together in no time."

Scrambling to her feet, she put her hands over his to prevent him from dialing. "No. No."

"Why not?"

"Besides the fact that it's not his job to put together cribs and it's almost ten o'clock," she said, "I want to do it myself."

He stared at her for a long moment. "Why?"

"Because I just do. I put this crib together after I bought it. I should be able to do it now."

"Why is it so important that you be the one to assemble it? The baby isn't going to know."

She lifted her chin. "Someday he will. Someday he will know that his mother loved him so much and was so excited that he was coming that she put her time and energy and money into making a nice place for him."

Her heartfelt determination tugged at something inside him. "That never would have occurred to me. I'm certain my mother didn't assemble my crib. I had a string of nannies and was shipped off to boarding school before my parents divorced."

"My mother could sew and knit and she made blankets and caps and booties for me. I'm going to use some of them on my little one."

"But not anything pink," he said.

She smiled and laughed. "Nothing pink. I have a few white and yellow things. After my father left, it was just my mom and me." She bit her lip. "I wish she was still around. I have a feeling I'm going to have a lot of questions."

"I'm sure you'll do an excellent job and when he goes to boarding school—"

Lilli gaped at him. "I'm not sending my child to boarding school."

"There's no need to automatically reject the idea. A

young man can get an excellent education and important connections at an elite boarding school."

"And they end up with warm, affectionate family ties just like you," she said.

He opened his mouth then closed it. "Mr. Steel haunts me again." He shook his head. "There's no need to discuss boarding school. That's years away."

"Never," she corrected.

He loosened his tie and unfastened the top couple of buttons of his shirt. "Let me help you put this crib together. Where are the instructions?"

Lilli winced. "That's the problem. I threw them away after I put it together the first time."

He couldn't swallow a chuckle at her stymied expression. "Okay, then we'll just look it up on Google."

"Google it?" she echoed. "I never thought of that."

"So I'm good for something," he said in a wry voice. "My laptop is in my quarters. Come on. I still haven't given you that tour. From the way you act toward me, I wonder if you still think I have a woman tied to my bed."

Her face bloomed with color and she groaned. "When are you going to stop teasing me about that?"

"When you stop calling me Mr. Steel," he said and led her to another wing of the house.

When Max opened the door to his suite, all Lilli could do was stare. Lush carpet covered the floor, cushioning every footstep. A gas fireplace featuring a stone mantel provided instant warmth. On either side, stone shelves held books, electronic items and a full bar. A large bed covered with luxury linens provided the centerpiece, but what captured her attention was the dramatic arched window that showed the starry sky in all its glory.

"I have shades to cover them if it's too bright," he said.

"How can you bear to do that? It's so beautiful," she said.

"Thank you. I like it. I also have a flat-screen television that comes down from over that wall." He walked through one door and motioned for her to follow. "Personal gym and lap pool."

Lilli blinked at all the equipment. "But you already have a pool."

"That one is for being lazy. This one is for exercise." He glanced her. "You can use it anytime you like. It's okay to swim during pregnancy, isn't it?"

She nodded. "Yes."

He led her to another room, which held a desk, sofa and more electronic equipment. He turned on his laptop. "There's another office suite downstairs, but I tend to accomplish more up here. Would you like some juice or sparkling water?"

She shook her head. "No. I'm fine. All you need to live in here are a kitchen and washer and dryer."

His lips twitched. "There's a galley kitchen across the hall. Laundry chute in my closet."

Tugging off his tie, he released another shirt button. Lilli was struck by the sight of his tanned fingers against the white shirt. He truly was an amazing male. She wondered how many women had shared his bed. No chains needed for him.

She cleared her throat and tried to move her mind in a different direction as he tapped on the keyboard. "Just curious, but do you even know *how* to do laundry?"

He glanced at her and gave a cryptic smile. "Yes, I know how. We were required to learn in boarding school, along with basic mechanics, financial management, survival skills and cooking."

"You can cook?" she said in disbelief.

"I make a damn good omelet, can broil a steak with the best of them and I was recognized for making the best grilled cheese sandwich in my class."

She couldn't stifle a laugh from his defense of his culinary abilities. "Nothing chocolate in your repertoire?"

He shot her a level glance. "I buy only the best." He looked at the screen. "Here we are. Instructions for assembling your crib."

She joined him to look at the screen, surprised at how fast he'd found the instructions. "How did you know what kind?"

"I looked at the brand and model before I left the nursery." He hit the print button and seconds later, they returned to the nursery armed with instructions.

An hour later, they proclaimed victory as Lilli put in the final screw. "We did it," she said, punchy with excitement. She lifted her hand for a high five. "I hate to say it, but I couldn't have done it without you. Thanks."

"My pleasure," he said, his hair mussed from raking his fingers through it. She'd known he'd spent the entire time itching to do the work himself. He'd offered and insisted every five minutes, but she'd demurred. "If only everything were this easy," he said, offering his hand to help her up from the floor.

Her knees cramped from staying in one position too long, she wobbled as she stood. Strong arms wrapped around her and pulled her against his warm body.

Bracing herself on his arms, she was immediately distracted by the sensation of him, smooth skin over hard muscle. Her breasts pressed against his chest, her belly meshed with his and her thighs just barely touched his trousers.

"Are you okay?" he asked in a low voice.

Her heart pounding a mile a minute, she nodded and barely managed a whisper. "Yes. I guess I sat a little too long."

He slid his hand through her hair, surprising her with the sensual but tender gesture. "You stopped seeing my brother months ago. How is it that you don't have a man in your life now?"

She swallowed hard. "I'm pregnant."

"And no man has approached you?"

"No." She closed her eyes, trying not to sink into a helpless puddle on the floor. He felt so strong, so good. The intimate sound of his low voice both soothed her and wreaked havoc with her nervous system. "I didn't want a man in my life. I don't know if I ever will," she said, remembering how victimized she'd felt.

He gave a low laugh that caught her off guard. "You've got to be kidding."

She looked up at him, searching his face in the low lighting. "No. I'm not."

"Every woman has needs," he said.

"I don't," she told him, because it had seemed all her sexual needs had disappeared. "Not for a long time."

"How can you say that? You're attracted to me," he said and slid his fingertips from her hair to her throat.

"That doesn't mean I want to have sex with you," she said, but her skin was heating and her heart was racing.

"I could make you want to be with me," he said. "I could make you want it more than you ever have."

For a sliver of a moment, she believed him and the possibility sent her into turmoil. She had to shut this down once and for all. She took his hand and put it on her belly. "There will always be this between us," she said. "Always."

Max returned to his suite and poured himself a glass of red wine. There was something electric between him and Lilli. He could feel it in his skin and deeper in his gut. She was a little afraid of him, but still determined to hold her own. That attracted him even more. She was resolved to push him away, but she was fascinated by him. He could see it in the way she looked at him, hear it in her quick intake of breath and he felt it in her response to him.

The passion she tried to hide got to him more than any other woman's overt seduction had. He was still aroused from being so close to her.

Plowing his fingers through his hair, he walked to his office and pulled out another legal proposal from his attorney. After watching what had happened to his brother because his guardian had been permissive and irresponsible, Max couldn't stand the idea of another De Luca plunging down the same path.

He suspected Lilli would never sign a document giving him guardianship unless she became ill, and she might not even sign it under those conditions.

There were other options, though. Other ways to make sure this De Luca was raised properly. His attorney had outlined each of them. Some were more costly than others, and not just in terms of money. Rubbing his chin, he remembered when he'd got the news of his brother's death. The feeling of loss and despair had slammed into him like a concrete wall.

He would never let the same thing happen to another De Luca. Never.

Four

The next evening, after a full day at work, Lilli entered the De Luca house to the sound of jazz music, tinkling glasses and animated conversation. She'd noticed a few extra cars in the driveway, but she hadn't known what to expect once she got inside.

The scent of grilled food permeated the house, making her mouth water and her stomach growl. Then she remembered. This must be the barbecue gathering Max had mentioned the other day. All she wanted was a sandwich and she could fix that herself. Heading for the kitchen, she found two men and two women preparing food and placing it on serving trays.

A large bald man barked orders from one end of the large kitchen island. The man pinned her with his gaze as she approached the island. "No guests in the kitchen, *bella,*" he chided and pointed to himself. "Louie can't have you stealing secrets."

This was Max's fabulous chef. She hadn't had a chance to meet him yet because he seemed to cook and disappear.

"I'm not really a guest and I won't steal your secrets. I just want to make a peanut butter sandwich. It won't take a minute."

He gasped in horror. "Peanut butter sandwich, when you can eat this?"

"I need to make this quick," she said, more than ready for the solace and quiet of her room. She stepped behind the island. "I just want to take it to my room. Upstairs."

Louie's eyebrows shot upward. "Upstairs? You are a special friend of Mr. De Luca. Only the best—"

"No, no, I'm sure he doesn't think of me as a special friend."

"I don't know why not," a man said from behind her.

Lilli whipped her head around to look at a tall, muscular man with brown hair and luminescent green eyes. "Alex Megalos," he said with a smile as he stood on the other side of the kitchen island.

"Nice to meet you. Lilli McCall."

His eyes crinkled when he smiled. She liked that. She liked that he smiled at her instead of frowning. But she felt the need to disappear. She didn't want to call attention to herself. "I really should go," she said. "This is a business gathering."

"No reason we can't mix business and pleasure. Let's get you a drink. Come out on the patio."

Lilli shook her head again. "Thank you, but I—"

Max stepped into the kitchen and Lilli felt her heart take an extra beat. "When did the party move in here?"

"Max, you've been holding out on us. How did you lure this angel into your dark castle?"

Max met her gaze and she took a deep breath. A snap of electricity crackled between them. "Just lucky, I guess," he said.

"Well, if you need anyone to take her off your hands," Alex ventured.

Max shot him a sideways glance. "Always competing," he said, then turned to the chef. "Louie, the lady is hungry."

"We can't have that," Louie said and quickly put a plate together.

"Max, don't be so greedy. You've already got Kiki," Alex said. "Share her with the rest of us. She should join us tonight."

Lilli stared at Max in panic.

"If you would like—

"I wouldn't," she said. "Like," she added, gulping and shot Alex an apologetic look. "I'm a little tired. Thanks, though."

"I'm crushed," Alex said. "Maybe I could give you a call when you're rested."

Confusion rolled through her as she watched a beautiful brunette appear from behind him. "Max, sweetheart, you disappeared," the woman said.

He turned to the woman. "Kiki, I'll be back before you finish your next drink. I need to take care of a personal matter."

The woman looked at Lilli and lifted one of her perfectly arched eyebrows. "Is this the personal matter?" She narrowed her eyes.

"I—uh—need to go," Lilli said.

"No need to rush," Alex said.

"Exactly," Kiki said.

Lilli felt as if she were suddenly surrounded by vipers. There were too many competing agendas for her comfort. "All I wanted was a peanut butter sandwich," she murmured.

Kiki snickered. "How charming."

"Here's your plate, bella," Louie said.

"Bless you," she said. "Thank you. It looks delicious." She turned to Alex and Kiki. "It was nice to meet you. Have a lovely evening."

"I will," Kiki said and slid her hand around Max's well-developed bicep.

Lilli nodded, feeling an odd combination of emotions, most of which she didn't want to examine. "Good night," she said and stepped from behind the kitchen island.

Kiki's jaw dropped. Alex blinked.

They were looking at her pregnant belly.

"Want Lilli all to yourself for the rest of the evening?" Max asked, shooting Alex a sly grin. He winked at Lilli and his humor helped her get through the incredibly awkward moment.

"Uh…uh…" Alex seemed unable to pry his gaze from her belly. He cleared his throat and closed his eyes then forced his gaze upward. He exhaled and smiled. "Hell, I bet she would be more fun than you are. And trust me, Lilli, I'm a lot more fun than Max."

"Who is the lucky father?" Kiki asked in a strained voice.

Lilli glanced at Max. "Um, it's—"

He met her gaze. "That's between me and Lilli."

Kiki's face tightened with suspicion. "That's a little vague, darling," she said with an edge to her tone.

"Kiki, this is not the place for this discussion," he said. "Louie will be upset if we don't enjoy his meal. I'll talk to you later," he said, looking at Lilli.

"That's okay," she said, feeling her nerves jump in her stomach. "I'm hitting the sack early tonight. Very tired. Thank you again, Louie. G'night. Enjoy your evening," she said and scooted out of the room, thankful that Kiki wasn't armed. Otherwise, she was certain she would be so dead.

While Lilli ate, she watched a boring show on her flat-screen television. Afterward, she took a shower and went to bed, but didn't fall asleep. Pulling a book about newborn care from her nightstand, she added to the list of items she would need to purchase for the baby.

A knock sounded on her door and she tensed, but didn't answer. The knock sounded again and she held her breath.

"I know you're not asleep," Max said. "I heard you walking around three minutes ago."

Lilli frowned. She'd gotten a drink of water from the attached bathroom. Sighing, she rose from the bed and opened the door.

Max stepped inside and closed the door behind him. His gaze fell over her body, and he gave her a bottle of water and a cookie. "You've charmed my chef. Louie said you looked like you could use a cookie."

"Thank you," she said, appreciating his kindness. "But I'm sure it's because he thinks I'm a special friend of yours, even though I told him I'm not."

"It's safe to say we have a special relationship," he said. "A bond, in a way."

His tone made her stomach dip. "Speaking of special friends," she said. "Just curious, was there a particular reason you didn't tell Kiki the real father of my child?"

"Yes. For safety reasons, I've decided it's better not to comment on your relationship with Tony. There are too many people he owes."

"Oh," she said, remembering the threat and feeling a sinking sensation in her stomach. She sat down on the bed. "I keep trying to forget about that."

"Don't," he said, moving toward her. "You need to be on guard when you go out in public. People will try to take advantage of you if they know of your association with the De Lucas."

"I don't think my real friends would dream of taking advantage of me," she said and put the cookie and bottle of water on the nightstand. The soft glow of the bedside lamp intensified the intimacy of the moment. He was close enough that she could smell a hint of his cologne and masculine scent. She could almost feel him.

He gave a cynical smile. "People will always try to take advantage of you when you have money."

"You forget," she said. "I don't really have any money."

He sat down beside her on the bed and studied her. "That could change," he said.

Feeling his gaze on her, she looked at him. The expression on his face affected her in a strange way. "How?"

"There are options," he said.

"If this involves that crazy contract," she began.

"We won't discuss it at this late hour," he said. "Alex

asked me to give you his card. He couldn't stop talking about you."

"That didn't have anything to do with me," she said, her hair drooping over one of her eyes. "I could tell he was only interested because he liked the idea of taking something away that he thought was yours. Just a game."

"You're right that Alex is very competitive with me, but you underestimate your appeal," he said and lifted his hand to her hair.

Her heart fluttered. She could have pushed him away if she'd had the inclination, but she couldn't find it anywhere inside her. He slid his hand over her cheek and then down to her mouth, rubbing his thumb over her bottom lip.

Her skin tingled everywhere he touched. She swallowed hard. "Why are you touching me?"

"You don't like it?" he asked, his dark gaze meeting hers. "There are so many reasons you should be off-limits." He moved closer. "But I like the way your skin feels. I like the way you look at me when I touch you."

She inhaled a shallow breath and caught another draft of his spicy scent mixed with cologne. In some corner of her mind, it occurred to her that she'd never been this close to such a powerful man. He knew who he was and what he had to do, and he was the kind of man who would make whatever he wanted a reality.

For Lilli, it was like getting up close and personal with a wild tiger. At the same time, he was solid and strong and she knew he would never force a woman. He wouldn't need to. And to have him looking at her as his object of desire made her dizzy.

"There's something about you," he said, gently urging her mouth open so he could slide his thumb just inside to her tongue. "Wide blue eyes with secrets, a sweet smile." He glanced downward. "You make me curious."

Lilli was shocked at how quickly her body responded. She'd considered herself sexually dead, but she felt her skin heat and the tips of her breasts tighten against her white cotton gown.

He saw it, too. She knew it by the expression on his face.

"I shouldn't want you," he muttered and slid his hand around the back of her neck. "But dammit, I do." He lowered his mouth to hers and took her lips in a kiss that made her lose track of time and space.

His tongue slid over hers and she felt herself respond. It was all instinctual. Her heart pounded in her head and her blood pooled in secret, sensitive places. Every second that she felt his warmth, his touch, she was shocked by her immediate response to him. Something inside her could not push him away.

She felt him lower one of his hands to her breast. Air caught somewhere in her throat as he caressed her through her gown. He rubbed the palm of his hand over the side of her breast and she shivered, pressing up against him.

He gave a low groan of approval and drew his hand closer to her nipple, but not quite touching it. She felt the peak of it stiffen against her nightgown, aching for his touch.

Full of wanting, she held her breath.

He finally pushed the top of her gown down and slid his thumb over her nipple. She couldn't swallow a moan of relief with a twinge of frustration.

He pulled his mouth from hers and slid his lips over her skin, down her throat and collarbone. A riot of sensations shot through her. She wanted him everywhere at once.

His other hand slid over her back, massaging her, holding her in a solid embrace. The combination of security and caresses hit her physically and emotionally.

He looked up at her, dark desire in his eyes. Swearing under his breath, he shook his head.

Pulling back, he rose from the bed and prowled toward the window. Moonlight spilled over his profile as he raked his hand through his hair.

Lilli drank in a gulp of air, trying to clear her head. Shocked at herself, she tugged her gown back in place and tried to make sense of what had just happened. That night after she'd broken up with Tony, the night made doubly awful because she couldn't recall it, she'd changed. She'd known she would never be the same. She would never be able to let a man touch her again unless she trusted him.

Why should she trust Max? There was no good reason. But something inside her did. Either that or she was crazier than she'd thought she was.

"You're so responsive. I wonder...were you this responsive with my brother," he ventured in a low voice.

"I wasn't," she said, the words popping out before she could stop them.

He turned to look at her. "Why not?"

She bit her lip. "I can't explain it. It's just different."

He continued to hold her gaze. "Did you leave my brother before or after you found out you were pregnant?"

"Before." She looked away from him. "Something happened one night. I knew I couldn't stay."

"What was it?"

"I don't like talking about it," she said, twisting her fingers together. "I knew I had to get away from him and his—" her stomach clenched with nausea "—his world."

"And you weren't tempted to go back with him when you found out you were pregnant?"

She shook her head vehemently. "Oh, absolutely not. If I didn't belong in his world, there was no way a baby would."

"Did he ask you back?"

She nodded. "Several times. But I think he was relieved when I said no. Tony wasn't ready to be a father."

"What about the baby? What will you do about a father figure for him?"

"I'll deal with that later. Right now, I need to get through the pregnancy and delivery. My girlfriends have promised to help me through the scary first few months." She felt a sense of dread in the pit of her stomach. "Then I guess I'll have to move."

Feeling his gaze on her, she looked up at him, wondering what he was thinking, what judgments he was making. "You probably don't understand any of this. How I could end up with your brother and then pregnant with no husband? You would never get yourself into such a crazy situation because you don't let emotions make your decisions."

"You're completely correct."

"I'm also completely human. Are you?"

His mouth lifted in a half smile. "Unfortunately, yes. Human enough to want to finish what we started a few minutes ago." He moved toward her, and she felt her heart jump into her throat. "Don't worry. I won't. I may be human, but I'm not ruled by my hormones. Good night, Lilli."

Staring after him in surprise, she took a ragged breath. She felt totally off balance.

I'm human, but I'm not ruled by my hormones.

That was part of the reason she'd responded to him. She had a gut feeling that he had maintained control of himself. He wouldn't lose it unless he chose to do so. She'd never been around such a man but she could sense it about him and it made her feel secure at the same time that it knocked her sideways. She closed her eyes and pushed her hair from her face. She needed to stay on guard.

Five

Lilli's hands were shaking as she turned onto Max's street Saturday after working at the free dental clinic. She'd been so careful at work lately, always making sure to have someone walk her to her car. Afterward, she'd stopped to visit Devon Jones, one of the hospice workers who had helped her mother during her last days. Devon was now caring for his own father during the end stages of a long illness.

After she'd left, she'd noticed a black car in her rearview mirror. Even after making a few turns, the car remained behind her. She became so nervous that she'd taken some wrong turns and had got lost.

Glancing over her shoulder as she pulled into the driveway, she shook her head. Surely they wouldn't follow her all the way to Max's house. Biting her lip, she grabbed her purse and rushed into the house, leaning against the door as she closed it, and took a deep breath. She closed her eyes for a moment to calm herself. When she opened them, Max was five feet away from her, pinning her with a searching gaze.

"And you look like you've had some excitement," he said. "Anything you want to tell me?"

She tried to shrug, but shivered instead. Despite the way he'd left her feeling last night, she couldn't deny feeling ten times safer in his presence. "Not right now," she said and headed for the kitchen. "Water sounds good."

Her heart still racing, she took another deep breath and put her hand to her chest.

"Lilli," he said from behind her and she thought she heard a note of concern in his voice. Hallucinating, she told herself. "Are you okay?"

"I will be," she insisted, getting a glass and filling it with filtered water from the refrigerator.

He moved in front of her and studied her. "Where have you been?"

"Work, well, not really work," she corrected.

"Your office isn't open on Saturday," he said, his expression growing suspicious.

"That's right. But we volunteer for the free clinic downtown. I filled in for one of the other hygienists."

"Downtown? Where?" he asked, clearly not pleased.

She winced. She had expected he wouldn't approve of her driving downtown by herself, but no one had bothered her for days.

She told him the address and his mouth tightened. "Afterward, I stopped by to check on a hospice assistant who worked with my mother." She shook her head. "Poor Devon. His own father is dying now."

"Devon? What did this guy want? Did he ask you for anything?"

"No, but if he did, I would try to help him. He helped my mother and I during a very difficult time."

"This is what I warned you about. You need to be careful because people will come out of the woodwork playing on your sympathy and asking for *help*."

"That hasn't happened," she said, folding her arms over her chest.

"Then what happened to make you so upset? Did one of Tony's buddies show up?"

"Aside from getting lost, the only thing I can tell you is that someone in a black Mercedes followed me most of the way home."

He swore under his breath. "That's it. You're quitting."

She gaped at him. "Quitting?"

"It's the only rational thing to do. Each day that passes I learn more about how deeply Tony was in trouble. You can stay here until the baby is born and you're ready to move and say goodbye to your contacts here. I've told you before. You need to be on guard in every way. People will try to take advantage of you."

She shook her head. "I can't quit. I need the income for the baby. As you said, babies aren't cheap."

"Money won't be a concern after you sign the agreement."

She supposed she should have been intimidated by him and part of her was, but she refused to give in to it. "I'm not signing that stupid agreement and I'm not taking your money."

"You would turn down a good life for your child in exchange for pride."

She scowled at him. "That was low. The point is that I'm not giving control of my child to you or anyone else. I don't know you well enough. You may give the impression of being very responsible, but at the same time you're bitter, cynical and a workaholic. I want my butter bean to be happy. You may be loaded, but you don't seem very happy."

"Butter bean?" he repeated.

"Yes, butter bean. An affectionate nickname. Something you wouldn't understand."

Exasperation crossed his handsome face. "Most women would kill to have the equivalent of an extended vacation here, but you're fighting it every inch of the way. Have you always been this disagreeable?"

"I think you just bring it out in me," she said.

"Do you have a will?"

"Yes, I do," she said.

"Have you chosen a guardian for you child?"

She resisted the urge to squirm. "I'm working on it."

"Why don't you name me the guardian?" he demanded.

She bit her lip. "Because you don't smile enough." As soon as she blurted out her answer, she knew it sounded a little crazy. "I think kids need smiles and lots of hugs."

He moved toward her. "I think you trust me more than you admit."

Her heart flipped. Maybe she did. There was something so solid about him. "I trust you to be rational, but some decisions should be more emotional."

He lifted an eyebrow. "Are you saying your emotional decisions have turned out well?"

"Not all, obviously," she said. "But it was at least partly an emotional decision for me to take a leave of absence from work to take care of my mother during her last months. I wouldn't trade anything for the time I had with her, because I won't have a chance for that again."

A trace of sympathy softened his hard gaze.

"If you were my son's guardian, what would you do if you had to choose between attending an important business meeting or going to his T-ball game?" She shrugged. "I'm going to make a wild guess and say you'd choose the former because it would be the more rational decision."

"You make a good point, but most parents have to balance career and children's needs. There's no reason I couldn't learn to do the same thing."

She crossed her arms over her chest. "How would you do that?"

He looked surprised that she would question him. "Why do I feel as if I'm being interviewed for a position?"

She nodded. "Maybe you are," she said. "You've pretty much asked, no, demanded to be the baby's guardian in case of my death or path to self-destruction. If someone asked you to give them the most important job in the world, wouldn't you interview them? Probably conduct a background search. Ask for references."

He gave an incredulous laugh, his teeth gleaming brightly in contrast to his tanned skin. "I don't know whether to be offended or—" A cell phone rang and his smile fell. He pulled the phone from his pocket and checked the number. "Excuse me," he murmured. "Yes, Rena?" He paused and shook his head. "I've sent a donation for the event tonight, but won't be attending." He listened for a moment. "I'm sorry they'll be disappointed. Hopefully the money I sent will soothe some of their pain. Okay. Have a good day."

He turned off the phone and turned back to Lilli. "Sorry that was my cousin Rena. She thinks I'm a recluse and she's determined to get me more socially involved."

"But you don't want to," Lilli included.

"This will be a boring chicken dinner with a silent auction afterward. I get enough social involvement at work. And I'm not stingy with my donations."

"But maybe Rena thinks that more people would be more generous with their contributions if they actually saw you show up at the charitable functions sometimes. You would be a good example," she said.

"Maybe," he said, clearly not convinced. "Do you know how painful these things can be?"

"Probably not," she said. "But it's not like you're making a lifetime commitment."

He sighed and met her gaze. "Okay, I'll tell you what. I'll go to the fund-raiser for the children's wing of the hospital if you'll go with me."

"Me?" she said, shocked. "But I'm pregnant."

"Does that mean you're disabled?"

"No, but—" she shook her head "—why would you want me to go? You're bound to have a dozen other women on the line who would want to go with you."

"Meaning you wouldn't," he said in a dry, amused tone.

"I didn't say that," he said. "What about Kiki?"

"I didn't invite Kiki," he said. "I invited you."

Her heart sped up. She cleared her throat. "I don't have anything to wear."

"I can have someone take care of that within an hour."

He was shredding her protests more effectively than a paper shredder. She stared at him, her mind spinning.

"Think of it as an opportunity to continue your interview," he said, as if he weren't at all worried that he would meet and exceed her expectations.

Must be nice to have that kind of confidence, she thought. "This is crazy. I can't believe you want to take me to this kind of event. Aren't you concerned about the gossip?"

"With my father, his mistress and my brother, I've been dealing with gossip most of my life. This will be a cakewalk."

Lilli took a shower and as she was fixing her hair, a knock sounded on her door. She opened it to Max's housekeeper, Myrtle, who held a large box. "For you," the older woman with iron-gray hair said and carried the box to the bed.

"Already?" Lilli asked, glancing at the clock. When Max said an hour, he meant an hour. "Thank you very much, Myrtle," she said, opening the box and pushing aside layers of tissue paper. "Omigoodness, this is beautiful. Did you see it?" she asked the chief housekeeper. She held up the black gown with the fitted bodice and deep V-neck. Just under the bustline dotted with tiny embroidered pink flowers, the remainder of the dress fell in a swirl of silk.

The woman nodded. "It's beautiful. Perfect for you. Mr. De Luca is always very generous."

"Yes, he is, isn't he?" She looked in vain for a price tag, wishing she could reimburse him for the dress. "Do you think he would let me pay him—"

Before she even finished, Myrtle shook her head. "Never," she said.

Sighing, she met Myrtle's gaze. "I don't want to be on the long list of people who sponge off of him."

Myrtle gave a slight smile that softened her usual stern expression. "You will have a difficult time outgiving Mr. De Luca."

Lilli frowned thoughtfully. "How long have you worked for Mr. De Luca?"

"Six years. One of those years, my husband was ill and he allowed me extra time off with pay. I'll always be grateful to him for that."

"I don't know how to ask this, but does Mr. De Luca have any *real* friends?"

"Very few," Myrtle said. "He keeps very busy with his company and socializes very little. And there are his godchildren."

Lilli blinked. "Godchildren? I didn't know he was a godfather."

"With such wealth, he's a natural choice. I should go," she said. "You'll look beautiful in your dress. Mr. De Luca would want you to enjoy it."

"Just on more thing," Lilli said as the woman headed for the door. "When is Mr. De Luca's birthday?"

"Next month, the fifth," she said. "But he never celebrates it."

Lilli's mind immediately flew with possibilities. *He*

never celebrates it. Well, maybe this year should be different. And he was a godfather? Who would have guessed? Sheesh, she should talk to Myrtle more often.

She glanced at the clock again and felt a kick of nerves. She would think about that later. Now she needed to get ready for the charity dinner. She wanted the rest of her to measure up to that beautiful dress.

It occurred to Lilli that perhaps she could have used a team of hairstylists and consultants to get her up to snuff for this event. Instead she would need to rely on the cosmetic tips she'd gleaned from the last fashion magazine she'd read and that had been two or three months ago.

One hour and ten minutes later, Max checked his watch again and wondered if he should sit down and review some reports while he waited for Lilli. Just as he headed for his downstairs office, she appeared at the top of the stairs. He stared for a long moment as she descended the steps. Her blond hair flowing in loose spiral curls to her shoulders and fair skin made her look like an angel. The cut of her black halter dress dipped into a deep V that drew his gaze to her breasts, and the way the fabric bonded lovingly to her curves made him hard.

Her pregnancy was obvious. The dress made no attempt to hide it. He wondered why he was so attracted to this woman. It made no sense at all, especially knowing the baby she carried belonged to his dead brother.

He clenched his teeth and nodded. "You look lovely."

"Thank you," she said with a smile. "So do you."

His lips twitched. He chuckled. "Thanks." He extended his elbow. "Ready?"

"As ever," she murmured and slid her arm through his. "You can still back out if you want. I mean, unless you've changed your mind about having me tag along."

"Not a chance," he said, guiding her through the doorway. "You're not backing out, are you?"

She shot him a sideways glance. "Not a chance. It's not as if I'm ever going to see these people again."

"You never know," he said, escorting her to the luxury sedan parked out front. He opened the car door for her. "You may enjoy yourself."

"I just hope the food is good. If it's not, we can always stop for a cheeseburger with everything on the way home."

He just grinned and got into the car. Adjusting the sound system to play an operatic aria, he noticed Lilli began to fidget after a few minutes. "Problem?" he asked.

"No, no, not really," she said, pushing her hair behind her shoulder as she moved her foot in a staccato beat at odds with the aria. He heard the soft jangle of her anklet with every movement. It was difficult to keep his gaze from straying to her sexy legs.

"Are you sure there's nothing wrong?" he asked.

"Do you know what she's saying?" she asked, pointing toward the CD player.

"It's from a German opera by Mozart called *The Magic Flute.* I didn't study much German, but if I remember correctly, she's saying something along the lines of 'The vengeance of hell boils in my heart. Death and despair flame about me.'"

"Cheerful little ditty, huh," she said. "That's why I'm not crazy about opera. Someone is usually pissed off, plotting to kill someone or getting killed."

"True. But some are more upbeat than others. I'll

have to take you sometime," he said, amused at the image of sharing such an experience with Lilli. "Have you thought about what kind of music is good for the baby's development?"

She nodded vigorously. "I want him to enjoy a variety of music, so I play instrumental Mozart for him. Based on what you just told me about the translation to that aria, I think I'll skip most opera for a while. I've also already started him on the Baby Einstein series."

"You've done some research," he said and felt the weight of her gaze on him.

"You sound surprised."

"Maybe I was," he admitted. "Since this pregnancy was unplanned—"

"Doesn't mean I'm not going to be informed. I've signed up to take an infant care class in a couple of weeks, and I've been researching pediatricians. Since I've changed where I'm living, I may need to do some additional research."

"I can get you the best pediatrician in Las Vegas anytime you want," he said finally, determined that Lilli and his nephew would have no less. "What kind of preschool you want him to attend?"

"I'm leaning toward a Montessori school but they can be expensive, so I'll have to see."

"Money won't be an issue—"

"As long as I sign your agreement, which I won't," she said.

"Yet," he corrected, feeling a twist of impatience. He'd made sure he didn't do anything that would cause his character to be called into question. Not after his father. "You can change your mind after you know me better."

"Maybe," she conceded. "But I still don't like the idea of signing my butter bean over to anyone."

"It's the job of a parent to make sure the child is taken care of in the event of the parent's death."

"I know."

A swollen silence followed, and he sensed she was thinking about things that made her sad. His gut twisted. He couldn't explain it, but he didn't want Lilli sad, so he changed the subject. "You didn't say anything about sports. The De Lucas are naturally athletic, good with any competitive sports. I could teach him soccer, tennis, basketball."

"That's nice, but the important question is can you play peekaboo?"

Max blinked and glanced at her. From the glow of the dashboard, her eyes gleamed with a combination of innocence and sensuality. "Peekaboo?"

She nodded. "Yes, and how good are you at giving hugs and pats on the back? A kid needs hugs and pats on the back more than soccer."

Max digested her comments for a long moment. "You think I may not be affectionate enough."

"I didn't actually say that."

"But you thought it."

She opened her mouth then closed it. "I think a child needs someone who means safety and security, home. That person will love you whether you make the goal or not. That person will teach you how to take a bad day and make it better. I think a child needs compassion."

He pulled in front of the resort where the event was being hosted. "We'll continue this discussion later."

"Okay," she said and lifted her mouth in a sexy smile. "Are you ready for your grand entrance?"

He looked at her for a long moment, unable to tear his gaze away from her. With her sunbeam hair and eyes full of life, she literally sparkled. She took his breath away. "Sweetheart, they're not going to be looking at me," he said, and gave his keys to the valet.

Six

Lilli felt curious gazes fastened on her as she sat next to Max at the dinner table. Chandeliers lit the luxurious ballroom, warming the red carpet and creating a glow on faces belonging to the who's who of the Las Vegas elite. Walls lined with elegant mirrors reflected women outfitted in designer gowns swishing alongside men dressed in expertly tailored suits. Servers refilled her glass of water before she had an opportunity to make a request.

It was by far the most luxurious event she'd ever attended and she constantly reminded herself not to put her elbows on the table. She noticed many people made a point of stopping to speak to Max. Even the mistress of ceremonies introduced him and thanked him for donating the resort's grand ballroom for the night's festivities.

Just as Max picked up his fork to take a bite of coq

au vin, a man stopped and touched his shoulder. "Good to see you here, Max. And congrats on the success of your latest refurbishment project in your Luxotic resorts in the Caribbean. I understand they're often booked over a year in advance."

"Thank you," Max said. "It takes a team. Good to see you too, Robert."

The man walked away and Lilli leaned toward Max and whispered, "Would you like me to put a sign on the back of your chair telling people not to talk to you until you finish eating?"

His lips twitched. "There are only three words appropriate for that question."

"What?"

"I told you," he said and took a bite.

"True," she said. "But maybe people wouldn't feel it necessary to try to talk to you if you attended more of these. Think about it. If they know this is their only shot at actually speaking to the mighty Max De Luca, they've got to grab it. If, however, they know you'll show up at some other events, maybe they won't feel the need to speak to you every time they see you, which is almost never."

"You're saying the attraction to me is how rarely I appear. It has nothing to do with me or my position. If I showed up more often, I would be old news."

She realized he could take that as an insult. "I never used the word *old news.* I'm just saying maybe some of the attention could be spread out over several appearances instead of concentrated on just one."

"Spread the torture out over several evenings instead of getting it done in one."

She sighed and shook her head. "Maybe it wouldn't feel as much like torture if it was spread out." She glanced up and saw a familiar woman walking toward them. "Is that—"

"Max, what a surprise. You told me you weren't planning to come tonight," the woman said and Lilli recalled who she was. Kiki.

Lilli felt a nervous twitch at the back of her neck.

"Last-minute change of plans," Max said, rising to his feet. "Are you enjoying the event?"

Kiki shot Lilli a venomous glance. "Not as much as if I were with you," she said and touched his arm.

"Oh, I'm sure I would have bored you to tears. I'm doing the same to Lilli. Just ask her," he said, glancing down at Lilli with a devil's glint in his eyes.

"I'm sure *Lilli* would never call you boring," Kiki said. "No woman in her right mind would."

"Let's ask Lilli. Tell the truth," he said.

She searched his gaze, wondering why on earth he was putting her on the spot like this. "Kiki is right. I wouldn't have described you as boring."

"See?" Kiki said.

"But he can complain right up there with the best of them," she added.

Kiki's eyes narrowed in disapproval. Max stared at her in surprise and Lilli heard the clatter of sterling silver hit the floor beside her followed by the sound of nervous laughter from the woman sitting in the chair beside her.

Fighting a twinge of nervousness and regret, Lilli lifted her shoulders. "You told me to be honest."

"Yes, I did," he said, giving the distinct impression he wouldn't make the same request again.

Kiki cleared her throat. "I need a quick private word with you, Max. It's urgent. Do you mind?"

He shot a longing glance at his food and Lilli. "Oh, go," she urged him. "If you're not back soon, I'll ask the server to wrap it up to take home."

He bent down and whispered in her ear. "At this rate we may be stopping at Wendy's for me."

She smiled. "Drive-through is open until midnight."

He gave a rough chuckle and turned toward Kiki.

"He's so hot," the young woman beside her said. "How could you send him off with that beautiful woman? You must be confident of your relationship with him," she said in admiration.

Lilli turned to the pudgy young woman with the sweet face. "Max and I have an unusual relationship," she said wryly.

The woman nodded, glancing at Lilli's pregnant belly. "You don't have to tell me anything. I've heard him dodging questions the entire dinner. I know what it's like to be surrounded by people with hidden agendas. Oh, I'm sorry. I should have introduced myself. I'm Mallory James."

"I'm Lilli—"

"McCall," Mallory said, then blushed. "I overheard him introduce you several times. I'm not usually nosy, but since I'm here by myself tonight, and the two of you were more interesting than the almost-dead and completely deaf eighty-seven-year-old beside me…well…"

Lilli smiled. "I'm glad we at least provided a little entertainment. Nice to meet you, Mallory."

The other woman glanced past Lilli's shoulder. "Good grief, you're surrounded by them," she murmured.

"Lilli, you're looking delicious tonight," a male voice said just behind her.

Lilli turned around to meet Alex Megalos's friendly gaze. She couldn't help smiling as she shook her head. "Do you give lessons on flirting on the side?"

"No way. Gotta keep my edge. Where did Max go? Not wise to abandon a woman as beautiful as you."

"You're so right," she said. "I'm bracing myself for the stampede any minute."

Mallory cleared her throat loudly.

Lilli glanced back at the woman whose expression clearly said *please introduce me.* "Oh, Alex Megalos, have you met Mallory James? She's new to town. Alex works for Megalos-De Luca Enterprises."

Alex extended his hand to Mallory and lifted it to his lips. "Enchanted. Have I heard of your father?"

"Perhaps," Mallory said, stuttering. "James Investments and Wealth Management."

Alex nodded in recognition and gave a roguish smile, dipping his head toward hers. "Yes. I bet he keeps you under lock and key. I hear he's excellent. I'd love a chance to chat with him. Is he here tonight?"

"Not tonight," Mallory said and pulled out a card. "But I'd be happy to introduce you. Give me a call?" she asked, rising, bumping into a server carrying a tray of drinks.

"Oh, no." Lilli watched helplessly as the drinks tumbled, splattering Mallory's pink gown and at least one leg of Alex's pants.

The server's face froze. "I'm so sorry."

"Club soda," Lilli said, quickly standing. "Club soda works magic for stains. And we need more napkins," she called after the waiter as he left. She gave her napkin to Alex and blindly accepted one that someone else offered her.

She gave the other napkin to Mallory, meeting the horrified gaze of her new acquaintance. "Mallory, go ahead to the powder room. I'll bring the club soda, sweetheart. These servers move so quickly," she said.

As soon as Mallory was out of earshot, she turned to Alex. "Shame on you for causing all this trouble."

"Me?" Alex said in an incredulous voice, wiping his slacks.

"You're such a flirt. I'm sure you know what kind of effect you have on most women. You really should be more careful doling out those kisses and smiles."

Max appeared at her side and glanced at Alex. "Did someone finally decide to douse him?" he asked, half-joking.

Alex met Max's gaze and gave a heavy sigh. "No. it was the server. Dammit, Lilli can explain it to you," he said and left.

"He didn't hit on you again, did he?"

She shook her head. "He's a flirt. I introduced him to the woman beside me and he got her all flustered. She bumped into the server and there was a spill. Ah, here comes the club soda," she said, smiling at the server as he delivered the bottle and some extra napkins.

"I'm so sorry," he said.

"Accidents happen," she said then looked at Max. "I need to do a little emergency stain removal."

"Saving the day?" he said, his gaze glinting with something that looked like approval.

"That's a stretch, but I would hope someone would do the same for me in the same situation."

He lowered his head toward her. "I could kiss you right this very minute."

Lilli's heart slammed into her rib cage and she gaped at Max. "You—"

"You heard me," he said and his voice was so seductive she immediately felt hot and flustered. "Now go do your good deed."

Stepping backward, her gaze still trapped by his, she nearly stumbled. Max's hand shot out to steady her. "You're worse than Alex."

His eyes widened in outrage. "What the hell—"

She pulled away. "I need to do my good deed," she said and forced her gaze away from his so she could regain her equilibrium. *Men,* she thought and headed for the powder room.

As soon as she entered the luxurious room with a sitting area separate from the stalls, she looked for Mallory, but couldn't find her. Lilli walked into the connecting room filled with stalls and tentatively called, "Mallory?"

"I'm here," she said, covering her face as she exited one of the restrooms. "I can't believe I did that. I'm so embarrassed. I can't go back in there."

"Of course you can. It was just a little spill. They happen all the time," Lilli said, urging the young woman into the sitting area. "Come on. Let me work on your dress."

Mallory moaned. "Why did I have to make a server spill wine on the most amazing man I've ever met?"

"Alex can afford to be taken down a peg or two." She poured a little club soda on the worst spots.

"But not by me," Mallory said. "Do you think he'll run from me every time he sees me from now on?"

Lilli shook her head, dabbing at the dress. "Of course he won't. If nothing else, your meeting was memorable. He'll probably talk to dozens of people tonight, but not many—"

"None," Mallory corrected and gave a reluctant laugh. "None will have gotten his slacks wet." She smiled and met Lillie's gaze. "You've been very kind to me. Would you mind getting together with me sometime for lunch if I promise to try not to spill anything on you?"

Lilli laughed. "I'd love to," she said. "You know this is the same kind of thing that could have happened to me."

"I can't see it," Mallory said. "You look so graceful."

"Thank you, but it's true. Now it's time for us to get back to dinner. The auction should start soon."

Mallory sighed and stood. "Okay, let me put on a little more lipstick."

While Mallory took a couple extra minutes to primp, Lilli walked out into the hallway. She'd gone no more than three steps when she nearly ran into Kiki.

Lilli immediately backed away. "Oh, excuse me. How are you?"

Kiki narrowed her eyes. "I could be a lot better." She stared at Lilli for a long moment then cocked her head to the other less busy side of the hallway. "Do you have a moment? I'd like to talk with you."

"I probably should get back to—"

"Max," Kiki said, her beautiful face tightening with displeasure. "He can wait. This won't take long."

Lilli reluctantly followed Kiki.

"You probably don't know this, but Max and I have

a very close relationship. *Very* close," she emphasized. "In fact, no one would be surprised if we were to get married. We've been seeing each other for a couple of years."

Lilli nodded. "I see."

"A man like Max, well, a woman just has to accept that he may stray every now and then. It doesn't really mean anything. Men, especially powerful men, have women throwing themselves at them all the time."

Lilli wondered what this had to do with her.

"Now Max hasn't wanted to admit anything," Kiki continued with a determined smile that didn't reach her eyes. "I'm sure he doesn't want to hurt my feelings. But I'm not stupid. He obviously feels obligated toward you and I can understand why you would want to take advantage of the situation."

"Not really," Lilli said.

Kiki waved her hand. "You don't need to deny it. I can't imagine any woman in your position who wouldn't exploit the situation to her advantage."

Lilli felt a spurt of anger. "I'm—"

"Just hear me out," Kiki interjected. "What you need to understand is that you won't be able to hold him. Sure, he'll be a great father to the child, but Max is a special man and trust me, he requires special handling. I know he will provide financial support for your child. But you seem like an independent-minded woman, so I thought you might like some additional support of your own."

Confusion and wariness mixed inside her. "Additional support?"

Kiki lowered her voice. "Here's the deal. You leave

Max, never come back and don't get in my way and I'll give you fifty thousand dollars."

Lilli blinked at the woman in disbelief. "Are you serious?"

"Dead serious," Kiki said. "Max is very important to me."

Incredulous, Lilli shook her head. "I can't—"

"Sure you can. Think about it. Imagine getting all that money and a clean break to do what you want where you want." She paused a half beat. "If you make the move within a week, I might even throw in a bonus. You could buy yourself a little condo or house and be in charge of your own life. Trust me, if you stay with Max, he'll have an opinion about everything you say and do." She pressed a card into Lilli's hand. "Call me. I'll make it worth your while."

Lilli stared after the woman as she strode away. She couldn't believe what had just happened. The conversation ran through her mind again, but it was almost too much for her to comprehend.

"Hey, Lilli," Mallory said, moving her hand in front of Lilli's face. "Are you okay? You look a little sick. Should you sit down?"

Lilli shook her head to clear it. "No, I just—" She sighed and headed back to the table.

"Are you sure?" Mallory asked as she followed after her. "You look pale. Like you're sick or you just had a close encounter with an alien or something. Some people don't believe in that stuff, but I do."

Lilli shook her head at the irony. "That's a pretty good explanation," she said.

"What is?" Mallory asked.

"A close encounter with an alien," Lilli said, crumpling Kiki's card into a little wad and tossing it onto a passing waiter's empty tray.

Mallory nodded and whispered, "The place is full of aliens tonight, isn't it?"

Still shaken from her encounter with Kiki, but trying to get past it, Lilli returned with Mallory to the table just as dessert was being served. Max immediately stood and helped both Lilli and Mallory into their chairs while Lilli introduced Mallory.

After they all sat down, he turned to Lilli. "Everything okay?"

She gave a circular nod, but mustered a smile.

"You want to explain that remark about Alex?" he asked.

She felt her cheeks heat with embarrassment. "I was just commenting that it's not fair for him—or you—to use your—" she searched for an appropriate word "—appeal to put a woman off balance."

His lips twitched. "Are you admitting I put you off balance?"

She reached for her glass of water. "I'm not saying anything else. I offered my explanation."

"Sounds like you're pleading the fifth."

"How is Kiki?" she asked, changing the focus off herself.

Irritation crossed his face. "How is it that a woman can appear perfectly sane and rational at the beginning of a relationship then turn totally insane and irrational at the end?"

"It's all the man's fault," she said. "Men turn women

into raging lunatics. They hint, they promise, they mislead."

"I am always up-front in my relationships with women. I make it clear that I'm not interested in marriage and—"

"Why not?" she asked. "Why aren't you interested in marriage?"

"It needs to be the right woman at the right time. I've never found the right woman."

"Why not Kiki?" she asked, keeping her voice low.

"This isn't the best place for a private discussion, but I've never been serious about Kiki. She's a beautiful, intelligent woman, but not right for me in the long run. I told her that from the beginning."

Ouch, Lilli thought. That couldn't have gone over well. "Is there anything you did that might have led her to believe that you'd changed your mind and that you and her were getting close to a commitment?"

He narrowed his eyes. "Why are you asking these questions?"

She shrugged. "Just curious. She seems a little..."

"A little what?"

"I don't know. Maybe possessive."

"I made it clear tonight that we're through. Now, don't you want to eat some of this dessert? It's chocolate cake."

Lilli's stomach twisted. "I'd love to, but I'm full."

He studied her for a long moment. "Something's not right," he began.

"Ladies and gentleman," Ann Wingate, the mistress of ceremonies announced, saving Lilli from replying to Max. "It's now time for the Silent Auction. Please make your way to the display tables and loosen your purse strings. And remember, it's all for a good cause."

"You're sure you don't want your cake," Max said.

She shook her head. "Thanks, no. I'm curious what they've put up for auction."

He nodded and stood, pulling her chair back for her to rise. "Pick a couple things you like and make a bid on my behalf."

"Oh, I couldn't do that."

"Why not? It's for charity."

"Yes, but—" She broke off. "It wouldn't feel right."

He gave a heavy sigh. "Then pick out something I can donate to a good cause."

She liked that idea much better. "That could be fun."

With the exception of several interruptions, Max actually enjoyed himself during the next hour. Lilli's careful assessment of the items amused him. He noticed she spent an inordinate amount of time studying an expensive baby stroller before she dismissed it and moved along.

"Which should I buy to give away?" he asked, curious what her answer would be.

"The spa and makeover packages for the women's shelter downtown. The deluxe computer system for the homeless shelter."

"That's all?"

"I think they'll provide good bang for the buck."

"You didn't see anything you like? Jewelry? A luxury cruise?"

She shook her head and he continued. "Baby stroller."

She gave a start then shook her head again. "That thing costs almost as much as a car. Crazy expensive."

Max couldn't help wondering how long her attitude would last if she were exposed to luxury all the time. In his experience, women tended to easily grow accustomed to the finer things. She amused him at the same time that she attracted him. Her laughter affected him like a strong jolt of java and her determination not to brown-nose him startled him. He was surrounded by yes people and she didn't hesitate to tell him no. Even though she was pregnant, or perhaps partly because of it, she drew his attention the way no other woman had.

How could she possibly be so innocent and sexy at the same time? He couldn't believe his half brother's damn good luck in finding her. She couldn't be perfect, though, he reminded himself. No one was, and he'd never met a woman who didn't have the capacity for deceit and manipulation. Still, he wanted her. And he wasn't inclined to resist her.

Seven

"You absolutely shouldn't have gotten that baby stroller," Lilli said in a huffy voice. "It was insanely expensive."

"Butter bean will like it," Max said.

She threw him a sideways glance as he opened the door to the house for her. "He would have been just as happy with a less costly model."

"You don't know that," Max argued. "The cutting-edge aerodynamic design, which features an unparalleled smooth ride," he quoted from the manufacturer, "may make a huge difference."

"In that case, he'd better be flexible because my compact car gives a high five to every bump in the road."

He chuckled.

She turned to face him. "But seriously, I cannot accept the jewelry."

"It's just sterling silver."

"David Yurman's top-of-the-line." She shook her head. "I don't understand why you bought it for me. I told you I didn't want anything."

"I'm sure that was part of it," he said.

"You mean you gave me this just to be disagreeable?" she asked, her eyes rounding in surprise.

"It contributed, plus as the hostess kept saying, it's all for charity."

Her lips twitched. "You don't believe any of it. You don't believe the manufacturer's brag about the stroller and you think it's stupid to hold an auction to get donations."

"It's a lot easier to just guilt people into giving money through the mail," he said.

"But for some people, it's more fun to give it away at an auction."

He nodded. "Depends on the people."

She bit her lip and her expression changed. "Maybe." She paused. "I still don't understand why you got me the jewelry."

"The blue topaz reminded me of your eyes," he said.

He saw a hint of something deeper than desire flash through her eyes before she took a quick breath and looked away. "Oh."

His gut twisted with a surprising instinct to pull her against him and kiss her. Take her. He swore under his breath.

She cleared her throat. "Well, you shouldn't have, but it was very nice of you."

"I surprised you," he said. "You thought I was a selfish miser like Scrooge."

"I never thought you were like Scrooge." She paused and seemed to decide that she shouldn't elaborate.

He would love to know what she was really thinking.

"Thank you again. I should go up to bed," she said and paused. "I was wondering," she began and abruptly stopped.

"Wondering what?"

"It's really none of my business."

"I won't know if that's true until you ask the question."

"I was wondering," she ventured. "Do you have any godchildren?"

He narrowed his eyes. "Why do you ask? Did someone mention that to you tonight?"

"At the auction?" she said. "Of course not."

He tugged at his tie. "The truth is I have five godchildren."

Her eyes rounded. "Omigoodness. So many."

He waved his hand in a dismissive gesture. "I'm not expected to do any real parenting. I'm actually a co-godparent. The parents just want my financial management in case anything should happen to them. Along with the gifts and tuition," he added.

"Gifts and tuition?" she echoed, her brow furrowing in confusion.

"They're counting on me to provide a significant college fund."

"For five children?" she said. "Isn't that a bit much?"

"I've got it," he said. "But I've started dodging the opportunity to add any more godchildren."

"I can't blame you for that. My goodness, no wonder you're so cynical."

"No need for flattery," he said, chuckling at her assessment.

Her gaze softened. "But it is very generous of you to accept the responsibility."

"Financial responsibility," he corrected.

She gave a slow nod. "Whatever would you do if, for some unforeseen reason, you became the guardian of five children?"

"Boarding school," he said.

Her face fell. "Oh. That's why I'll never sign your agreement for butter bean."

"You don't really have anyone in mind to be the guardian for your child, do you?" he asked.

She looked away. "I really am working on it."

He touched her arm. "Lilli, tell me the truth."

She bit her lip. "The closest I have is my good friend Dee. She's loving and affectionate and adores children. But she's also a free spirit and loves to travel." She sighed and lifted her lips in a smile that didn't reach her eyes. "Maybe I should place a want ad."

"Never," he said.

"That's what I have to say about boarding school," she replied. The silence hung between them, thick with pent-up desire and emotion. It was so strong he could taste it.

"I should go to bed. Thank you again for an amazing evening. Good night," she said and turned to go upstairs.

He felt the same twitchy sensation he'd felt the first time he'd met her. It was the same feeling of intuition he had just before he made a successful business move. He'd never felt it about a woman, he thought, shaking his head. Loosening his tie, he picked up the weekend edition of one of his newspapers and sat down for a few minutes.

Restless, he decided to pour a glass of red wine. Taking it outside on the patio, he inhaled the scent of the flowers his gardener kept in meticulous condition year-round and listened to the soothing sound of the waterfall in the pool.

Max wondered what would have happened between him and Lilli if they'd met under different circumstances. If she'd never been involved with his brother and gotten pregnant. For just a moment, he indulged himself. He would have seduced her immediately. He would have talked her into quitting her job so she could travel with him at a moment's notice.

The image of her pale naked body available to him at all times made him hard. She was a passionate woman and he would want to learn all of her secrets. He would find out what made her moan, what made her sweat and what would make her come alive in his arms.

He would want to mark her as his with jewelry, but not marriage. Although he'd never invited a woman to live in his home, Lilli may very well have been the first.

Of course, he would have asked her to sign a financial agreement that would protect both her and him for the time when their relationship ended. Every good thing came to an end, Max knew that. He suspected she would have refused to sign the agreement, he thought with a twinge of humor, and he would have had the affair with her anyway.

He swallowed a drink of wine and ruthlessly cut off

his little mental fantasy. With the impending birth of his brother's child, there was far more at stake than Max's libido. Even though he was encouraged by how seriously Lilli was taking her maternal duties, he knew that attitude could change for a variety of reasons.

His own brother's guardian had started out well, but when Tony had hit his teens, the guardian had seemed to give up. She'd allowed Tony way too much freedom and Max was convinced the lack of parental influence had sent Tony down the road into trouble and eventually to his death.

Max refused to allow that to happen to another De Luca. If Lilli continued to refuse to sign an agreement with him, there were other ways. More drastic, more costly, but perhaps ultimately necessary.

Two days later, Lilli left work a little early because Max had invited her to join him for dinner at The Trillion Resort's rooftop restaurant. His assistant had made the arrangements with her, and she had no idea why he'd invited her. Since the auction, Max had worked such late hours she hadn't seen him at all.

She fussed over what to wear and finally chose a pair of maternity slacks and a silk top with varying colors of sea-blue that featured an Empire waist and fell nearly to her knees.

She wore the sterling jewelry Max had purchased for her at the auction and had gone a little more daring with her makeup by giving her eyes a smoky look.

Although she cursed herself for it, she wanted to look nice for Max. She rolled her eyes at the way she minimized her feelings. The truth was she wanted to make his head spin. It was only fair since the man could turn her upside down with just a glance.

Max's chauffeur drove her in one of the luxury sedans. As he pulled in front of the palatial resort, a valet rushed to her door to open it. "Good evening. Mr. De Luca's guest?"

She nodded in surprise as she accepted his assistance out of the car. "Yes, how did you—"

The young man smiled. "We know all of Mr. De Luca's vehicles."

"Oh," she said, nodding. "Thank you." She turned back to Max's chauffeur, Ricardo. "Thank you for the ride."

Ricardo smiled at her and waved. "My pleasure, Miss McCall. Enjoy your evening."

Lilli made her way to the glass elevators that whisked her up to the top level of the resort. Walking into the restaurant, she looked for Max. A man beside her said, "May I help…"

Her gaze collided with Max's across the room and she didn't hear anything else. He rose from the table where he sat, his gaze fixed on her.

The intensity with which he watched her made her feel as if she couldn't breathe. Her heart felt as if it were tripping over itself. Why did this man affect her on so many levels?

She walked to his table and he extended his hand, taking hers. "You look beautiful."

"Thank you," she whispered and took a shallow breath. "This is lovely."

"I thought you might enjoy a night out," he said and glanced down at the necklace she wore. He touched the pendant and his warm fingers brushed her bare skin. "I like the way my gift looks on you."

The hint of sensual possessiveness in his tone gave her a surprising, forbidden thrill. She was a liberated woman. For Pete's sake, what was wrong with her?

"Have a seat," he said before she could reply. "I already ordered orange juice and seltzer for you."

"Thank you." She sat down and felt the hum of anticipation and electricity wind a little tighter between them.

The waiter appeared at their table, offered suggestions and they placed their orders. Max was all charming conversation, pointing out different sights from the restaurant's breathtaking view as the sun slid lower on the horizon.

Tonight interruptions were kept to a minimum. Although Lilli felt plenty of gazes on her and Max, no one approached the table. The waitstaff were perfect, appearing to refill drinks, clear plates and provide nearly invisible but courteous service.

"I told the maître' d I wanted as few interruptions as possible tonight," Max said as if he'd read her mind.

She nodded. "I couldn't help comparing this experience to the auction."

"The auction was a free-for-all. Now you understand why I don't attend many," he said and lifted his hand. "Although I must say I enjoyed it much more because you were there."

"It was fun and I made a new friend," she said.

"Who?"

"Mallory James. She invited me to lunch on Saturday."

He nodded his head in approval. "Good. You'll be occupied."

Strange response, she thought. "Occupied for what?"

"I'm going out of town for three weeks."

Her heart sank. Crazy. She would have to think about that later. "Oh, wow. That's a long trip."

"Yes. I knew it was coming. We have several grand reopenings in different locations scheduled over the next few weeks and my presence is required at all of them."

"The bane of being the boss," she said, forcing a smile because, heaven help her, she would miss him.

"These arrangements were made before I knew you existed. I'll be out of the country," he said, clearly displeased. "I'm not comfortable leaving you at this stage."

His confession made her feel as if the sun came out from behind a cloud. "I've got six weeks until my due date. Everything's been perfect so far. There's no reason to think I'll have any problems."

"Still," he said. "It's best to be prepared for everything. Give me your cell phone."

She blinked. "Why?"

"So I can program in my contact numbers," he said.

"Oh, I can't imagine that I would need to call you while you're out of the country," she said.

He waved his fingers impatiently and she gave him her phone. "Of course, you'll be talking to me. I'll be checking in with you on a regular basis. For any immediate emergencies, you're to call my assistant, Grace. I've told her to be on twenty-four hour call."

"That's ridiculous. I wouldn't call your assistant. I've never even met her."

"If you're not comfortable, I can arrange a meeting."

Overwhelmed, Lilli shook her head. "No. That's not

necessary." She lowered her voice. "None of this is necessary. I'll be fine."

He met her gaze. "It's my job to make sure you stay that way."

"Why?" she demanded. "It's not as if you're my hus—" She broke off, horrified that the words had just popped out of her mouth.

Unable to tear her gaze from his, Lilli felt something snap and shimmer between them. A forbidden possibility neither of them would consider. What if Max *was* her husband? What if… Feeling as if the circuits in her head had scrambled and misfired, she looked away from him.

She took a mind-clearing breath. "That was stupid. This is about the baby. You feel responsible because you're the uncle. It's not about me."

He cleared his throat. "It's all connected. The baby, you, me. And since your delivery date is growing closer, you must make a decision about guardianship if something should happen to you."

She glanced back at him and watched him pull a manila envelope from his suit jacket pocket. "I've asked my attorney to come up with an agreement that should be more palatable for you. While I'm gone, I want you to look at this and take it to another attorney if that will make you more comfortable."

Her heart twisted. This entire meal had been a setup. Max wanted one thing and one thing alone from her. Control of her baby. Although she wanted to toss the agreement back at him, she felt forced to take the envelope for the sake of civility.

Max seemed to sense the change in her mood and signed for the check and escorted her from the dining room. She hated sharing the close space of the elevator, but getting into the Ferrari with him was far more excruciating. The darkness closed around them, creating a veil of intimacy.

Every time he shifted gears, her gaze strayed to his hand tightening around the knob. His long legs flexed as he accelerated and pushed in the clutch. Despite her hostility, she couldn't help noticing a commanding sensuality with the way he drove the luxury sports car. He would be a commanding, demanding lover, she knew, but he would also make sure his partner was satisfied. In fact, she suspected a woman might never be the same once she'd shared a bed with Max.

As soon as he pulled into the garage and came to a stop, she turned to unlock her door. The second after she hit the button, the automatic lock clicked again, effectively trapping her in the car with Max. Inhaling a shallow breath, she caught a draft of his masculine scent with just a hint of cologne.

Although she fought its effect on her, she couldn't deny feeling light-headed and entirely too aware of him as a man. "What do you want?" she asked without turning to look at him.

"You haven't had a chance to read my attorney's proposal, so you can't be upset about it. But you haven't said a word since we left the restaurant. Why?"

She stiffened her resolve against his gentle, reasonable voice. "You don't seem to understand. My baby is not for sale."

Three seconds of silence passed before she felt his hand on her arm. "Look at me. You can't really believe that I intend to buy your child."

She reluctantly faced him. "Why should I believe anything else? You've been trying to cram money down my throat since the first time I met you. In exchange for control of my child." She willed herself to keep her voice from wavering. "You said I should find this agreement more palatable. You don't seem to understand that it doesn't matter how much money you pile onto the agreement, I'm not giving up my baby to you."

He stared at her in shock. "Is that what you think? That the new agreement is about money? It isn't. It gives you far more rights than the previous one. Good God, do you really think I'm that much of an ogre?"

Glimpsing his sincerity, she bit her lip in confusion. "I didn't know what else to think. You invite me to a fabulous dinner where you act as if you're actually enjoying my company then slap me with a contract."

"Of course I enjoyed dinner with you. Otherwise, I could have left the contract with one of my staff to give to you. And I wanted you to have my contact numbers. This is my last night in town for a while. I wanted to spend it with you."

Her heart hammered against her rib cage and she shook her head. "You're confusing me. I don't know what you want from me," she said. "Other than to sign your agreement."

He looked into her eyes for a long moment then his gaze traveled to her lips and lingered. He lifted his gaze again to hers and she felt scorched by the desire she saw there.

"You want to know what I want from you?" he asked in a low voice. Then he lowered his head and took her mouth. He slid one of his hands under her jaw and cupped her face as if she were both precious and sensuous. The gesture undid her.

He devoured her mouth in dizzying kisses as he gently rubbed his hands down her neck, massaging her taut muscles.

His kiss turned her body into a bow of tension, eager for him. His massaging fingers gentled her, clouding her mind, making her willing to do whatever he wanted.

His mouth continued to take hers while his fingers drifted across her collarbone and lower to the tops of her breasts. She felt her nipples strain against the cups of her bra. Restlessness and need swelled inside her.

He paused a half beat then slid his fingertips beneath the top of her blouse, brushing them over her sensitized nipples. She gasped in pleasure at the sensation.

He pulled his hands from her breasts and placed them on her shoulders. He pulled his mouth a breath away from hers and it was all she could do to keep from asking him not to stop.

"I want you," he said against her mouth. "I want you in every way you can imagine and probably a few you can't. But now is not the time." He slid one of his hands through her hair. "Promise me that you'll take care of yourself while I'm away. No taking chances. And call me if you need me."

Lilli closed her eyes. She'd felt the power of his desire. What frightened her was the fact that her desire for him matched his. What frightened her even more was the very real possibility that she could need Max in ways *he* would never dream.

Eight

Two and a half weeks later, Lilli dragged herself from her little car up the steps from the mansion's garage. Her back and legs had been aching all day. She felt tired and cranky and, heaven help her, she missed Max. He called frequently, and every time, she felt the tension between them twist a little tighter.

She'd spent more than one night flirting with the forbidden fantasy of Max being the father of her child. Right now, though, all she wanted to focus on was getting a sandwich, taking a shower and going to bed.

Stepping into the foyer, she stopped and drank in a moment of peace and quiet then walked toward the kitchen.

"Surprise!" a chorus of voices called, startling her so much she dropped her water bottle and purse.

Her friends clapped in delight.

"We did it," her best friend Dee crowed. "We surprised you."

"Yes, you did." Lilli felt some of her weariness fade away and smiled. "How did you pull this off?"

"Because we're your brilliant friends, of course," Dee said. "And I think Mallory here has a magic wand. She knew how to deal with the staff, and just wait until you see the cake she brought."

"Cake?" Lilli echoed and gave Mallory a hug as the woman walked toward her. She'd enjoyed a few lunches with Mallory during the last two weeks and Lilli already had a soft spot for the woman. "You shouldn't have."

"It's nothing. I'm just glad to be a part of all this. Now come in and sit down. Let me get you some sherbet punch."

After Lilli opened the gifts for her and the baby, Mallory presented Lilli with a large sheet cake decorated with a baby in a blue buggy inscribed with frosted letters, "Happy Baby, Lilli!" The cake was lit with one candle.

"Make a wish and blow out the candle," Mallory said.

"But it's not my birthday."

"It's your first baby. You can add more candles when you have more babies."

Lilli looked at her in horror. "More?"

"Okay, let's just focus on one, then," Mallory quickly amended. "Make a wish and blow out the candle."

Lilli closed her eyes and wished for a safe and easy delivery and good health for her baby. Secretly, she wished for a father for her child. An image of the man she would choose appeared in her mind. She blinked, pushing aside the thought. Crazy and impossible, she thought. Must be the hormones.

Just after she opened the last gift, the room abruptly turned silent.

"Major hot guy alert," Dee whispered.

Lilli turned to see Max standing in the doorway, a wrapped package in his hand. "Max," she said, stunned. "I thought you were still traveling."

"I just got back thirty minutes ago. You didn't tell me you were having a baby shower," he said in a lightly chastising tone.

Lilli drank in the sight of him. Holding her breath, she wondered if he had looked forward to seeing her again as much as she had looked forward to having him back home. She wondered if he still wanted her the same way he had before.

Dee cleared her throat. "It was a surprise shower," she said to Max. "What's in the box?"

He gave a brief glance to Dee then moved toward Lilli. His gaze dipped to her belly.

"I've gotten bigger," she said, unable to keep herself from smiling.

He gave a half grin. "So you have. And still glowing." He gave her the small but beautifully wrapped box. "Myrtle left a message for me about the shower. I thought you could use this."

Her hands trembled and she wished they would stop. She hadn't seen Max in weeks and she would just like to sit down and talk with him. She managed to open the box and found a gift certificate inside. "One mother's helper of your choice from Personalized Nanny Services for one year."

Mallory nodded in approval. "PNS is the very best."

"A nanny?" Lilli said, staring at Max. "I hadn't planned—"

"Oh, no," Dee said. "You're not turning this one down. She loves it," Dee said to Max. "Perfect gift. Thank you very much." She turned back to Lilli. "If you get tired of having her around, you can send her over to my place. I would love for someone to make peanut butter and jelly sandwiches and chocolate chip cookies for me."

Several of the women moaned in agreement. "Will she do laundry? Will she grocery shop?"

Max met Lilli's gaze. "She'll do whatever Lilli wants her to do."

There was another group moan followed by a collective sigh.

"Can I see you privately for a moment?" he asked.

Lilli felt a combination kick from the baby and a flutter from her heart. "Sure," she said, rising from her seat.

"Ask him about Alex," Mallory whispered.

Tearing her gaze from Max, she glanced at Mallory. "Ask him what about Alex?"

"Where he hangs out after work. I introduced him to my father and haven't seen him since."

"From what Max says, that could be for the best. Alex is supposed to be a major player."

"I'd just like the opportunity to find out for myself," Mallory said.

"Okay. I'll see what I can do," she said, but her mind wasn't on Alex or Mallory. It was dominated by Max.

She followed him into the foyer, noticing subtle changes in his appearance. His hair was just a little longer, more wavy. When he turned to face her, she noticed his eyes looked a bit weary as he studied her.

"It's a nice surprise to see you," she said. "I had no idea you'd be back so soon."

"I'm glad I could make it. Are you okay? Any of Tony's friends hanging around?"

"I'm fine and I haven't seen any of Tony's friends in a long time."

"Good," he said and held her gaze. "I have another event I'm expected to attend tonight, but we need to talk sometime soon. Have you looked over the agreement I left with you?"

She felt a rush of disappointment. "Yes, I have."

"Good," he said again. His gaze seemed to say so much more, but Lilli wondered if she was imagining it. "I won't keep you from your friends."

She felt another twist of disappointment. That was it. No *I'm glad to see you, I want you...* Nothing. She stared, waiting, wanting.

"Good night," he said and turned toward the door.

Lilli continued to stare after him, starting to feel like a fool. Had she misunderstood? "Wait," she said.

He stopped just as he reached the door and turned around. "Yes?"

Her heart raced. Confused, she didn't know what to say. "I...uh..." She groped for something to say. "Mallory asked me to ask you about Alex."

"Alex Megalos?" he said with a frown, walking back toward her.

"Yes. I think she'd like to get to know him better. She

was wondering where he usually hangs out after work," she said, suddenly feeling like a middle schooler.

He shook his head. "I have no idea."

She gave a slow nod. "Okay" she said. "I'll tell her."

He shrugged. "I can probably find out something from my assistant."

"Thanks." She hesitated a half beat, hating the awkwardness between them. "Are you okay?"

"Yeah. Just tired and harassed. I've been on longer trips, but this one felt like it went on forever."

She nodded again. "Yeah, it did—" She broke off before she added *for me, too.* Feeling her cheeks heat from his knowing gaze, she cleared her throat. "Why do you think it felt so long?"

"I think you know," he said and moved closer to her.

"You want me to sign the agreement about the baby," she said in a husky voice.

"That's part of it." He lowered his head. He inhaled sharply and closed his eyes then stepped back. God help him, if he started kissing her, he wouldn't stop. Being away from her hadn't cleared his perspective or dampened his desire for her. And Max knew there wasn't a damn thing he could do about wanting her at the moment. He'd missed the sound of her laughter and knowing she would be there at home for the end of the day.

Maybe it was a good thing he had to attend the charity fund-raiser tonight after all. Being with Lilli was a constant reminder of what he couldn't have.

"I should go," he said in a low voice. "We can talk more on Friday. Tomorrow will be a busy day."

"Okay, thank you for the gift."

"You're welcome," he said and held her gaze for a long moment before he left.

The following evening, Lilli flipped through the newspaper as she put up her feet at the end of a long day. She glanced at the bad news on the front page, skipped the Sports section and stopped at the Lifestyle section. The front page featured photos of a charity function sponsored by Max's company. In one of the photos, Kiki stood next to Max, her arm looped through his. He didn't look as if he were suffering at all.

A surge of something dark twisted through her and when she realized what it was, she felt more stupid than ever. She was jealous. Maybe it was hormones. Oh Lord, she hoped so. Because if it were hormones then at some point, when her hormones straightened out again, the crazy longing would go away.

Restless after reading the article, she took a long bath and listened to soothing music. She sipped herbal tea to calm herself and tried not to think about that photo of Max with Kiki.

She slept horribly, unable to get comfortable. Giving up on sleep, she rose earlier than usual. When she got out of bed, she felt exhausted and noticed her abdomen tightening. As she prepared for work, the sensation didn't go away. Were these contractions?

Although she had a few weeks left before her due date she called her doctor's office. The doctor on call asked a few questions then, erring on the cautious side, instructed her to go to the hospital.

Lilli grabbed her purse and went downstairs. Max

stood poised to leave. He met her gaze. "Good morning. How are you?"

Lilli burst into tears.

Alarmed by her response, Max dropped his briefcase and immediately took her in her arms. "What is it? What's wrong?"

She choked back a sob. "I may be in labor. My doctor told me to go to the hospital. Max, this is happening too fast." Her blue eyes filled with tears of desperation. "I'm not ready."

"Of course you are," he said firmly even though his own gut was clenching in apprehension. "I'll drive you to the hospital and—"

"Are you sure that's what you want—?"

"Of course I'm sure," he said, appalled that she would expect anything less of him. "We'll take the town car." He ushered her to the garage. "I'll drive. You can sit in the backseat and stretch out."

His own heart hammering in his chest, Max helped her into the car and sped to the hospital. He shot a glance at Lilli in the rearview mirror and the expression of fear on her face tore at him. "You're going to be okay. The baby is going to be okay."

"Do you really believe that?"

He nodded. "Yes, I do." He had to believe it.

Pulling the car to a stop outside the emergency room door, he helped Lilli inside. An admission clerk took her information and Lilli was whisked away. Just before she disappeared behind the double doors, she looked back at Max. "Are you leaving?"

He shook his head. "I'll be right back after I park the car." Returning to the hospital, he was consumed with concern for Lilli and the baby. He would get the finest doctors in Las Vegas to care for her. He would do whatever it took to keep Lilli and the baby safe and healthy.

He strode toward the emergency room double doors, making a mental list. A woman stepped in front of him. "Excuse me, sir. You're not allowed inside unless you're a member of a patient's family."

Frustration ripped through him. He needed to take care of Lilli, but it wasn't his official duty or his official right. At that moment, he made a life-altering decision. He knew there would be no going back. But never again would he worry about being barred from taking care of Lilli or the baby. He would make her his wife. That way, taking care of her and the baby would always be his right. "I'm the baby's father," he told the woman, and she allowed him to pass.

Two and a half hours later, a mortified Lilli left the hospital with Max. "I'm so sorry," she said, shooting a wincing glance at him. His hair was ruffled from plowing his fingers through it and his tie hung loose from his collar. He was more gorgeous than ever and she felt like a lunatic. "I should have realized it was false labor."

"Like the doctor said, it's an easy mistake to make. This is your first pregnancy."

"Maybe," she said. "But now you've lost half a day of work because of my mistake."

"A half day of work is nothing to make sure you and the baby are safe," he said, his words barely softening the harsh sound of his voice as he drove them home. "Stop apologizing."

She bit her lip and looked out the window then back at him. "Are you sure you're not angry?"

"I'm not angry, but I am concerned. This underscores the need for you to provide for the baby if something, God forbid, should happen to you," he said and swore under his breath.

"I know," she said glumly. She knew she couldn't dodge it any longer. "I'm going to change my will today so that you'll be the baby's guardian."

He narrowed his eyes at her words. "That's a good start, but we may need to take that further."

Her chest tightened. He was talking about the agreement he wanted her to sign. Even though she understood the money in the agreement was designated for support, she still found it distasteful. "I don't want your money and I don't want to sign the agreement. It just feels totally wrong to me."

"I'm not talking about that agreement," he said, pulling the car into a bank parking lot and cutting the engine.

Lilli looked at him in surprise. "Then what?"

"I've been thinking. How do you feel about the baby's last name being De Luca?"

She frowned in confusion. "I thought I was going to try not to draw attention to the fact that Tony was his father. For safety's sake. That's the reason I'll be moving away."

"What if you didn't move away?" he asked, his gaze searching hers. "What if your last name became De Luca, too?"

More confused than ever, she shook her head. "How could that happen?"

"If you named me the father of—" he paused "—your child. And married me."

She gaped at him, feeling as if someone had turned the whole world upside down. "Married you? But you don't love me."

"Starting out in love isn't the best predictor of success in marriage."

Her head was whirling. "I don't understand. You don't want to get married. You're pretty cynical about marriage."

"I want to provide a good life for the baby. I feel responsible for him. For you," he said as if he didn't totally understand his own feelings.

"I don't think that's a good basis for a marriage."

"There's a lot worse," he said.

Her chest tightened. "I don't want to feel like a responsibility. Like a burden. And I don't want the baby to ever feel that way."

"It *wouldn't* be that way. I think you and I could make this work." He slid his hand under her jaw. "And there's the fact that I want you. And you want me," he said, his tone intimate.

"I wondered if maybe that had changed."

He slowly shook his head.

Her heart skipped over itself. "What about when that does change?"

"How do you know it will?" he asked, his dark eyes holding hers.

Lilli felt herself sinking into a delicious, forbidden pool of hope. "I don't know."

He caressed her jaw. "I think you know that you and I would be good together. In a lot of ways."

True. But that didn't mean they should get married. Lilli tore away her gaze to clear her head. If she put the baby's needs in front of hers, what would she do? She felt an immediate smack from her conscience. Who was she fooling? It wasn't as if being with Max De Luca would present a hardship for her. But this was a huge decision. Huge enough that she wanted to make it with a clear head.

"Could you give me some time to think this over?"

He met her gaze and nodded. "Sure." He paused a half beat. "Think about it. You'll realize it's best for everyone."

She felt a sliver of relief. She'd bought herself a little time.

"Do you have any questions you'd like to ask me?" he said, as if he sensed what was going on inside her.

She closed her eyes so she wouldn't be affected by his presence, but she still sensed him, still smelled the faintest scent of his sexy cologne. "If you raised the baby, would you blow bubbles with him?"

He didn't even pause. "Yes."

"Will you read him books at night? You can let the nanny do it every now and then, but you need to do it most nights."

"Yes," he said.

"Will you tell him he's wonderful?"

"Yes."

"Will you hold him when he cries?"

"Yes. And I'll hold you, too, Lilli, whether you're crying or not."

And Lilli felt her heart tumble a little farther away from good sense and sanity.

Nine

"I like it," Max said to Alex during a one-on-one meeting in his office. "At first glance, when you say West Virginia, I would think the local economy wouldn't be able to support this kind of luxury resort."

Alex tapped his pen on his outline. "Because it's close to Washington, D.C., there's great transportation access. D.C. residents will be rushing there every weekend."

"The sticking point with the board will be the midweek challenge," Max said. "Who wants to go to West Virginia in the middle of the week?"

"We can hold meetings and conferences. Plus, if we do it right, this place will have a spa, golf course, special events and all kinds of luxury amenities that will draw people year-round."

"Like I said, I like it. You've got my—" His intercom

beeped, interrupting him. Surprised because he'd told his assistant no interruptions during his meeting, he picked up his phone. "Yes."

"I'm terribly sorry to interrupt you, Mr. De Luca, but security downstairs has called and they said a very pregnant woman insists on seeing you."

There was only one very pregnant woman in his life. Immediately concerned, he frowned. "Lilli," he said. "Is she okay?"

His assistant, Grace, made a sound between a cough and swallowed laughter. "She sounds quite healthy, sir. Just very determined to see you. Security was unsure what to do with her."

He nodded, feeling a twinge of amusement at the notion of the beefy guys downstairs trying to handle a demanding pregnant woman. "Send her up immediately."

Alex stood, lifting his eyebrow. "Does this mean our meeting is over?"

"For now," Max said. "Let's set up a time to discuss a strategy for approaching the board about this."

Alex extended his hand. "Sounds great." He gathered his report and headed for the office door. Just as he reached for it, the door flung open and Lilli burst inside. Her cheeks bright red, she carried a large rectangular plastic food container.

"Good grief," she said. "Do you train your security to suspect that every pregnant woman is a nut or did I just get lucky today?"

Max chuckled under his breath and moved toward her to take the container. "It won't happen again. Here, let me help—"

"No," Alex said and grabbed the container before

Max could. "Allow me and let me say you look gorgeous as ever."

Flirting again, Max thought with more than a pinch of irritation. Did the man ever stop?

"I look like a blond beach ball," she told Alex. "But thanks for the effort. Would you do me a favor and call a few of the assistants into the office?"

Max frowned. "What—"

"Sure," Alex said and set the container down on a table.

Lilli smiled nervously as she met Max's gaze. "This won't take but a few minutes. Then you can get back to whatever you were doing."

Max shook his head. "But what is *this?*"

She gnawed her lip. "Just a little something."

Her expression made him uneasy. *What the…*

Alex reappeared in the doorway with several members of the staff, their faces filled with curiosity. "Ready for service," Alex said.

"Thank you," Lilli said and went to the table where the plastic container sat. "I just need to borrow your voices for two minutes. Today is Max's birthday, so I was hoping you would join with me in singing 'Happy Birthday.'" She whipped off the top of the container to reveal a collection of frosted cupcakes decorated with sprinkles. "Sorry you can't blow out the candles," she said with a moue. "Security took my matches. Okay, let's go."

Max stood in stunned disbelief as she led the small group in song. Alex laughed the entire way through the tune.

When they finished, Lilli shot him a wary glance and a tentative smile. "Happy Birthday, Max."

Max met her gaze and felt his heart swell to at least twice its normal size. He hadn't celebrated his birthday in years. It was just another day to him. "How did you know?"

"That's a secret," she said. "But I didn't know your favorite kind of cupcake, so I made a variety. Vanilla with chocolate frosting, chocolate with chocolate frosting, chocolate with vanilla—"

Alex extended his hand into the container. "I'll take the chocolate with—"

Lilli lightly swatted his hand. "It's Max's birthday. He gets to choose first." She glanced at Max. "What kind do you want?"

I want Lilli with Lilli frosting, he thought and cleared his throat. "Chocolate and chocolate," he said and nodded toward the staff. "Go ahead, help yourself."

Each of his employees took their treats and wished him a happy birthday before they left. Alex lingered an extra moment. "For your information, my birthday is November 16 and I love cupcakes."

Max felt a surge of possessiveness. "Call a bakery," he growled.

Alex laughed and shook his head. "You're a damn lucky man, Max. Happy birthday," he said and left the office.

Closing the door, Max turned toward Lilli, who was sitting in a chair across from his desk, biting off the top of a chocolate cupcake. He walked to the chair across from hers and sat down. "What possessed you to do this?"

"You're not angry, are you?"

He shook his head. "Off guard. Surprised." And a

few other things he didn't want to name. "You didn't answer my question."

She licked her lips and he wished he could do it for her. "It occurred to me that you may not have celebrated your birthday very much when you were in boarding school. That was a bad habit to start at such a young age," she said in a chastising voice that made his lips twitch. "So I thought I should get you back on track."

"Why?"

She met his gaze and he saw a flash of deep emotion shimmer in her eyes. Max could identify things that held a high value and what he saw in her gaze was more precious than all the gems in the exclusive jewelry store down the street.

"I think you are an amazing man. So the day you were born should be celebrated."

Her simple explanation held no false flattery. He heard the sincerity in her voice, saw it on her face, and it was the most seductive thing anyone had ever said to him. Lilli, pregnant or not, made him hungry for more of her. Standing, he took her hand and pulled her close. "Marry me."

He saw the desire and fear collide in her gaze. "It's right," he said. "For all of us."

"How can you be so sure?" she whispered.

"Be honest, Lilli. Underneath it all, you want it, too."

She closed her eyes for a long moment and he could feel her heart hammering against him. She took a small shallow breath and opened her eyes. "Yes, I'll marry you."

Max made the arrangements so quickly Lilli barely had time to catch her breath, let alone her sanity. Three days before he'd scheduled a private wedding ceremony with a judge who was a friend, he and Lilli shared late-night conversation on the patio.

"I picked this up today. Let me know if you like it." He casually slid a box across the table toward her.

Curious, she opened the box. Shocked at the diamond ring winking back at her from the velvet fold of the box, she choked on the water she had just swallowed.

Max patted her on her back. "Are you okay?"

She coughed, tears coming to her eyes, then waved her hand. "Yes." She coughed again and shook her head. "I didn't expect an engagement ring."

"Of course I'd get you a ring."

She stared at the ring, almost afraid to touch it. "The stone is huge."

He was silent for a moment then laughed under his breath. "You're complaining about a large diamond?" he asked in disbelief. "That's a first."

"I'm not complaining," she quickly said. "I just didn't expect it. When I think about us getting married, I haven't thought about diamonds, or even rings."

"Then what have you been thinking?"

She bit her lip, reluctant to reveal the fact that she was wondering if it was such a smart thing to marry Max. She shrugged, not meeting his gaze. "More about how all three of us will adjust to family life." She hesitated. "Wondering how you and I will adjust to being married."

"I think we've demonstrated we won't have any problems," he said, sliding his hands over her neck, making her feel as if her collarbone was a sensual hot spot for the first time in her life. It amazed her that he could make her feel so sexy with just a touch.

She closed her eyes for a second. "In bed," she said in a voice that sounded small to her own ears.

His hands stilled. "What do you mean?"

"Well, it may be a rumor," she said, trying to keep a light tone, "but I hear married couples tend to spend a lot more time out of bed than in bed."

"Damn," he said. "So you may actually have to join me for dinner most nights and we'll have to do things together." He walked around her chair and bent down over her, meeting her gaze. "Sounds rough, but I think I can do it. What about you?"

She smiled reluctantly. "Probably," she said.

"But you're still bothered."

"You have to admit this isn't the typical romantic wedding. We don't even have a honeymoon planned. For that matter, how did you find out my ring size? I didn't know yours."

"While you were sleeping," he said and added, "in your bed. Say what you want, but sex between us will take away a lot of your doubts."

The notion filled her with a combination of anticipation and anxiety. Would she have any leftover reactions to that last experience with Tony? So far, Max seemed to push everything from her mind, but him.

"So try on the ring. Maybe you'll like it better on your finger," he said casually and plucked the ring from the box and slid it onto her hand.

It fit perfectly. It sparkled like a bright star. "It's beautiful," she said and wiggled her finger. "Does it come with a crane?"

* * *

Lilli woke up the next morning full of anticipation and hope. She was just two weeks from her delivery date, two weeks from when she would hold her baby in her arms. The excitement inside her seemed to build with each passing hour. And she was getting married in just two days.

Glancing at the diamond ring that felt heavy on her finger, she fought the slivers of trepidation that stabbed at her. She felt as if she were on the precipice of falling completely in love with Max. What if she spent a lifetime waiting for him to love her and he never did? What if he fell out of lust with her and left her? Or worse yet, what if he never allowed himself to love her, but stayed with her even though he was miserable?

Lilli shook off the thoughts. She had every reason to hope everything would work out well. The sun shining brightly outside seemed to invite her to take a short stroll along the driveway that led to Max's home and then down the block. The fresh air cleared her head and the sunshine gave her a boost of optimism.

Returning from the stroll, she spotted a car parked in the driveway. It was a Jaguar, so she knew it didn't belong to any of her friends. Mallory drove a BMW.

Curious, Lilli entered the house and overheard a woman talking with Ada, the assistant housekeeper. "I left some of my things here several months ago. I just want to pick them up."

Recognizing the woman's voice as Kiki, Lilli stiffened. She turned away to quietly climb the stairs. She didn't want a confrontation with the woman.

"Oh, look, the sweet mother-to-be. Don't run off. It's been too long. We should visit for a little bit," Kiki said.

Lilli reluctantly stopped and turned. "Hello, Kiki."

Looking as svelte and perfect as ever in a fashionable black-and-white sheath, Kiki moved past the housekeeper. "Omigoodness, you look like you're ready to go any minute. Positively glowing," she said. "Babies are pure magic, aren't they? They make the impossible seem possible. I mean, look at how your life has changed."

"I just want what's best for my baby," Lilli said.

"Of course you do," Kiki said. "I was surprised that I never heard back from you after we met at the charity auction. Did you lose my card?"

"Yes. I think I did," Lilli said.

"You seem like a smart woman. I thought you might take me up on my offer. But rumor has it you're placing your bets somewhere else."

Lilli and Max hadn't announced their decision to marry, so Lilli refused to confirm or deny any implications. "I should go upstairs. I have a doctor's appointment this afternoon."

"You can at least show me the nursery," the other woman said with a fake pout. "I'll go upstairs with you. I need to pick up a few things I left here."

Ada stepped forward. "I'm sorry, Miss Lane, but I'm not sure Mr. De Luca would be comfortable with you going through his private quarters. If you'll wait, I can call him."

Alarm shot across Kiki's face. "That's not necessary. I'll give him a call myself. It's just so awkward to ask a man to return lingerie," she whispered. "But it was

La Perla. One of my favorites," she said with a sigh. "One of his, too, as I recall. Oh, well. Lovely seeing you. You can still give me a call if you change your mind about anything, but don't wait too long."

Watching Kiki leave, Lilli told herself not to trust the woman. Kiki was clearly desperate and would do anything to get Max back. She shouldn't let the woman generate any doubts about her decision to marry Max. Her rebellious mind, though, hung on to Kiki's description of lingerie. She remembered the photo of Max and Kiki in the newspaper just recently. Perhaps she had underestimated their relationship.

Ten

Lilli's day went from bad to worse when Max presented her with a prenup agreement late that evening. With the exception of the clause that gave Max custody of the baby if they separated and she was determined to be an unsuitable influence, the prenup was very generous. Financially, anyway.

Lilli slept on the agreement, not wanting to overreact. The day before she was scheduled to marry Max, she rose and looked at her large diamond engagement ring and took it off. In a calm voice completely at odds with the turmoil raging inside her, she called Max and asked him to meet her at the house as soon as possible. He arrived an hour later.

"I'm not going to sign it the way it is," she told him and set the ring and the agreement on the patio table in front of him.

His mouth twisted as he glanced down at the ring and the unsigned agreement. "You want more?"

"No. I'm not going to leave the judgment of my ability to parent up to a court that could be bought or skewed by your influence.

He met her gaze. "It's not money?" He paused a half beat. "Are you sure this isn't about Kiki's offer?"

She couldn't hide her surprise.

He walked toward her, dressed in a suit that emphasized his height, power and attractiveness. "You didn't know that I knew? The housekeeper told me she came to visit. She seemed to imply she'd made some prior offer and I can only imagine it was meant as a buy off."

"Apparently she came by to collect some expensive lingerie she'd left," she said, refusing to give in to his effect on her.

"That was a lie. I've never invited Kiki to stay in my bedroom. Why didn't you tell me that she was trying to buy you off?"

Trying to digest the fact that Kiki's La Perla lingerie had never made it into Max's bedroom, she fought another wave of confusion. "I didn't know if you were still in love with her."

He lifted a dark eyebrow. "I've told you my opinion of romantic love. It doesn't last."

His words cut, but she didn't want to show it. "I didn't feel comfortable telling you. I felt like I should handle her on my own."

"Or maybe you were holding out for a better offer than I gave you in the prenup."

Lilli felt a spurt of anger. "If you really believe that, then we definitely shouldn't get married."

Max met her gaze. "What do you want?"

"Strike the clause about my being an unfit mother."

"Done," he said. "If Kiki contacts you again, you must tell me."

She paused a brief second. "I will," she said. "Are you sure you don't have some leftover feelings for her? She is more beautiful than I am," she impulsively blurted.

He stared at her in surprise. "I disagree."

Perhaps she should have felt affirmed. Instead her insecurities seemed to bubble up from deep inside her. "She knows how to operate in your crowd."

"She's manipulative as hell. Do you really think I want to be married to a woman like that?"

Lilli realized she needed to get her questions answered, or she would be victimized by her doubts forever. She took a deep breath and braced herself. "I think I need to know your stand on fidelity in our marriage. Since this isn't a love match, do you consider yourself free to have—" she forced the word from her tight throat "—affairs?"

His face turned to stone. "Absolutely not. Once we marry, you will be the only woman in my bed and I will be the only man in yours. I take my vows very seriously. If you can't make the same kind of commitment, then you'd better tell me, because I'll expect the same complete fidelity that I'll give."

His fierce response took her breath away. Perhaps she should have known. A man like Max wouldn't make a marital commitment easily and he would not only give, but expect to receive complete loyalty from his wife.

"I can't even imagine being unfaithful to you." What woman would want to?

His expression gentled a millimeter and he picked up the ring. "Then you won't need to take this off ever again," he said and slid the diamond on her finger. "I'm giving you and your baby my name and adopting him. Our marriage will work. I've decided it will," he said. "Understand?"

Even though there was no judge or minister present, at that very moment, she felt as if they were exchanging vows. He was making a promise he would keep and she was doing the same. "Yes, I understand."

The following day, Max arranged for the prenup to be changed. Lilli signed it and put on a cream-colored silk dress with a voluminous amount of material beneath the Empire waist that allowed for her advanced pregnancy. Her stomach jumped with butterflies. She told herself to put aside her fears, but in the back of her mind, although she feared that Max would take his commitments seriously, she knew he might never grow to love her.

A dull nagging ache in her back and those dancing butterflies continued to distract her, but she was determined to be as beautiful a bride for Max as possible. She clipped her hair back in a half up-do and added a fresh pink rose above the clip.

The ceremony was truly private with only the judge and Jim Gregory and Myrtle serving as witnesses. The weather was beautiful as usual and she and Max said their vows on the patio where they'd shared dinner the first night she'd stayed at his house. There was something right about that, something right in knowing they would share many more dinners on the very spot where they'd made lifelong promises to each other.

She told herself not to worry, but her hands were cold with nerves as Max held them.

"I pronounce you husband and wife," the judge said. "You may now kiss the bride."

Max drew her against him and slowly covered her mouth with his in a kiss that echoed the promises they'd just made.

Afterward, they shared a private lunch on the patio, just the two of them and toasted their marriage with sparkling water and orange juice.

"To us and our life together," he said.

She nodded. "To us." She took a long sip then another, her mind reeling with what she'd just done. She'd just married a man who cared for her, but didn't love her.

"You're very quiet."

She nodded again. "It's a big day. A lot to think about," she managed.

"You can relax now. We'll have more to think about after the baby is born. After your recovery."

He was talking about sex, she realized. There would be no night of passion tonight. One more way this day was odd. "The doctor told me that's usually four to six weeks," she said, feeling her cheeks heat.

He covered her hand with his and her heart took an extra beat. "Where would you like to honeymoon? We can go anywhere you like."

"I haven't even thought about it," she said.

He stroked the inside of her wrist. "You should. By the time we go on ours, we will have both earned it. Yes?"

Her chest tightened at the sight of his hand caressing hers. "I guess you're right."

"So tell me where you'd like to go," he said.

She fought a sudden shyness. "Somewhere with a beach?"

He nodded. "The company has resorts all over, but I also have access to some private spots. We would have staff, but no one else around to intrude."

"That sounds nice," she managed. "I wish it could be sooner."

He gave a rough chuckle. "You and me both, sweetheart." He sighed and lifted her hand to his lips. "The anticipation will either kill us or make the experience explosive."

"Or both," she said.

He laughed again. "We should eat."

Her stomach still doing dips and turns, Lilli picked at the meal. Her back was hurting like the dickens. She shifted uncomfortably in her chair.

"Is something bothering you?" he asked.

"I hate to complain, but may back hurts and—" She sighed. "I don't know. Maybe it's the excitement, but I don't feel very hungry at all." She felt a sudden telltale surge of liquid and stared at him startled.

"What is it?"

"I think I'm in labor. Real labor, this time," she added. "I think my water broke."

Her announcement galvanized Max into action. The wide-eyed expression of fear on her face clutched at his gut. He immediately told his driver to start the car and grabbed the suitcase Lilli had packed after her experience with false labor.

Hustling her into the backseat of the town car within three minutes, he slid in beside her and made the call to Lilli's doctor. He got the answering service since it was a Saturday. "Lilli McCall is going to the hospital right now. I don't care who is on call. I expect to see Dr. Roberts at the hospital. My name is Max De Luca. I'm her husband."

He disconnected his cell and turned to find Lilli staring at him. "That's not how on call works. If you deliver on a weekend, you don't necessarily get your specific doctor."

"Not my wife," Max said.

She blinked and shook her head. "I'm not used to the idea of being your wife."

"I'll help you," he said in a dry tone. "Do you need to lie down?"

She shook her head and winced. "I'm too uncomfortable to lie down. The contractions are much stronger than they were with the false labor." Fear glinted in her eyes. She bit her lip and reached for his hand. "Max, I'm going to have a baby. I want him to be okay."

He pulled her into his arms. "He will be."

Within two hours of arriving at the hospital, Max could tell that Lilli was suffering. Her body tensed in pain. With each contraction, she stared straight ahead and did the breathing she'd learned in her prepared childbirth classes.

Her fingernails dug into his hands during the height of the pains. The sight of her dealing with such pain horrified him. He'd never known modern childbirth was so barbaric. A newfound respect for Lilli grew inside him.

"I think I want an epidural," she announced breathlessly after what looked like an excruciating contraction.

Relieved, he immediately called the nurse and demanded the medication.

After what felt like forever, the obstetrician checked Lilli's progress and shook her head. "Too late for an epidural."

Outraged, Max stood. "What do you mean too late? She's in pain. She needs medication and she'll damn well have it."

The doctor shot him a long-suffering look. "Mr. De Luca, the baby is crowning. Your wife is ready to deliver."

His wife. His son. The knowledge hit him like a ton of bricks. Within thirty minutes and what had to be a thousand pushes, the baby, a small squalling mass of humanity, made his entrance into the world.

The baby cried. Lilli cried. Max swore. Seconds later, Lilli held her son, *their son,* in her arms. "You're here," she said to the baby, touching each of his tiny fingers and toes. "You're really here." She looked up at Max, her eyes filled with tears. "Look. We did it."

Max shook his head. "You did all the work. I didn't do anything."

"Yes, you did," she said. "You were here for me. For him. You watched over me. I want you to hold him."

Max gingerly took the baby in his arms and looked down into the infant's face. "Nice hat," he said of the tiny blue cap the nurse had placed on his head. "He's—" Max paused. "He's pink."

Lilli laughed. "That's a good thing. It means he's healthy."

Max gave a slow nod and studied the baby. "Little hands. Soft skin. What are we going to call you? There's got to be something better than butter bean." He glanced at Lilli. "Do you know what you're going to name him?"

Lilli felt something inside her quiver and shake. Watching Max hold her son made her bones shift.

The baby waved a hand toward Max and he looked surprised. "Hi there," he said in a low voice. "Looks like your mom did an excellent job."

Lilli bit her lip as she felt another stabbing urge to cry.

Max returned the baby to her arms. "He looks perfect."

"Thank you," she said, blinking against threatening tears. "I think I want to name him David."

He nodded. "Excellent choice. Solid. Not trendy or ambiguous. He won't have to beat anyone up on the playground to defend his name."

She took a careful breath and watched his face. "And for his middle name, I was thinking of Maximillian."

He stared at her for a long moment in silence.

The longer the silence lasted the more nervous Lilli felt. Even the baby squirmed in her arms. "If it's okay with you," she added. "If you don't want that, then—"

"No, I do. I'm just surprised. I wondered if you would name him after Tony."

"You have already been more of a father to him than your brother could have ever been."

The next month passed in a blur of bottles, diapers and middle-of-the night interruptions. Lilli fell head over heels in love with her son, but when she showed the first sign of weariness, Max insisted she choose a mother's helper. Although she fought the idea at first, Lilli couldn't deny that getting a full night of rest made her feel like a new woman.

Since the baby had been born, Max continued to sleep in his room and she slept in hers. It seemed as though he was at work all the time. At first, she'd been too tired to focus on it, but now she was starting to get nervous. The more she thought about it, the more she realized he'd barely touched her during the last few weeks. Had his desire for her waned? Now that she was a mother, had she somehow become less sexy? The notion tortured her.

Unable to stand their polite distance any longer, she waited up for him one night. She sat in the dark, drinking her first glass of wine in ten months, rehearsing her conversation. She'd carefully chosen a silky camisole top and flowing blue skirt that made her feel feminine. She'd even put on a little makeup to perk up her features.

Sitting in the den, she turned on the lamp beside her and flipped through an architectural magazine. With only the soft glow from a lamp to keep her company, nine o'clock passed, then nine-thirty, then ten o'clock, but she was determined to wait for him.

It was close to ten-thirty when Max dragged himself through the door from the garage. He rubbed the back of his tense neck. These late hours were going to kill him.

But it wasn't as if he had any choice. He sure as hell couldn't hang around the house. Now that Lilli had delivered the baby, he had no visual reminder of why he couldn't take her to bed.

He would be an inconsiderate bastard to take her before she was fully recovered. That left him with the option of playing an exhausting game of keep-away. Sighing, he tugged his tie loose the rest of the way and unbuttoned the top few buttons on his shirt. Out of the corner of his eye, he noticed a light from the den. Curious, he walked into the room and found Lilli sleeping, her arms wrapped around a large throw pillow.

A stab of hunger twisted his gut. Lord help him, he was jealous of that damn pillow. He wanted her wrapped around him.

Her skirt had risen above her knees, revealing her shapely legs, and the material clung with sensual ease over her feminine curves. A strand of her hair had fallen over her cheek.

She was so inviting it was all he could do not to carry her up to his room right then. Instead, he tempted his self-control by lifting his fingers to touch that silky strand of hair and slide it away from her cheek.

Her lashes fluttered and she gradually opened her eyes. Her sexy, dazed expression lingered a few seconds before it cleared. "Hi," she said with a trace of self-consciousness and pushed herself up from the pillow. "I must have fallen asleep."

He nodded. "You're dressed up. Did you have plans?"

Her cheeks warmed with color and she pushed her hair from her face. "I was waiting up for you."

Surprise kicked through him and he sat down beside her. "Why? Is there a problem with David? Is the mother's helper still working out?"

"No problem with Maria. She's perfect. David is

perfect," she added and paused. "Although I would like you to spend a little more time with him."

He nodded. "I can do that. I just wanted to give the two of you time to get adjusted first."

She bit her lip and met his gaze. "Is that why you've also been avoiding me?"

"Caring for an infant is demanding, plus you need to recover from the birth."

She continued to look at him as if she were waiting for him to add something more. When he didn't, she sighed. "You're sure that's all there is?"

He frowned. "What else would there be?"

She bit her lip again. "I wasn't sure if perhaps you were having second thoughts about getting married. If, maybe..." She faltered then lifted her chin as if she were determined to go on. "If you didn't want me anymore."

Shock zinged through him like an electrical current. "You're joking, aren't you?"

"No, I'm not," she said, her voice husky. "You haven't touched me since the baby was born. You're always gone. What else should I think?"

"That I don't want to ravage you like some sex-starved bastard," he told her. "That I don't trust myself in the same room with you for more than five minutes."

Her eyes widened in surprise. "But you seem so detached."

"Lilli," he said, primitive need rising inside him, "I've been waiting to take you for a long time. I'm not sure how gentle I'll be."

Her gaze fixed on his, she licked her lips, sending another current of desire lashing through him. "So you really do still want me."

"Yes," he said in a voice he knew sounded rough around the edges.

Giving a sigh of relief, she moved closer to him and lifted her hand to his jaw. At her soft touch, he clenched his jaw. She rubbed her thumb over his mouth and he covered her hand with his. He slid that daring thumb of hers inside his mouth and gently bit the delicate pad.

He heard her soft intake of breath and put her hand away from him. "Don't push me."

She met his gaze for a long moment. "I go to the doctor on Friday."

"For what?"

"My follow-up visit. It's likely that I'll be released for all normal activity."

Wanting to remove any confusion on his part, he asked, "What does that include?"

"Everything," she said and lowered her voice to a whisper. "Including sex."

Max immediately felt himself grow hard with arousal. *Friday. Two days.* "I'd like you to give me a call after your visit," he told her.

"I know you told me not to push you," she said, moving closer to him again. "But can I kiss you?"

Max knew a cold shower was in his future tonight. "Come here," he said and pulled her across his lap.

She slid her fingers through his hair and gently pressed her mouth against his.

Desire raged through him. Her lips were petal soft, her body deliciously pliant. He wanted to touch her and take her every way a man could take a woman. When she dipped her tongue into his mouth, he thought he would explode.

A simple kiss, he thought, and he felt like a raving lunatic. Her breasts pressed against his chest and he wanted to tear off her dress, rip off his shirt and feel her nipples against his skin. He rubbed his hands over the side of her breasts and felt her shiver. With that small encouragement, he slid his fingers over her nipple and felt the stiff peak through her silky top.

Making a restless movement against him, she slid her tongue deeper into his mouth. His temperature rose and he began to sweat. She was so sweet, so tempting.

He knew he should stop, but he couldn't resist going a little further. He eased his hands under her top, surprised to find that she wore no bra. He wouldn't have thought he could get any hotter, especially knowing they couldn't finish tonight, but he did.

Taking control of the kiss, he slid one of his hands over her breast and swallowed her delicious gasp of arousal. "Do you want me to stop?" he asked against her mouth.

She shook her head. "It's been so—" She broke off and shuddered when he brushed her nipple with his thumb. "I never thought I could feel this way again."

"You couldn't have forgotten completely," he said in disbelief, nibbling at her bottom lip as he continued to caress her breast.

"I think I must have," she said and reached for the buttons to his shirt.

Not trusting himself any further, he covered her hand with his. "Later," he said. "Later."

Looking at her smoky eyes and lips puffy from their kisses, Max groaned. It took every ounce of fortitude not to take her mouth again.

She shook her head in disbelief. "After that last terrible time with Tony, I was sure I'd never want to be with a man again."

Max's arousal abruptly cooled. "You've mentioned this before. What was terrible about it?"

She glanced away. "I don't like to think about it. I don't like to talk about it. It's just that everything is so different with you."

"What happened with Tony?" he demanded.

She sighed. "He's your brother. There's no need to taint his memory any more than it already is."

"Lilli," he said. "I knew Tony had problems, most of which he made for himself. Heavy drinking, drugs, illegal deals. We weren't close. I'm your husband, now. You can't keep this kind of thing from me."

She twisted her fingers together. "I had already broken up with him once," she said in a low voice. "He promised things would be different, so I went out with him again. We went to a club and things were getting wild. I told him I wanted to leave. He begged me to stay for just one more dance, just one more drink. I just ordered soda."

Max got a dark feeling about what had happened with Lilli. "And?"

She bit her lip. "He put something in my drink. I woke up hours later and he had—"

Max felt a rush of nausea. He couldn't believe his own brother would do such a thing. "He took advantage of you without your consent?"

She closed her eyes and nodded. "I had told him I wasn't ready to be intimate again, that we had to take it slow. After that night, I broke things off permanently.

I realized I would never be able to trust a man who would do that to me."

Max's mouth filled with bitterness. He was so furious he wanted to break something. The strength of it caught him off guard.

Taking a mind-clearing breath, he reined in his anger and focused on Lilli. "I'm sorry he did that to you. I tried to steer Tony in the right direction, but he refused to listen." He slid his hand under her chin and guided her so she met his gaze. "I promise you I would never do something like that to you."

Her eyes were shiny with unshed tears. "You don't have to promise. I already know."

Max realized that Lilli would need to be seduced. It had been a long time for her and it would be his pleasure to remind her in every way that she was a desirable woman and that the passion between them would take her to a level she'd never experienced before. And as her husband, he would make damn sure no one ever hurt her again.

Eleven

Lilli envisioned that once she told Max the doctor had released her, the first thing Max would do was take her to bed. Instead he took her to dinner at the top of the premier Megalos-De Luca property in Vegas. With the baby in Maria's care, Lilli was free to enjoy herself.

Steeped in luxury, the resort featured an outdoor restaurant with a prized breathtaking view of the strip and beyond. "This is beautiful," she said for the umpteenth time after they enjoyed a delicious meal. "You really surprised me."

"I thought we both deserved a night out," he said, a cryptic grin crossing his face. "Think of this as the wedding dinner we skipped."

"For David," she said, laughing. Her heart skipped a beat at the sight of Max seated across the table from her. Dressed in a black suit, black shirt and tie, he looked dark and devastating. Tension and anticipation hummed between them. Every time Lilli thought about how the evening would end, her breath stopped in her throat.

She looked past the other empty tables at the nighttime view of Las Vegas. "It's so sparkly," she said.

"So it is," he said and poured her another glass of Cristal.

"Why are there no other people here?"

"I ordered privacy," he said. "We can do anything we want," he added in a velvet, seductive voice.

Her heart hiccuped and she stared at the table. It was the first possibility that came to mind. "Omigoodness, you don't mean doing it here in public."

He laughed. "I said it's not public."

She sputtered. "B-but—"

Rising, he extended his hand. "Let's dance."

She distantly heard the strains of a romantic melody being piped through an outdoor sound system and immediately identified it. She stood and walked into his arms. "It's hokey, but this is one of my favorite songs."

He drew her close to him. "Old Elvis song sung by Michael Bublé. 'I can't help falling in love with you.'"

"How did you know?"

"I swiped your iPod."

"You are diabolical."

"I'll make you like it."

She had an unsettling feeling he could make her like a lot of things. She felt an achy tug in the region of her heart as she breathed in his scent and clung to his broad shoulders.

He nudged her head upward and took her mouth with his. He slid one of his hands behind her neck and she felt a sensual possessiveness in his touch. Her body immediately responded to his.

The sexy romantic song continued to play and she couldn't help feeling a little sad knowing that Max might want her, but would never really love her. The knowledge didn't keep a fire from building in her belly. The touch of his tongue and the way his body skimmed the front of hers made her blood pump with a primitive beat.

He pulled back slightly. Although his eyelids were hooded, she could still see a naked passion in them. "I've never waited this long for a woman," he said and dipped his open mouth to her neck. He drew her against him and she felt his unmistakable hardness. Sliding his hand over her bottom, he guided her against him.

"I want to taste every inch of you," he muttered against her mouth as he lifted one of his hands to her breast.

Lilli gave an involuntary shudder of anticipation.

"You like that," he said, more than asked. "I'm going to touch you all over." He slid his hand down over her hip.

The prospect took her breath away and she instinctively tried to get closer to him. She wanted to feel his skin. She wanted to slide her mouth over his chest and taste him. She wanted to see if she could make him sweat a little. Her blood pounding through her body, pooling between her thighs, she pulled his tie loose and tugged at the buttons to his shirt.

"I want to be closer, as close as I can get," she whispered breathlessly.

He swore and caught her hands against him. "This is our first time. I'll be damned if it's over in five minutes."

"You make me—" She broke off and swallowed over her dry throat. "Want."

His nostrils flared as he took several deep breaths. "Good. We'll finish this back at the house."

Burning with frustration, she allowed him to lead her from the restaurant. On the way down the elevator, she concentrated on trying to calm down. What must he think of her? That she was so easily aroused by him that she forgot about time and space?

He led her to the car and tucked her into the backseat, instructing Ricardo to take them to the house. He pressed the button for the privacy panel and turned to her. "Why so quiet?"

"I'm a little embarrassed," she quietly admitted, looking out the window.

"Why?"

She shrugged, not wanting to meet his gaze.

He slid his hand under her chin and made her look at him. "Why?"

"Because I would have had sex with you on one of the tables, and you were just—" She broke off and tried to look away, but he wouldn't allow it.

"Just what?"

"Just kidding or teasing," she said.

His dark eyes widened in disbelief. "You think I didn't want you back there?"

She bit her lip.

He swore. "Lilli, I've wanted you since the first time I saw you. I've been to hell and back a dozen times trying to keep my hands off you. You haven't had sex since you got pregnant. I don't want to rush things. I don't want to hurt you."

"Oh," she said, surprised he was so concerned about her discomfort. She'd known he had been determined to wait until the doctor released her, but this went further and oddly turned her on even more.

She impulsively slid her hands behind his neck and kissed him. She rubbed her breasts against his chest, straining to get as close as possible.

Max immediately slid his arms around her and kissed her back just as eagerly. The kiss seemed to go on and on and Lilli felt her temperature climb along with Max's.

He pulled his mouth just a breath away from hers. "I'm not complaining, but what was that for?"

"It was so sweet of you to be worried about hurting me," she whispered.

"That's your way of rewarding me for being sweet?" Max said. "Hell, no one has ever called me sweet before. Maybe I should be sweeter more often if this is how you react."

He took her mouth again and teased both of them into a frenzy by the time the chauffeur pulled into the driveway. Ricardo opened the door for them and Max helped her out of the car. After they climbed the steps to the porch and he opened the front door, he swung her into his arms and carried her inside.

"Wow," Lilli said, shocked again.

"For luck," he said. "I'm not usually superstitious, but I want to hedge my bets this time." Then he carried her upstairs to his master suite. When he set her down on the floor, he allowed her body to slide intimately down his, not hiding his arousal from her.

Lilli felt a quick shimmer of nerves and nearly suffocating anticipation. This was it. No turning back. "I bought a negligee, but it's in my room."

"Another time," he said and took her face in his hands and began to kiss her. His mouth was warm and sensual; the touch of his hands made her feel precious and sexy at the same time. Lilli felt the room begin to spin.

He unzipped her dress and pushed it down over her shoulders, waist and hips until it pooled at her feet. She pushed his jacket from his shoulders and fumbled with the buttons on his shirt. This time he didn't stop her.

Unsnapping her bra, he filled his hands with her breasts. Lilli let out a breath she hadn't known she'd been holding. Skimming his hands down her rib cage and waist, he cupped her bottom and rubbed her against his hard erection.

Taking her mouth in a French kiss, he looped a thumb beneath the waistband of her tiny silk panties and pushed them down. Lilli had thought she couldn't get any hotter, but she'd been wrong.

His fingers did maddening things to her, and she felt herself grow so swollen she could barely stand it. He made her ache. He made her acutely aware of the empty, needy sensation that she knew he could fill.

Tugging his belt loose, she unfastened and unzipped his slacks. Meeting his gaze, she pushed down his slacks and underwear.

"Touch me," he said.

She did. He was huge and hard in her hands and she couldn't help wondering if perhaps his concern about her discomfort may have been valid. She stroked him and he let out a hiss of breath. He closed his eyes while she caressed him.

"Not too much of that," he muttered and pulled her against him. Pushing away the rest of their clothes, he picked her up and carried her to his big bed. He reached over to his bed table and pulled a condom from the drawer.

Lilli took a shallow breath at the sight of him. His eyes were dark with need, his body was well-muscled, his erection huge. He reminded her of a prize stallion and some secret, primitive part of her was proud that she was the one he'd chosen.

He groaned and lowered his mouth to hers. Lilli thought he would take her at that very second. He was ready. She was ready. There was nothing stopping them. Finally.

Instead, he dipped his lips to her nipples and started making her crazy all over again. He slid one of his hands between her legs. She thought about protesting or begging. She didn't know which, but then she couldn't seem to breathe let alone say anything except the whisper that squeezed past her throat. "Please."

He drew the tip of her breast deep into his mouth and she arched toward him. "Please," she whispered again.

"What do you want, baby?" he asked her.

Shameless with need, dripping with want, she closed her eyes. "You. In me."

"Open your eyes," he said in a low, rough voice.

She did as he asked and he thrust inside her with one smooth, sure stroke.

She gasped. He moaned.

"Too much?"

She waited a few heartbeats for her body to adjust to his and shook her head. "More," she said.

Swearing under his breath, he pumped into her, driving his pelvis in a rhythm she echoed. The sensation of him filling her, stretching her, making her secret, wet places contract and shudder was almost overwhelming.

The feeling intensified with every stroke and Lilli lost control, splintering, spinning into orbit. Seconds later, she felt him stiffen and thrust one last time, groaning in release.

He lifted his head and pressed his mouth to hers, his kiss both tender and seductive. "Now, you're mine," he said.

Max kept her in bed for the next eight hours with very little sleep. At that point, he took a shower and returned some business calls. Lilli grabbed a quick shower, then took David from Maria, fed him, held him and bathed him.

Wide-awake, her baby watched her with big eyes and moved his mouth and made little sounds as if he were trying to talk with her.

"You've been such a good boy," Lilli told him. "Sleeping through the night. Maria was so happy and I am, too." She pulled a book from the basket beside the rocking chair and began to read. "'Once upon a time…'"

She alternated between reading and looking at his sweet face. The rapt attention in his big eyes made her smile. She tickled him under his chin and he wiggled. She did it again and he lifted the corners of his lips into a smile.

Joy and surprise rushed through her. "You smiled," she said and stood, bursting to share the news. "David smiled," she called down the hallway to anyone who would listen. "His first smile. David smiled for the first time."

Max rounded the corner, his cell phone pressed to his ear. "Just a minute, Jim. Something wrong?"

"No," Lilli said, rubbing her thumb under David's chin again. "David smiled for the first time."

Max looked at her first then at David, who was not smiling now. "Are you sure?"

"Yes, I'm sure. I just distracted him because I got so excited. I probably scared him," she said.

"Maybe it was gas."

"It was not gas," she said. "He doesn't smile when he has gas. He grimaces."

Max looked at her and David skeptically. "If you say so. I should wrap up this call with Jim. If David does it again, let me know."

He didn't believe her, she realized, and it bothered her. She wanted him to be as excited about David's firsts as she was. She wanted him to love David as much as— She broke off the thought. She was expecting way too much too soon, she told herself.

After a little more time, Max would grow to love David. He wouldn't be able to resist the child. It would be no time before David would be looking at Max with hero worship in his eyes. Surely a child's adoration would be able to penetrate the steel vault protecting Max's heart. Lilli just wasn't sure she could make it into his heart and maybe it was best if she didn't try.

* * *

Later that night after she fed David once more and put him to bed, she turned on the monitor and cracked the door to the nursery as she left the room. Bone tired, all she could think about was going to sleep. Max met her in the hallway holding two glasses of wine.

"Time for the rest of the honeymoon."

Despite her weariness, her pulse quickened at the seductiveness in his eyes. "If I drink a sip of that wine, I'll fall into a coma."

"Tired?" he asked, nudging the glass into her hand and guiding her down the stairs. "Baby wear you out with all his gas?"

She shot a dark look at him. "It wasn't gas. He was smiling."

"Did he do it again?" he asked.

"No, but—"

"Like I said."

"I'm the mother. I know," she said defiantly.

He lifted his lips in a half grin. "Can't argue with that," he said and clinked his glass against hers. He dipped his mouth over hers. "A meeting of the minds. Next, a meeting of the bodies. I think you might like a soak in the Jacuzzi."

It sounded wonderful. "I need my swimsuit."

He shook his head. "No, you don't."

Her heart jumped again. "Won't one of the staff see?"

"They're paid not to see."

"But still," she began.

"If your modesty is screaming that loudly," he said. "I can turn off the lights. Come on." He tugged her out the patio door and into the cool night air.

She shivered.

"The Jacuzzi will warm you up in no time."

It was easier being naked in front of him when they were in bed, when she didn't have time to think. She took a shallow breath. "You go first."

"Okay," he said and set their wineglasses beside the tub. He shucked his clothes without an ounce of self-consciousness. His tanned skin gleamed in the moonlight. His shoulders were broad, his belly flat, his buttocks firm.

Why should he be self-conscious? He had a body that should have been chiseled in marble. His face was hard, but when he smiled, he could turn her world upside down. And his eyes did things to her heart rate, her temperature, and her whole body.

He stepped into the Jacuzzi and turned to look at her. "Your turn."

She fought a rush of self-consciousness. "Turn off the light."

After he killed the light, she pulled off her shirt and jeans, then her bra and panties. Fortifying herself with another breath, she stepped into the tub. Despite the hot temperature, she plunged her body under the bubbles.

"Better?" he asked.

"Hot," she said, although she was grateful for the semicover of water.

His laugh rumbled all the way down between her legs. "You sound like Goldilocks. Too cold. Too hot. You even have the hair," he said, touching her hair before he slid his mouth over hers. His mouth was warm, his tongue seductive.

She felt some of the tension ease out of her.

"You have a beautiful body," he said against her lips. "I love the way your breasts respond to me." He lowered his hands to her nipples and plucked at them, turning them into hard orbs of sensation.

Making a sound of approval, he pulled her onto his lap. She balanced herself with her hands on his chest. His skin felt slick and sexy beneath her touch. Her thighs were slippery against his and the steamy water mirrored the heat between them.

He dipped his forehead against hers. "This wasn't such a bad idea, was it?"

Her breasts brushed against his chest, keeping her nipples taut and sensitive. "It's nice."

"I thought you would like it." Reaching behind him, he grabbed a remote and the strains of a saxophone eased around them. "Are you hungry? I can ask the housekeeper to bring something out—"

"I would drown so she wouldn't see me."

He chuckled and slid his arms around her. "I'll help you get over your shyness."

"Maybe with you," she said, her breath hitching when he fondled her breasts again.

"I wasn't sure how I would like being married, but so far I'm liking it," he said.

"So far is all of six weeks. But that reminds me of something," she said and tried to focus on something other than his muscular chest or how his hands felt on her or how his hard thighs felt under her bottom.

"What?"

"If we're going to make this marriage thing work—"

"We are," he interjected.

She nodded. "It occurred to me that I don't know what you want from me as your wife."

His eyes glinted with an irresistible sexy humor. "You've done very well so far."

"I didn't mean *that.* I mean when we're not in bed."

"We're not in bed right now," he reminded her, shifting her legs apart and pulling her intimately against him. He slid one of his hands between her thighs and moved his hand in a sensual, searching motion.

"I mean when we're not—" She broke off when he grazed the most sensitive part of her. "You're making it hard for me to concentrate."

"That's because you're concentrating on the wrong thing," he said. "I want you to concentrate on what you're feeling right now." He sank deeper into the water and slipped his hand under her bottom, pushing her upward so that her breasts bobbed directly in front of his face.

He lowered his head and took one of her nipples into his mouth. The sight of his dark head against her pale skin sent a hot current to the most sensitive pleasure points in her body. His thumb found her again and a delicious haze fell over her.

It didn't matter that things between them felt so unsettled. It didn't matter that they were outside and if someone really wanted to watch them, they could. What mattered was that she was in his arms and the water made her feel both relaxed and eager. He was looking at her as if she was his first meal in a long time, and she knew firsthand that it hadn't been very long at all.

She slid her hand down between them and found him already hard. He gave a sensual groan and leaned backward on one of the graduated steps, looking at her through hooded eyes. "How am I supposed to go slow if you're going to touch me like that?"

"You want me to stop?"

"Oh, no," he said and pulled her over him and took her mouth in a kiss that made her feel consumed and restless. "You have no idea how sexy you look," he muttered and cupped her bottom, guiding her over him. His pelvis flexed upward and she sank down onto him. With her hair spilling forward, she kissed him. His tongue filled her mouth with the same rhythm he filled her lower body. Slow and easy, the erotic motion made her dizzy with pleasure.

He squeezed her bottom. She lifted her mouth for a breath and he drew one of her nipples deep into his mouth. "You make me so greedy," he said.

He made her desperate to please him. At the same time, though, he made sure she was pleasured. She'd thought she would be too sore, too sensitive, but the water cushioned their movements.

Steam rose around them. Tiny droplets dotted his face. His dark eyes were glazed with arousal. He continued to rub and she matched his pace, her nether regions tightening with every stroke. She felt the peak start in her breasts and shower down to where she convulsed around him, her muscles contracting around his hardness.

His eyes narrowed as he gasped in pleasure, surging into her. "Oh, Lilli."

When he said her name, an aftershock coursed through her, and she realized what she craved. She wanted this to be more than good sex for Max. She wanted it to mean something to him. *She* wanted to mean something to him. Fear prickled inside her. It wouldn't be a good idea to want these kinds of things from a man who didn't believe in romantic love. She needed to figure out how to stay safe and sane.

He took her mouth in a kiss and moved sideways in the bubbling water, still inside her, her legs laced with his muscular thighs. Sanity was the last thing she could muster.

Twelve

The following morning, Max rose early. He felt an itchy sensation in his back. He felt crowded, yet at the same time, he would have liked to stay in bed and enjoy his wife's charms. Instead, he took a shower and was putting on his tie just as Lilli awakened.

She rubbed the sleep from her eyes and glanced at the alarm clock. "It's only six o'clock. You're going into the office already?"

"There's a lot waiting for me. I'll be home late tonight."

"What's late?"

He shrugged. "Maybe nine."

She nodded slowly. "Can I get you some breakfast?"

He shook his head as he straightened his tie. "I'm going straight to the office. My assistant will bring something."

Pulling the sheets up to her shoulders, she met his gaze in the mirror. Her hair was sexily rumpled and she blinked her eyes as she obviously tried to make herself wake up. The skin around her chin was pink from the effects of his beard.

He would need to be more careful in the future, he thought as he rubbed his just-shaven jaw. Her skin was sensitive and he'd mauled her from head to toe during the last two days. The vulnerability in her eyes made him want to hold her, but something else made him want to run.

He walked toward her. "Have a good day, lovely Lilli," he said in a light voice and, not trusting himself, he dropped an even lighter kiss on her cheek.

"You, too," she said. "If David smiles, I'll try to catch it with my camera phone. I'll send you a message."

The offer made his chest feel tight. "You mean if he has gas?" he teased and opened the bedroom door to leave. But not before he felt a pillow hit him in the back of the head. He whipped around, staring at her in surprise. Her hand covered her mouth as if she'd surprised herself, too. It didn't help his concentration that she'd dropped the sheets and her breasts were bared to his sight.

Steeling himself against the distraction and the hard-on growing harder by the moment, he looked down at her and shook his head. "You had me fooled. I thought you were an angel except when I got you in bed."

She bit her lip, but couldn't seem to prevent the beginning of a saucy smile. "I'm still in bed."

"So you are," he said and wished like hell he were there with her. "See you tonight."

* * *

Maybe it shouldn't have felt abrupt for Max to leave so early, but it did. Lilli pulled the sheet over her head and told herself to go back to sleep. She tried to push aside her feelings, but she felt bothered, unsettled. Was this the future for their marriage? Strangers everywhere except when they shared a bed?

Groaning, she threw off the sheet and climbed out of bed. Sore and tired, she wished she could grab a few extra winks, but she knew her mind wasn't going to let her. Grumbling to herself, she took a shower. Her body was sensitive, and she ached in secret places. She allowed the hot water to flow over her, willing it to soothe the tenderness in her muscles. And her heart.

After she dressed, she gave Maria a well-deserved break and listened for David's cry. He'd barely let out a sound before she gathered him to her and fed him. As he devoured his bottle, she noticed tiny beads of perspiration break out on his forehead.

"You are very intense about your food, aren't you, sweetie?" she said.

Moments later, he finished and she squeezed a couple burps out of him. She looked down into his face and smiled at him. He smiled back. Delighted, Lilli drank in his joyful expression. Then she remembered she needed to take a photograph, so Max would believe her. Jumping up from the rocking chair, she ran to grab her cell phone and positioned it over David's face, ready to take a photo. David, however, was less interested in smiling and more fascinated with the object in her hand. The smile had disappeared.

"Well, darn," she muttered. She smiled again and he looked at her with solemn eyes as he blew bubbles. "That's just as cute as a smile," she said and took the photo and sent it to Max anyway.

She took David for a stroll around the block. Just as she was turning into the driveway, her cell phone rang. Her heart racing, she didn't bother to check the caller ID because she was sure it was Max. "Hi there," she said.

"Hi, Lilli," an unfamiliar voice said. "This is Devon."

Lilli stopped midstep and swallowed a sudden foolish twinge of disappointment. Devon, one of the hospice attendants to her mother, he had been with them until the very end. "Oh, Devon, I haven't heard from you in a while. How are you? How are your parents?"

"Dad's not doing so well. He's in the final stages of cancer and my mother was just admitted to the hospital. They want to put her on dialysis."

Sympathy surged through her. "I'm so sorry. Is there anything I can do?"

"I didn't want to ask, but you told me to call you if things got out of control. I'm staying with my father around the clock, so I'm not making any money."

"I understand," she said. "How much do you need?"

"It depends," Devon said, his voice choking up. "On how soon my father goes. Oh, God, I can't believe I said that."

"No, I understand. I took off a lot of time to be with my mother at the end."

"I don't want him to die, but—" He broke off again and sighed. "You would think that since I work in a hospice, I would be better prepared for this."

"It's much more personal," Lilli said. "It's your father. Listen, why don't I bring you some money to tide you over? I've forgotten your address. Give it to me again."

Devon gave her the address. "I'll probably need to call you back for directions. Would you like me to sit with your father so you can get out for a while?"

"I couldn't do that to you," he said. "I feel bad enough asking for financial help."

"You forget how great you were with my mother when she was so sick. You were there for us. I'd like to be there for you."

"But that was my job."

"Well, you did an amazing job and my mother and I couldn't thank you enough. So let this be a little token. I'll come over this afternoon around three. David should be napping."

"Ah, the baby. How is he?" Devon asked.

"Perfect," she said.

He laughed. "As if he could be anything else since he came from you."

She smiled. "Please keep your cell handy, in case I get lost."

"Will do, Lilli, and thanks," Devon said.

Lilli drove her little Toyota instead of the monster SUV Max had bought for her use. She left David in Maria's caring arms. After stopping by the grocery store to pick up a few things for Devon and his family, she only got lost twice, but finally arrived at Devon's apartment complex.

Devon greeted her at the door, but his father had taken a turn for the worse, so he refused to accept Lilli's offer to sit with his father so that Devon could get out for a little while.

Lilli gave the dark gentle giant a hug and left. The visit brought back memories of her mother's time in hospice. Lilli had been forced to hide the gnawing grief she'd felt in anticipation of her mother's death. Losing her mother inch by inch had been excruciating, but she wouldn't trade a moment of the time she'd had with her.

The familiar feeling of being all alone hit her as she stopped at a traffic light. She'd never known her father. Her mother was gone. Even though she was married, she sometimes still felt alone. Her chest grew heavy, her throat tightened and her eyes began to burn. Tears streamed down her face and she tried to comfort herself.

She had David. She had her little baby. She wasn't alone. The thought soothed her and she made a turn when the light turned green. Twenty minutes later, she realized she was horribly lost.

She reluctantly called Devon, but he wasn't picking up. She thought about stopping at a convenience store, but several men sat outside on the ground drinking from bottles in brown bags.

Lilli began to fuss at herself. "Should have done MapQuest. It would have taken three minutes. Three minutes." She rounded the corner and, spotting a small grocery store, she pulled into the tiny parking lot and went inside. The owner spoke very little English, but gave her directions to the interstate.

She followed the directions, or so she thought, but just found herself deeper into another area where she'd never been. At six-thirty, she gave up the fight and called Max's driver, Ricardo. He offered to come and get her, but she refused, embarrassed by her lack of a sense of direction.

Ricardo gave her turn by turn directions. Once she arrived at the interstate, she sagged with relief. Ricardo didn't want to hang up, but Lilli insisted she would be fine. She pulled into the garage an hour later and was surprised to see Max's car.

She smiled as she bounded up the stairs from the garage. Walking through the corridor, she looked for him in the foyer. She spared a quick glance into the den and noticed the patio door was open. Still dressed in his business attire, he stood outside with a bottle of water in his hand.

Lilli rushed to the patio. "Hi. You're home early," she said, unable to disguise her delight.

He turned to look at her. "And you're home late," he said in a voice that could cut glass. His eyes were cold. "Where have you been?"

Lilli winced when she remembered the discussion she'd had with Max about visiting suspicious areas of town. "I visited a friend and got a little lost driving back."

"Ricardo told me you called him from one of the worst neighborhoods in the city," Max said.

She could feel anger emanating from him. "Like I said, I got all turned around. I should have used MapQuest."

"If this was such a good *friend*," Max said. "Why would you need directions to their house?"

Lilli refused to squirm. She'd done nothing wrong. "I haven't been there very often. But I'm back now," she said cheerfully. "I need to check on David."

"Maria has him," he said. "Who was the friend?"

Lilli bit her lip. Darn, she'd hoped to avoid a confrontation. "It was Devon. His father has taken a turn for the worse, but he's lingering and Devon's mother is in the hospital."

"You didn't give him money, did you?"

"Yes, I did," she said without batting an eye. "I took him some groceries, too. I would have sat with Devon's father so he could get some fresh air, but his father was very ill this afternoon. Devon didn't want to leave him."

"You shouldn't let this guy take advantage of you."

"He didn't," Lilli said. "I was happy to write him a check." She paused a second and pressed her lips together. "I didn't take the money out of your account. I took it out of a savings account I set up with the small amount my mother left me."

"That's not the point. The point is that this man could be taking advantage of you," Max said.

"He's not. He has a heart of gold," she said, then corrected herself. "Maybe gold isn't the best description. He has a soft, sweet heart. No hard metals included."

"Unlike your husband with the steel heart," he said.

"I didn't say that," she said. "I just don't think you comprehend that Devon is a good soul."

"Who lives in a terrible area of town."

"Not everyone can afford to live up on the hill like you."

"We discussed this. You weren't going to visit him again without telling me."

"I never really agreed," she said. "But I'm an adult. I don't think I should be hassled because I want to help someone who was so good to my mother when she was dying."

"You can't put yourself in danger like that. You have a son to think about. You have people counting on you."

People? As in plural? Her heart stammered. She studied his face and moved toward him. "What are you really upset about?"

He met her gaze for a moment that seemed to last forever then let out a long breath. "I don't want anything to happen to you."

"It didn't."

"But it could have. Next time you feel the urge to go into a questionable neighborhood, will you please at least take Ricardo with you?"

"What if he's busy?"

"Then either wait until he isn't, or call me."

The worry in his voice took some of the air out of her defiance. "Okay," she said. "But if you start fussing at me, I'll stop listening."

He nodded and they stood silently watching each other. Wary. Lilli felt as if she were being pushed and tugged at the same time, as much from herself as from Max. The sound of David's cry broke the tension.

"I'd better check on him," she said.

"Have you had dinner?"

She shook her head.

"Neither have I. We can eat out here."

"Okay. I'll be back down in a little bit," she said and went upstairs to the nursery. Lilli did the bottle, bath and bed routine for David, but the baby was still wide-awake when she put him to bed. She read him some stories and rocked him, but he still didn't fall asleep.

Giving up, she took him downstairs with her and put him in a springy infant seat in a chair beside hers. Her stomach growled at the sight of the food in front of her. Max set down the newspaper he'd been reading. "Is someone not sleepy?"

"I think he wants to play soccer or basketball and he's very frustrated that he can't yet."

Max's lips twitched.

She turned on the Jacuzzi.

Max looked at her in alarm. "You're not really going to put him in the hot tub?"

"No, I was thinking the sound of the bubbles might soothe him."

"Good idea," he said.

"And if that doesn't work, maybe he would like to hear a male voice."

Max lifted his eyebrows. "Mine?"

She took a bite of her dinner. "You could read to him."

"What?" he asked, pointing at the paper beside him. "The *Wall Street Journal?*"

"Sure. That should put him right to sleep, don't you think?"

"If you say so," he said and began to read an article about the economy.

David kicked and wiggled. He made a neutral sound that Lilli suspected could turn into a fussy sound. "It would work better if you hold him."

Max looked at her. Her hair was fairy flyaway as usual and she had a crumb on the corner of her mouth. She gave him a huge, encouraging smile and damn if he didn't feel tempted to do anything for her. Including holding a potentially fussy baby.

"Okay, I'm game. Any tips?"

She set her fork down and jumped up from her chair.

"He likes to be held close," she said, picking David up from the infant seat and placing him in Max's arms. "He feels more secure when his arms and legs aren't flopping all over the place."

It presented a new challenge to hold the newspaper at the same time as he held David, but he was up for it. He'd conducted billion-dollar deals, and he'd been player of the year for his college soccer team. He had the right stuff for this. Max continued to read, but David still squirmed.

"Sometimes it helps if you jiggle him," Lilli said and took another bite from her plate, seemingly content to watch him struggle.

Max jiggled the baby and struggled to read the article from the newspaper that also jiggled from his movements. He made up a few of the words that got blurry. Actually, he began to make up entire sentences. "And then the economy got kicked on its ass due to the price of oil."

"I do not believe that statement was in the *Wall Street Journal,*" Lilli said.

Max glanced down at David, whose eyes were closed. The baby slept peacefully in his arms. He felt as if he'd just made a goal in soccer or landed a huge deal. "It doesn't matter," he said in a low voice, "because I have successfully put our son to sleep."

He glanced up and looked at Lilli. She stared at him, her eyes shiny. "Yes, you did," she whispered. "But can you put him into his crib without waking him up?"

Another challenge. His competitive spirit piqued, he ditched the paper and carefully rose to his feet. "And what do I get if I succeed?"

"A pat on the back?" she said, covering her mouth as she muffled a chuckle.

"Lower," he said. "And not on the back."

Her blue eyes lit and smoldered. "Okay. If you can lay him down in the crib and he stays asleep, you can have whatever you want. I'll warn you, though, that he usually wakes up and needs to be rocked or walked a little longer."

"We'll see," he said, more motivated than ever.

Lilli stood. "And you need to put him to sleep on his back or on his side placed against the crib rail."

"Okay," he said.

"And make sure the blanket doesn't cover his face."

"Got it."

"And kiss him good-night."

"Kiss him?"

She nodded. "It's a requirement for a good night of sleep."

"I'll remember that," he said.

He could see her cheeks bloom with color even in the moonlight. "I'll be back in a few minutes."

"If you have to pick him up again, then it doesn't count."

"For what?" he asked. "You won't go to bed with me?"

She bit her lip. "I didn't say that."

"Give me a couple minutes. I'm an amateur at this, remember?"

Her gaze softened. "Yeah, I'll be waiting upstairs."

"Don't you want to finish your dinner?"

"That won't take two minutes," she said.

He smiled and she immediately smiled in response. Then he turned and took the baby up to the nursery, coaching himself and David. "You want to stay asleep," he said to David. "You're tired. You're ready to sleep until morning. You're worn-out. You've got a full belly and you're ready for your nice bed. You'll dream of warm bottles and walks in the stroller and being held in Lilli's arms. Can't argue with that last one, big guy."

He carefully walked toward the crib and continued to hold David, studying the baby's face. The baby looked as if he were totally out. Leaning over, millimeter by millimeter, he extended his arms and David stirred. Max immediately stopped, suspended over the crib.

David quieted and pursed his lips. Max counted to twenty then moved a few more inches. David wiggled slightly and Max stopped again. Patience was clearly the name of this game. He counted to twenty and moved several more inches. This time, David didn't stir. He extended the last few inches and carefully laid him sideways on the crib, leaving the blanket wrapped around him.

David wiggled and wiggled, but Max kept his hand on the baby and surprise, surprise, his son settled down.

Then he remembered the kiss. Max swallowed an oath. Surely it couldn't be that important. The baby was asleep. That was what was important, right?

Bowing to a combination of his Type A personality and his conscience, because he knew Lilli would ask about the kiss, he carefully lowered the side of the bed. He bent over and pressed a silent kiss on David's head then rose and slowly, slowly lifted the side of the crib. It made a loud clicking noise when it locked into place, making Max grimace.

He closed his eyes, waiting for David to make a

sound. A moment passed and all was still quiet. Max opened one eye, looked down at his son and was thrilled to see that the baby was asleep.

He took a deep breath and sighed. Now to collect his reward. He left the nursery and left a sliver of a crack between the door and the jamb. Walking into his bedroom, he stepped inside and found Lilli sitting in the middle of his bed wearing a white lace teddy that managed to look both innocent and naughty. Her rosy nipples showed through the transparent lace, as did the shadow between her thighs. His fingers itched to pull the skimpy garment from her, to bare her body to his gaze. He curled his hands into a fist then forced himself to release them.

"Very nice," he said. "How did you know I would succeed in getting David to stay asleep?"

"Aside from the fact that you're an overachiever?" she asked.

He couldn't keep his lips from twitching. "Yes."

"I wanted to thank you for the effort."

He tugged his shirt over his head then shucked his jeans and underwear so he stood before her completely naked. He saw her gaze gravitate to his erection and felt himself grow even harder. "How do you want to thank me?" he asked.

"Come here," she said and opened her arms. The gesture was so artless and open that it took his breath. He slid over the bed, pulling her against him, enjoying every millimeter of her silky skin against his.

"You feel so good," she whispered.

"I was going to say the same about you," he said, and dipped his head to kiss his way down her throat. When he reached her collarbone, he gently nibbled. Her sigh made him feel as if he were ready to burst.

"You're going to make this hard for me, aren't you?" he muttered, lowering his mouth to her breast, pushing the delicate fabric aside. He slipped his hand between her thighs and found her already wet and swollen. She squirmed beneath him and he felt his heart hammer against his rib cage.

She slid one of her hands between them and captured his bare erection in her hand. "I think you already started out—" She paused and shoved him onto his back. "Hard," she said and flowed down his body like silk.

The sensation of her open mouth on his chest, followed by his belly, took his breath. She waited three breaths and the anticipation nearly made him insane. Then she moved lower and took him into her mouth. The sight of her with her fairy angel hair, good girl/bad girl teddy, and her lips wrapped around him was one of his sexiest fantasies come true.

He watched her until he couldn't stand it any longer, then rolled her over, unsnapped her teddy and plunged inside her. He couldn't get enough of her—her passion, her sweetness. It was crazy, but being with her made him believe in possibilities he hadn't considered before.

After Max took her over the top twice and finally gave in to his own release, he held her against him for several moments. Neither of them said a word, but the power and pleasure of their lovemaking vibrated between them. He gently turned her over and pulled her back against him, stroking her hair.

His touch mesmerized her and she relaxed to the point that she almost fell asleep. She felt safer and more cherished than she'd felt in her entire life.

"I missed you today," he whispered into her ear.

Her heart stopped. His admission was the closest he'd come to professing any emotion. In her heart, she hoped it was just a step away from *I love you.* It took everything inside her not to make her own confession because she knew it would only burden him. He wasn't ready to hear that sometime along the way, she'd fallen in love with him.

Max woke to the sensation of Lilli's hands on his face. "Hey, Mr. Sunshine, the alarm is on your side of the bed."

Max blinked, opening his eyes to the sight of Lilli, with sleepy eyes, sexy puffy lips and the sound of one of Beethoven's symphonies from his alarm clock. He shook his head to clear it. He must have slept so soundly that he didn't hear his alarm when it first went off. He reached over and turned it off.

He never hit the snooze button and he always got out of bed within ten seconds. Glancing over at Lilli, he paused a good sixty.

"If you're going to stare at me, you can at least make yourself useful and hug me, too."

He chuckled and rolled back toward her, pulling her against him. She snuggled her breasts to his chest and pressed a kiss to his neck. Her body felt like silk.

Growing hard, he groaned. "The problem with holding you when you're naked is that I want to do a lot more than hold you."

"What's stopping you?" she asked in a sexy sleep-husky voice.

She might as well have lit a match next to a gas pump. He took her with a thoroughness that left both of them gasping for air.

Reluctantly, he dragged himself from bed. He looked back at her, nude, with a dazed, just-taken expression on her flushed face. He couldn't resist going back for one more kiss from her petal-soft lips, then forced himself to pull away.

Just as he reached the door to the bathroom, he heard her voice. "You can call me during the day if you want. It's not required," she quickly added. "But you can if you want."

She heard him last night after all, he realized. His heart gave a strange stutter. He couldn't tell if it was pleasure or pain. He'd gone skydiving a few times, and this sensation reminded him of free-falling out of an airplane. Was this what it felt like to fall for a woman? He swore under his breath. He didn't have the time to think about it right now.

"Thanks for the invitation," he said and headed for the shower.

Over the next few days after Lilli moved into Max's bedroom, Lilli felt almost like a newlywed. Max arrived home early. They shared dinner and took care of David then retired to Max's bed for nights of amazing lovemaking. She began to hope that he would eventually love her.

Saturday night after they'd visited a park and enjoyed a gourmet picnic prepared by Max's chef, they returned home. David had been fussy most of the afternoon. She fed him part of an extra bottle, hoping he would settle down, but he continued to fuss. She noticed he felt warm to the touch and took his temperature. It was elevated, but not overly so. Still, every time she tried to put him in his crib, his little body stiffened and he cried until he shook.

Max stepped inside. "Does he need another dose of the *Wall Street Journal?*"

She shook her head. "I don't think he's feeling well."

His demeanor immediately changed. "Does he have a temperature?"

"Not much of one," she said, showing him the thermometer. "All the baby books say to keep calm. But I think I may need to take him to the doctor tomorrow."

Max nodded in agreement.

"It may be a long night," she told him. "He's only calm when I hold him."

"I can understand that," he said, meeting her gaze, making her stomach jump at his double meaning. "I'll take a turn holding him if you can't get him settled."

"Thanks," she said and sighed when he gave her and David a hug. His arms felt so solid, so strong.

"Wake me to take a turn," he told her again.

"Maybe later," she said, but she didn't ask him. She finally succeeded in getting David settled and crawled into bed. She kept the nursery monitor directly beside her and heard him when he awakened in the middle of the night with a heart-tugging wail.

Max stirred beside her. "What is—"

"No, I'll take care of it," she said, quickly climbing out of bed and heading for the nursery. She almost collided with Maria, who'd already picked David up.

"Oh, the little sweetheart, he's burning up with fever," Maria said. She made a tsking sound. "He got sick in his bed."

"Oh, no. Let me hold him," Lilli said, taking him into her arms and biting her lip at the heat emanating from his tiny body. She pressed the thermometer against his ear, aghast at how quickly it had risen.

Fear clutched at her. David began to cry. "I wish I knew what was wrong with you, sweetie. I wish you could tell me where you hurt." David gave a high-pitched scream and Lilli fought a rising tide of panic.

Max stepped inside the room. "What's wrong?"

"His fever has gone up and he got sick in his bed," Lilli said, holding him close to her as she stroked his forehead.

As David let out another scream, Max nodded his head decisively. "Okay, that's it. We're taking him to the emergency room."

Thirteen

There was no wait at the emergency room for David Maximillian De Luca. It seemed everyone knew that Max had made generous donations to the Children's Hospital. The admissions tech quickly took down the insurance information and escorted Max, Lilli and David behind a curtain.

Max looked at David, who was clearly in pain, and felt his gut wrench. His son. It was his responsibility to alleviate his pain.

A very young woman in a white coat stepped inside the curtained cubicle. She picked up the chart and glanced at it. "Are you the parents?" she asked.

"Yes, we are."

"I'm Dr. Jarrett." She extended her hand and shook his. "Let's see what's wrong with your son."

Lilli continued to hold David close, cradling his head as he let out cries and sobs. As Dr. Jarrett looked inside David's right ear, the baby howled and the doctor winced. "I think I've found the problem. An ear infection. A nasty one at that." She rubbed the baby's head. "We can take care of that, sweetheart.

"We'll start him on antibiotics right away, and I have some other recommendations for pain. The good news is that these little guys tend to respond to antibiotics within twenty-four hours or less."

"Thank goodness," Lilli said. "He's been miserable."

"And he made sure you knew it, too, didn't he?" the doctor said with a smile.

"Yes, I guess he did." Lilli met Max's gaze. "I'm glad we came."

"Me, too," he said and asked the doctor a few more questions. Dr. Jarrett left David's file open on the tray while she left the area for a moment. Max glanced at the file, seeing David's birth information, his height, weight and blood type. He digested the information without focusing on it. The doctor returned, apologizing for the interruption.

After picking up the medication from the hospital pharmacy, Max helped Lilli administer it to David. He ushered both of them to his car, and David fell asleep on the way home.

Max pulled into the driveway and Lilli put her hand on his elbow. "I'm afraid to take him out of the infant seat," she confessed.

Max chuckled. "We can't leave him in the car the rest of the night."

"It's almost morning," she said and reached closer

to touch his jaw. "You are so amazing. And I am so lucky."

His heart swelled in his chest. "Why do you say that?"

"Because I was ready to panic over what to do about David, and you knew what to do immediately."

"You would have figured it out."

"Thank you," she whispered and kissed him. "I know you don't believe in love, but you're making me fall in love with you."

He didn't say anything, but she made him feel ten feet tall. She made him feel as if he could conquer anything and he wanted to do it for her and David.

He took a breath to clear his head. "We need to put him to bed," he said.

"Yeah," she said reluctantly.

"We can do it," he encouraged her. "We can do it together."

She nodded as if she found strength in his words. "Sure we can. Okay, let's go."

Surprisingly enough, David only gave a few peeps between the car seat and the crib. He made just enough sound to reassure Max and Lilli that he was uncomfortable, but okay. Lilli placed him in the crib and appeared to hold her breath.

David continued sleeping and Lilli let out a sigh.

"Time for Mama to get some sleep," Max said, taking her hand and leading her to bed.

She insisted on brushing her teeth then fell asleep as soon as her head hit the pillow. Max wasn't so lucky. Something nagged at him. He couldn't quite put his finger on it, but something he'd seen or observed at the hospital still bothered him.

Propping his hand behind his head on his pillow, he mentally backtracked his way through the evening.

Finally he remembered viewing David's file, his birth record, his weight. His blood type. His brother's blood type didn't match David's. Lilli's blood type had been listed above David's. David's didn't match hers, either.

He shook his head in disbelief. There had to be something wrong, a mix-up. But insidious doubts poked at him. If not Tony, then who was David's biological father?

The next question hit him so hard his chest squeezed tight with the pain. If not Tony, then who had been Lilli's lover?

Max felt nausea back up into his throat. Realization coursed through him like a slow-moving poison. Sitting up, he felt himself break into a sweat. Had she deceived him? Had sweet, angelic Lilli who'd baked cupcakes for his birthday pulled off the ultimate charade?

She'd made him believe she was going to give birth to his brother's son. With her wide blue eyes and fairy hair, she'd looked so innocent, so pure. And she'd played him to the hilt when she hadn't accepted his repeated offers for money.

He looked over at her sleeping in his bed as his wife and nearly drowned in disgust for himself. Shaking his head, he rose from the bed and thought of the way his father had acted like a fool over a woman. Max had made a vow to himself never to lose his head over a woman. But he'd gone and done just that.

Caught in semisleep, Lilli struggled to open her eyes. They felt as if someone had placed sandbags on top of them. She forced them to open. It took several minutes for her to become conscious.

Her first thought was of David. Her second was of Max. She looked beside her on the bed to find her husband gone. Type-A overachiever, she thought then glanced at the clock—8:00 a.m. She immediately pushed aside the covers and headed for the nursery. No one had called her, she reminded herself, as she stepped inside to find David being fed by Maria.

The nanny smiled. "He's much better this morning. Just a little cranky. A few more doses of his medication and he will be good as new."

David was focused on his bottle, clearly intent on getting every last drop. Lilli gave a sigh of relief. "Thank you for getting up with him."

"My pleasure," Maria said. "Mister De Luca is downstairs. He asked for you to go see him after you wake up."

"He's not at work?" Lilli asked, surprised.

Maria shook her head. "No. He's downstairs."

"Thank you again," Lilli said and returned to the bedroom to throw on some clothes, wash her face and put on some concealer. She didn't want to make a practice of looking like a hag first thing in the morning.

She went downstairs and spotted him on the patio. He sat on one of the plush chairs, staring at the fountain next to the Jacuzzi. Admiring his strong profile, she felt a rush of love. She gave herself a mental pinch. *This was her husband.*

She walked toward him and smiled. "Good morning, Mr. Amazing." She shook her head. "I don't see how you can go to sleep after I do, and still get up earlier than I do."

He met her gaze, but his eyes were cold. "I have things on my mind." He set his coffee cup on the patio table. "I saw David's medical file at the hospital last night."

"Is he okay? Is there something wrong that they didn't tell us?"

He lifted his hand. "No, no. Not that. What I noticed was David's blood type. It didn't match yours."

Max watched her carefully.

"Then it must match Tony's," she said, as if she were certain.

Feeling his gut begin to twist and turn, he shook his head. "No, it doesn't."

Lilli frowned. "It has to. There must be some mistake."

Max sat silently for a long moment. Awed by her ability to lie without so much as a twitch, he continued to study her. "There's no mistake, Lilli. David's blood type doesn't match Tony's. Tony cannot be David's biological father."

She stared at him for a long moment. "He is," she said her voice rising. "There's no other possibility. There's no—"

"Are you sure?" Max asked. "Who else did you have sex with while you were seeing my brother?"

Her mouth dropped wide in horror. "No one, I mean—" She broke off. "I wouldn't—"

She was still sticking to her story, but he was beginning to see some cracks in her composure. "Funny, that's what I thought, too."

"No, really," she said, knitting her fingers together. "I didn't have sex with anyone else. Tony has to be David's biological father. There's no other possibility."

she said. "There was no one else. How could it be anyone else?"

Max stared at her in silence. Disappointment stabbed at him. Some part of him had held out hope that she would be honest with him. That she would give him that much.

Panic shot across her face and she ran to him. "You must believe me. You must. That blood test is wrong. It has to be. It has to—"

He stepped aside before she could touch him. He didn't want her to touch him. He didn't want his body to betray him. There was only one explanation for her hysteria. She had indeed lied to him and she was terrified of losing her meal ticket.

"I need to leave," he said and headed for the door.

"Max," she called after him, her voice full of tears and desperation.

But Max kept on walking.

Watching him leave, Lilli felt her throat and chest close so tight she could hardly breathe. He didn't believe her. He thought she had deceived him. Her heart died a little with each step he took away from her.

She sank into her chair, feeling as if she were going to splinter into a million pieces. How had this happened? *What* had happened? *Who* had done this to her?

Her mind reeled and she tried in vain to remember more details of that last fateful night with Tony. It had been hard enough for her to deal with the idea of Tony taking advantage of her, but knowing some anonymous faceless monster had done this to her made her feel more victimized than ever.

How could Max believe her when she couldn't believe it herself? And now he hated her. She'd read it on his face as clear as the writing on their prenup, on their marriage certificate and on the adoption papers.

She closed her eyes and felt her stomach and chest twist so hard she feared she would get sick. She broke into a cold sweat. Her mind raced. If he hated her, then how much more would he hate David?

Her first instinct was to leave. To get as far away from Max and this house as she could.

But why? She had done nothing to be ashamed of. She was the victim.

But she wouldn't be the victim any longer.

All day at work, Max tried to wrap his mind around the idea that Lilli had deliberately deceived him. But as his anger had cooled, he had trouble believing it. If she was acting, she could win an Academy Award.

She'd been stunned when he'd confronted her, certain there'd been a mistake. Her face had been full of confusion, horror and disbelief. Everything he'd been feeling.

If she'd truly been after his money, wouldn't she have insisted on more in the prenup agreement? He sat in his office, gazing blindly at the mountains in the distance. None of this added up. She had looked at him in complete disbelief when he told her Tony couldn't be David's father.

Pinching the bridge of his nose, he knew what the only explanation could be. Tony had not taken advantage of Lilli that night she'd been drugged. Some other man—some perverted stranger—had violated her. The only consolation he could find was that at least Lilli had no memory of the event.

He thought of little David and felt a surge of protectiveness. The baby *was* his. In every way that mattered. That child had burrowed into Max's heart so deeply he'd never be able to extricate him. Nor would he ever want to.

And Lilli. Max took a deep breath.

They'd made irrevocable vows to one another. He'd sworn to care for David as if he were his own. Now that the harsh emotions of the moment had passed, he knew he needed to go to her again. This time, he *would* listen.

After Lilli brought David back from his stroll, she rocked him for a long time. His soft warm body and sweetness were the only thing that reminded her she was alive. Setting him into his crib, she bent over to kiss his forehead and stared at him for a long while.

Softly closing the door to the nursery, she walked downstairs. Halfway down the steps, she heard a sound and saw Max standing just inside the front door. Her breath just stopped. She stared at him for a full moment, wondering if he was real.

"We need to talk," he said.

Her heart squeezing tight with dread, she followed him out onto the patio. The sunny afternoon provided a stark contrast to the desperation she felt inside her. She swallowed over a lump in her throat. "I understand if you want David and me to leave. I don't expect your support, especially now."

He held up his hand. "Lilli, I'm sorry I jumped to so many conclusions. I can guess what happened."

She closed her eyes. She couldn't look at him as she

recalled that terrible night she'd tried to forget. "Like I told you before, I told Tony I wanted to leave that night. He begged me to stay for just one more song, one more drink. I ordered a soda. I remember feeling dizzy, then nothing…until I woke up hours later in the back room of the club. I could tell something had happened," she said in a halting voice. "Tony was passed out next to the door. I couldn't get out of there fast enough. I got home and sat under the shower until the water turned cold." Opening her eyes, she shook her head, her tight throat reducing her voice to a whisper. "I'm so sorry, Max, but I swear I didn't know. I don't remember anything. And now there's this image of a faceless monster—"

"That's enough." He moved toward her and wrapped his arms around her. "No more," he said. "You've been through enough."

Lilli was afraid to believe her ears. Yet his strength surrounded her. His warmth, the scent she knew and loved. Could it be real?

Swiping at her tears, she cautiously searched his face. What she saw there almost made her knees buckle in relief. He believed her. She could see it clear as the sunlight. "You believe me, don't you?"

He nodded. "Yes, I do. I should have given you a chance to explain, but—"

She sniffed. "You thought you were looking after your brother's child and—" She lifted her shoulders. "And you're not." She took a deep breath and tried to steady herself. "If you want David and me to leave, we will."

"No," he said, the word as hard as steel. "I want you and David to stay. You two belong to me."

Lilli felt a surge of relief, but had to make sure. "But

won't you resent us? Won't you feel as if we're a burden that's been pushed on you?"

He shook his head. "I chose to marry you. I chose to adopt David. None of that has changed." He paused, slicing his hand through his hair. "The only thing that has changed is that now I know how vital you are to me, to my life. I never thought this would happen to me, but I love you. I don't want to live without you. Either of you."

Lilli felt as if the room turned upside down and this time her knees did buckle. Max caught her against him, sank into a chair and pulled her onto his lap. She lifted her trembling hands to his hard, but precious face. "I thought I was going to be all alone in my feelings. Loving you, but never having your love."

"But you married me anyway."

"How could I not? If there was a chance that I could make your life happier by being in it, then I wanted to be there for you. I love you so much."

He closed his eyes and shook his head as if he was overcome with emotion. "I kept saying I didn't understand how Tony could have been so damn lucky to find you. But I'm the lucky one. I get to keep you. Forever," he said, sealing the words with a kiss.

"Forever," she echoed, "But I'm the lucky one. I got the man of steel who has a heart of gold."

* * * * *

TYCOON'S ONE-NIGHT REVENGE

by
Bronwyn Jameson

Dear Reader,

If you've read my previous books then you may remember Susannah Horton. Although she didn't appear on the page, Susannah played a vital, indispensable role as Alex Carlisle's intended bride. In *The Ruthless Groom*, she was the catalyst that brought Alex and Zara together…and one of the obstacles that kept them apart.

The possibility of creating a happily-ever-after for Susannah only struck after I'd finished writing *The Ruthless Groom*, and during the final edits I hurriedly added some hints of her future story. At that stage I had no idea what her story would be, only that she'd run away from her wedding because of "a mystery man." That man would have to be very special, I knew, and her reason for running high-stakes. And that was all I knew.

To those readers who've been eagerly awaiting Susannah's story – here it is! I hope you enjoy her journey from a conveniently arranged engagement to a marriage based purely – and inconveniently – on love. I also hope you enjoy your reading journey to Tasmania, Australia's southernmost island state. Stranger's Bay and Charlotte Island are both fictitious but, I hope, reflective of the wild natural beauty and dramatic scenery for which Tasmania is known.

Cheers from the Land Down Under,

Bronwyn Jameson

BRONWYN JAMESON

spent most of her childhood with her head buried in a book. It seemed only fitting that she turn her love of romance fiction into a career, creating the kind of stories she's always loved to read. Her books have won many accolades, including an Emma Darcy Award, an Aspen Gold, a Write Touch Readers Award, an Anne Bonney Readers' Choice, and in 2006 she was a triple RITA® Award finalist and nominated as *Romantic Times BOOKreviews* Series Storyteller of the Year.

Bronwyn shares an idyllic piece of the Australian farming heartland with her husband, three sons, three dogs, a few thousand sheep, several horses and the occasional wallaby or echidna. She still spends most of her time with her head stuck in a book, sometimes writing, sometimes reading and always avoiding housework.

You can contact Bronwyn via her website at www.bronwynjameson.com.

With heartfelt thanks to the mates who talked,
and at times walked, me through this story in
one or more of its many incarnations.
Trish, Yvonne, Emilie, Fiona, Anne:
you guys rock!

One

So, she'd come. Sooner than Donovan Keane had anticipated, given the weather and the travel necessary to reach the resort's remote location. And, Van noted with satisfaction, she'd come alone.

Good.

A grim half smile tugged at the corners of his mouth as he watched her dismiss the bellhop's substantial umbrella and jog up the steps toward reception. Under the shelter of the portico she paused to acknowledge the doorman, and something in the swing of her red-gold hair and the lift of her hand triggered a weird flash of déjà vu. For a fraction of a second, time vacillated from present to past, between dream and reality.

Then she disappeared inside the building, gone in a

flurry of long legs and designer raincoat, leaving Van alone and stripped of his satisfied smile.

Punching gloved fist against palm, he searched his memory but came up blank. "Big surprise," he told a captive audience of weight stations and treadmills.

He'd identified Susannah Horton the second he caught sight of her arrival through the rain-streaked window. But that recognition was due to the number of photos he'd viewed during the past weeks of intensive research—Australian society cameras loved the local hotel heiress—and not from the weekend she'd spent in his company. Shoving away from the window, Van shook the tight grip of frustration from his muscles and circled the punching bag he'd deserted minutes earlier.

He'd flown in from San Francisco the previous morning, but twenty-four hours at The Palisades at Stranger's Bay, the Tasmanian resort where they'd supposedly spent that weekend, had done nothing to fill the dark hole in his memory. Hell, he'd come within a whisker of buying the place, yet nothing rang any bells. Not his flight into Australia's island state, not the helicopter transfer to the isolated retreat. Not even his first stunning view of the scattered villas perched high on a rocky promontory overlooking the southern ocean.

Nothing. *Thud.* Nada. *Thud.* Zilch. *Thud.*

Van hit the punching bag with a lethal barrage of punches that did little to soothe his frustration. The insistent internal burn came from more than the forgotten weekend, more than losing the prime property to an Australian hotel group. It stemmed from *how* he'd lost out.

The below-the-belt punch had been thrown while he

lay unconscious in an ICU, incapable of defending himself let alone fighting back. *Thud.* A knockout counter-bid, perfectly timed and perfectly presented. *Thud.* And all due to a treacherous redhead named Susannah Horton. *Thudthudthud.*

Despite the veiled threat in the voice mail he'd left last night, he hadn't expected her to turn up so promptly. At best, he'd expected a return call. At worst, another don't-you-dare-call-again reply from her mother. The fact that Susannah had scurried down here without any advance warning or any entourage in tow, suggested he hadn't misread the signs.

She'd come because he'd hit a vein, and she hadn't wasted a minute seeking him out here in the resort's state-of-the-art fitness centre.

He hadn't heard her entrance, but he caught a glimpse of reflected movement in the expansive window. And a jolt of awareness travelled the length of his spine, strong enough that his next punch miscued and slid off the side of the bag. Recovering, he delivered a final combination of punches, sharp, swift, relentless, until his breath rasped in his lungs and his inner physical therapist barked, *enough!*

Then he dispensed with the boxing gloves and pulled on a T-shirt. Snagging his towel and water bottle he turned, and, dodging the arc of the still swinging bag, started toward the plush reception area. As he walked, he drank from his bottle and he drank in the woman.

Up close Susannah Horton packed even more punch than that first glimpse through glass and rain. She wasn't a bombshell; her beauty was more about class than flash. Tall, willowy, feminine. Generous lips balanced by a long, straight nose. Red-gold hair and the kind of redhead's complexion that would burn in the sun. Green eyes that tilted upward and smoked with wariness.

Until that second, he'd harboured a lingering doubt over how they'd spent their days, and nights, that July weekend. He couldn't recall one damn detail. All he had to go on was Miriam Horton's word—and hadn't that been one helluva phone conversation!—and his own instincts. Those he trusted. And when his eyes locked on hers, when he detected the suppressed heat in their sea-green depths, his body responded with a powerful jolt of elemental recognition. As he came to a halt in front of her, his instincts hummed like a mesotron.

Oh, yeah, she'd slept with him, all right.

And then she'd really screwed him over.

Susannah thought she was ready for this moment. Since hearing his voice mail last night, she'd had enough time to prepare. More than once she'd cursed herself for her impulsive, panicky reaction to his voice mail. More than once she'd considered turning straight around and flying back home.

But what good would that have done? She hadn't imagined the aggressive edge to that recorded message any more than she'd misheard the threat inherent in his words. She may not have adopted her usual analytical approach before deciding to fly down here—impulsiveness seemed to be a feature of her dealings with Donovan Keane—but she had made the right decision.

And after five hours of travelling and analysing, Susannah's initial anxiety had developed a decent head of indignation. After weeks of ignoring her calls, he'd turned up, two months later, making threats that sounded ominously close to blackmail. She had many, many regrets about that weekend and its aftermath, but she was not the guilty party. And the more she thought about his message, the more questions it raised.

In that frame of mind she'd marched into The Palisades' gym and found Donovan naked from his low-slung sweatpants up, muscles rippling with lean strength as he pummelled that unfortunate hunk of leather into submission. All the simmering indignation had deserted her mind. She was left empty, hollow, underprepared, and so *so* susceptible to the flood of sensations that came from seeing him again.

When he turned and his eyes locked on hers, the blow to her senses was more powerful than any he'd thrown against the leather bag.

It was just like the first time they'd met, the first time she became the sole focus of that riveting silver-grey gaze. She experienced the same rush of awareness, the same slow somersault in her stomach, the same sweet explosion of warmth in her skin.

Instantly entranced. At a loss. Slow to react.

So slow that he'd come to a halt in front of her before she realised what was wrong with this picture. It was too much like that first meeting. The way he was silently taking her all in, not like a lover, not even like an acquaintance, but almost like a stranger.

What was going on? Did he not remember her? Was

this even the same man she'd fallen for with such uncharacteristic haste on that wintry July weekend?

"Donovan?" she asked in a second's uncertainty.

"Were you expecting someone else?"

Head tilted at a slight angle, he narrowed his eyes in an expression as familiar as the defined angle of his cheekbones and the fullness of his bottom lip. Oh, yes, this was Donovan Keane. His hair cut ruthlessly short, his face sharper and harder, his expression as cold as an Antarctic wind, but definitely Donovan.

"After the tone of your message, I wasn't sure what to expect," she replied, battling to collect her scrambled composure. "Although I must say I didn't expect you to look me over as if you were having trouble remembering me."

He'd lifted the towel slung around his neck to wipe the sheen of perspiration from his face, but that didn't disguise the flicker of emotion deep in his eyes. Not belated friendliness. Not the teasing humour that had caught her off guard so many times the weekend they'd met.

"My message wasn't clear?" he asked.

"Frankly, no, it wasn't."

The towel paused midswipe and in the hard set of his jaw and the thin line of his lips, Susannah recognised the signs of restraint. He wasn't cold and distant; he was struggling to hide his anger. "What part do I need to make clearer?"

Bewildered by his hostility, she shook her head. "The part where you're so angry with me."

"You can drop the innocent act, Goldilocks. You know what this is about."

Innocent act? Goldilocks?

Susannah's confusion sharpened with irritation. "I can assure you, this is no act."

"Then let me spell it out for you. Right after our weekend together—a weekend you spent in my well-paid employment—my bid to acquire this resort was rejected."

"Your bid was bettered."

"By Carlisle Hotel Group, which is headed by your close friend and business ally, Alex Carlisle."

Was he implying that things weren't aboveboard? "Alex's bid was legitimate."

"So I was led to believe. Imagine my surprise when I discovered, a week ago, that he's also your fiancé. Tell me," he continued conversationally, "did he suggest you sweet-talk me into revealing details of my proposal? Was that how he perfected a counterbid so quickly?"

"That makes no sense," she fired back, her composure splintered by that outrageous accusation. "Your recollection of that weekend appears to be seriously flawed."

A muscle in his cheek jumped but he replied in the same deceptively even tone. "Perhaps you had better refresh my memory."

"*You* hired *me*. You had to sweet-talk me into changing my schedule to take the job. I warned you there could be a conflict of interest with my mother owning a significant stake in The Palisades, but you insisted. You wanted me."

For a long moment, their gazes clashed. The air between them crackled with animosity and with a different kind of heat, the kind that flared from those last three words. *You wanted me.* And he had—there'd been no disputing the physicality of his desire—but it had been secondary to the real reason he'd sought the services of her private-concierge business.

"You wanted me," she said tightly, "because of my mother's shareholding. You wanted my recommendation in her ear to ensure all the board voted yes to your proposal. But once you'd had me, you got complacent. You only had to play nice a little longer and your bid would have won approval."

His eyes narrowed. "I didn't play nice?"

"When you went back to America, you shouldn't have screened my calls. I wasn't about to make a pest of myself. All you had to say was 'We had fun, Susannah, but we're not looking for the same thing here. Let's leave it at that.' If you hadn't thought your bid was in the bag…if you'd taken my calls instead of hiding behind your assistant—"

She broke off, annoyed at revealing how much she'd let that stonewalling silence hurt. For letting the emotion seep into her words and to rasp the edges of her voice. But she straightened her shoulders and met the stillness of his gaze with quiet dignity. "All you had to do was pick up the phone, Donovan. Just once."

For a short beat his eyes remained on hers, their depths stark with what looked like frustration, and Susannah braced herself for his next attack. But he only shook his head briefly before turning to pace the short distance to the window. Hands on hips, he stared out into the sodden landscape and belatedly she realised that the rain had relented to a thin drizzle, painting the glass a misty grey.

The same colour as his morning eyes, she recalled with a jab of regret, and when he swung around, those eyes fixed on hers without a hint of that remembered softness. "Let me get this straight. You're saying I lost an eight-figure deal I'd spent months pursuing because I didn't return your calls?"

Put like that it sounded like a game of school-yard pettiness, and when Donovan exhaled a disbelieving huff of breath, Susannah knew he was thinking the same. The awful truth churned sickly in her stomach. He was right. There had been an element of "the hell with you" in her decision, but there'd been a whole lot more going on, as well.

Lifting her chin, she met his gaze across the blue-matted floor. "It was more complicated than that."

"The complication being Alex Carlisle. Your fiancé."

"That was one thing," she replied carefully. One thing that Donovan Keane should not have known.

"And it brings us to my original question."

With the same slow, deliberate pace as he imbued the words, he started back toward her and the new determination in his expression caused a shiver of disquiet in Susannah's skin. When he stopped right in front of her, her heartbeat skittered with anxiety. She didn't have to ask which question. She knew he referred to the one he'd left on her voice mail last night.

Does your fiancé know you slept with me?

The unspoken question arced between them for several seconds in the tense stillness. Susannah didn't have to say a word. She knew he'd read the answer in her eyes and that any denial wouldn't be worth the breath it took, yet one thing needed saying. One very important thing.

"I wasn't engaged to Alex then."

"Yet you hared down here today. I can only assume you want to protect your dirty little secret."

Susannah's eyes widened with the sting of those words. They cheapened what she'd once thought special, but then she'd been a prize fool to think they'd shared anything other than a one-weekend stand. "Since you haven't contacted Alex, I can only assume you want something from me in return for keeping quiet about my…error in judgment?"

Something flared in his eyes, a brief indication that he'd noticed her choice of words. *Score one, Susannah.* Her battered ego rallied instantly.

"Why did you come back here, Donovan?" she asked. "What do you want from me?"

"I want to know how and when Carlisle became involved in this deal. The Palisades wasn't officially on the market, I did all the legwork, I convinced them to sell." His gaze locked on hers, gimlet sharp and merciless. "Did you take the deal to him?"

"Yes," Susannah admitted after a moment. "But only—"

"No buts or onlys. You brought him into this deal, you can take him out again."

"How do you expect me to do that?" Her voice rose, incredulous. "Horton's management accepted the Carlisle offer. The contracts are drawn."

"Drawn, but not signed."

Of course the contracts weren't signed—they wouldn't be until both sides of the deal she'd negotiated with Alex were fulfilled.

"As for how—" he paused to pull on a sweatshirt "—I don't care. That's your problem."

Stunned by the audacity of his demand, Susannah took several seconds to realise what the sweatshirt meant. By then he'd gathered towel and water. "You're leaving?" she asked on a note of alarm.

"We've said all that needs to be said for now. I'll leave you to make your phone calls."

Every instinct screamed at her to stop him, to explain the impossibility of what he asked, but as much as she railed against admitting it, he was right. She needed to think, to chart her options, to decide who to call.

Her mind had started to chew over that conundrum when he paused at the door.

"One of those calls should be to your mother," he said, as if he'd read her mind. "Ask her what she knows about me returning your calls. And while you're chatting, you might want to get your stories straight about your engagement."

He *had* called.

A week ago, according to Miriam Horton, who'd taken the call at the Melbourne office of Susannah's concierge service. Her mother wasn't a permanent employee, God forbid, but she helped out when necessary. Sometimes the need wasn't Susannah's, but more often Miriam's. Despite her many charity committees and her directorship at Horton Holdings, Miriam still needed more to fill the chasm created by her husband's death three years ago.

She needed to be needed, a condition Susannah understood all too well.

What Susannah didn't understand was Miriam's failure to pass on the news of Donovan's call. *A week ago.* A week of days spent working alongside her mother every day, preparing her for Susannah's absence over the next two weeks.

In the manager's office of The Palisades, Susannah released her icy clutch on the phone and paced to the window. How could her mother have kept this to herself?

"You were about to leave with Alex, to visit the Carlisle family's ranch," she had justified. "I know how uptight you were about meeting his mother and convincing his brothers he'd made the right choice of wife. On top of your business stress, I didn't want to load you with another burden."

"A client is never a burden," Susannah had reminded her.

"A client?" Miriam tsked her disapproval. "We both know Donovan Keane transcended that boundary."

Susannah ignored the jibe and concentrated on the question at hand. "You should have told me he called."

"What good would that have done, darling?"

I would have been warned of his imminent reappearance, I could have prepared my explanation, I might not have made an ill-informed goose of myself. "I would not have been caught out when he called back."

There'd been a moment's pause, the sound of air being drawn through delicate nostrils. "I told him, in no uncertain terms, never to call you again."

"That was not your place."

"It is always a mother's place to protect her child," Miriam countered, "as you will discover once you are a mother. That man used you, darling, and then he cast you aside. Now you're engaged to marry an honourable man whose word you can trust. Surely I don't need to remind you of that?"

Of course she didn't, but Donovan's final sling about getting the facts straight rang in her ears. "What, exactly, did you tell him about my engagement?"

"I don't recall my exact words."

"Did you mention when I accepted Alex's proposal?" When her mother *hmmed* vaguely, Susannah went very still. Miriam Horton did not do vague. Her sharp-as-a-whip recall of names, places, facts was legendary in Melbourne society circles. It also made her a valuable, if aggravating, member of Susannah's *At Your Service* team. "Did you tell him I was engaged when we met? When we came down here for that weekend?"

"He may have gleaned that impression, but I don't see why that should be an issue."

Caught between exasperation and a sinking sense of acceptance, Susannah pinched the bridge of her nose. At least now she understood why he'd looked at her so differently, why he'd been so scathing, why he'd sensed collusion between her and Alex.

"You said he called," Miriam continued.

"Last night. He's here, Mother. In Australia."

"Please tell me you're not seeing him, Susannah. Please tell me this isn't why Alex called, asking if I knew where you'd gone today. He sounded very unlike himself, edgy and short and slightly…annoyed."

More than slightly, Susannah predicted, turning away from the window with a heavy sigh. And she didn't blame him. After deciding to fly down here in the early hours of this morning, she'd tried to call him, to tell him she was going away to think things over, but he hadn't answered his phone…and wasn't *that* becoming the story of her life?

In her frantic rush to organize travel and get to the airport in time for her flight, she'd left the task of contacting him to her half sister. Zara would have delivered the message, Susannah had no doubt. She also wouldn't have been daunted by Alex or bullied into revealing anything more than the message.

However, Susannah had learned in the last thirty minutes how easily the message-delivery system could go pear-shaped…and the consequences of miscommunication. The idea of dealing with another thwarted alpha-on-a-mission filled her with trepidation, but she had to call Alex. She had to let him know she was all right, that she hadn't walked out on him, that she'd simply panicked when faced with a tricky problem from her past. She still intended to marry him just as soon as they could schedule a time and a celebrant.

In several decisive strides, she crossed to the desk and picked up the landline phone. There was no cell coverage in this remote corner of the country, which was a plus or a minus for the resort depending on the client. She imagined both Alex and Zara would have tried to contact her, that they would both be puzzled by her uncharacteristic "disappearance," since she'd left no clue as to her destination and never went anywhere without her phone.

With all the misunderstandings swirling in the air,

protecting her location had turned out to be a smart move. A face-off between Donovan and Alex could only end in an ugly confrontation. She had created this twisted mess and she needed to unravel it.

Starting with a phone call to Alex, and finishing with the explanation Donovan deserved.

Two

From a sheltered perch in his villa's hot tub, Van tracked the bobbing progress of the yellow umbrella as it dipped in and out of sight behind clusters of brush and jutting outcrops of rock. As well as sealed roadways that provided vehicular access to the accommodations, a series of rustic walking paths traversed the steeply sloped headland…although he didn't think Susannah was taking a nice, invigorating stroll in the rain.

Van had tried that himself after leaving the fitness centre—more at a run than a walk—before easing his overworked muscles into the swirling water. To help him relax, a bottle of pinot noir sat open at his side. The combination had been working a treat until he spotted the zigzagging umbrella zeroing in on his ridgetop location.

It had been ninety minutes since they spoke. Ninety

minutes to make her phone calls, to compare notes, to concoct whatever comeback she brought back to the table. And that's what she would do. Van had no illusions about that. If her stake in this deal wasn't high, she would not have hared down here today. She wouldn't have reacted so strongly to his accusations. She would have shrugged them off or called his bluff by handing him Alex Carlisle's business card.

Earlier he'd been tense and on guard, wary of giving away his one point of weakness. If she'd latched on to his deficient memory of that weekend, she could have grabbed a huge advantage. Instead she'd handed him the gift of her knowledge and the desire to unwrap it. If he asked the right questions or made suitable leading statements, she would fill in some of the memory gaps...and after meeting her, he wanted more than ever to fill in those gaps.

It wasn't only her beauty—expected, given the pictures he'd seen—but her attitude. He didn't recall if she'd used the phrase *how dare you accuse me,* but that was the message trumpeted by her defensive stance and haughty gaze.

Who would have thought that affronted dignity could be so damn arousing? Or that wintergreen eyes could light a flame in his blood?

Despite the miles he'd run through the rain, despite the blast of icy wind against his exposed skin, the heat of their encounter still licked through his body. It was no surprise that she'd lured him into her bed on that forgotten weekend. Or, if he wanted to believe her version of events, how much he'd have enjoyed doing the luring. He could imagine how easily the seduction would have gone down.

Hello, I'm Susannah, a few seconds tangling in those deceptively cool eyes, and she could have led him away…or pushed him down to the floor and taken him there.

The fact that he didn't remember any of the *wheres* or *whens* or *how many times* kicked through him, but not with the same impact as before. Now the frustration was tempered by satisfaction with how their first meeting had played out, as well as anticipation for their upcoming encounter.

He'd done the hard work, now he intended treating himself to a little entertainment.

When she disappeared behind the casuarinas that screened the approach to his villa, he planted both hands on the timber deck and hauled himself out of the water. For an evil beat of time, he contemplated walking to the door as he was. Naked, wet and, now he'd started thinking about who he'd be greeting at the door, aroused.

But he wrapped himself in one of the resort-issue robes, not through any sense of modesty, but for the same reason he'd donned a shirt before facing her in the gym. He didn't want her eyes drawn to the scars or her mind to their cause. He preferred to keep that in reserve, to play only if absolutely necessary.

With the bottle and emptied glass swinging from one hand, he headed for the sliders that separated terrace from living area. Despite the shelter afforded by the surrounding garden, a wet southeasterly gusted in and plastered the towelling to his damp thighs. It was the kind of unruly blast that could turn a woman's umbrella inside out, but when he opened the door, Susannah Horton stood on his doorstep, looking disappointingly dry in her tightly buttoned and belted raincoat.

She also wore a look of determined poise, although that faltered slightly when she took in his state of dress. It was the barest glance, before her eyes fixed resolutely on his face, but the trace of heat in her cheeks and eyes gave away her discomfiture. "I'm sorry," she said quickly. "I've caught you in the shower."

"The hot tub, actually. Would you care to join me?"

She blinked once in surprise before recovering swiftly. "Thank you, but I'll take a rain check."

Beautiful, poised *and* a sense of irony. Van's appreciation of Susannah Horton grew by the second. "The tub's sheltered, the water's warm, the wine's open." He saluted her with his glass. "I highly recommend it."

"I didn't bring my swimsuit."

"Nor did I," Van said evenly. "I don't see that as a problem."

The colour in her cheeks sharpened, but she held his gaze steadily. "Nor would I, but we've done all the tubbing we will ever do together."

"I gather it's my company you object to, and yet here you are."

"Briefly. I'm leaving at four."

"Do you always schedule your time this precisely?"

"Only when I have a flight to catch," she replied smartly, and Van realised she was talking about leaving the resort rather than his villa. All day, the weather had been iffy for the necessary helicopter transfer. He wouldn't bet on anyone going anywhere until after this storm front passed, but he figured she would find that out for herself soon enough.

Opening the door wider, he waved his wineglass toward the cosy interior. "I'm disappointed you're passing on the tub, but there's still the wine. Why don't you come in and I'll get you a glass?"

Her elegantly shod feet remained rooted to the spot and, by the look on her face, he might as well have invited her into the wolves' den. He managed to refrain from baring his teeth. "You might be all snug in your buttoned-up coat, but I'm freezing my ass…ets off here."

"Perhaps you should put some clothes on," she suggested. Taking obvious care to avoid contact with anything close to his assets, she edged through the doorway.

No, Van decided with a perverse little smile as he closed the door. *I prefer the robe, just to keep you on edge.*

And just to keep himself on edge he watched her walk away in skinny-heeled boots that were designed to highlight the sexy arch of her calves and the sway of her hips. "Why don't you take your coat off," he said, following her through to the living room. "Make yourself at home. I'll pour your—"

"This isn't a social visit," she replied crisply, still walking, circling the room as if she couldn't decide where to plant her sexy heels. "No wine for me."

"So it's business." Van deposited glass and bottle on the table. "I'm impressed. I didn't think you'd have managed to talk Carlisle around in such a short time."

That brought her up short in front of a leather sofa. She didn't sit. Shoulders straight and chin high, she turned to face him. "I haven't spoken to Alex yet. I may not be able to reach him until Monday."

Van settled his hips against the edge of the dining table and crossed his arms across his chest. Playtime was over…for now. "You can't reach your fiancé on weekends?"

"He isn't answering any of his phones, which means he is not in his office or at his home. I will continue to try his cell, but if he's out of the coverage area—" she shrugged "—there's nothing else I can do."

"Convenient."

"Not particularly," she countered without missing a beat, although her gaze sharpened as his barb found its mark. "I would prefer if I could reach him."

"How about your mother? Is she answering any of her phones?"

"Yes, I have spoken with her and she told me about your call last weekend. I'm sorry that she didn't tell me about that and I'm even more sorry that she mislead you about my engagement."

Van studied her closely for a second. Playtime was definitely over. "Are you telling me you're not engaged to Alex Carlisle?"

"I wasn't in July. I am now." Her gaze narrowed on his. "Why do I get the feeling that you don't believe me?"

"Because, apart from your mother, I haven't managed to find anyone who knows about it. Scores of mentions of you and Carlisle in business and society columns, yet no mention of pending nuptials."

"Which is exactly the way we like it," she said with bite. Then, as if annoyed with that minishow of temper, she pressed her lips together and composed herself before continuing in a more measured tone. "Both our families are high profile, especially the Carlisles, and we don't want a media circus surrounding our wedding plans. Alex decided—we both decided," she amended quickly, "not to make an announcement until after we're married."

"And when will that be?"

For the first time, her eyes shifted nervously and she lifted a hand—her left hand—in a vague fluttery gesture. "I…we haven't settled on a definite date."

Van's eyes shifted to her hand and a grim punch of satisfaction drove him to his feet. "Soon?"

"Yes," she said, her uneasy gaze steadying and settling. "Very soon."

Ever since he'd opened the door, Susannah had been at a distinct disadvantage. Everything from the carelessly knotted robe, to the teasing glint in his eyes, to the suggestion they get naked together in the hot tub, rang with unwanted memories. Inside the villa it was even worse. How could she concentrate when every place they'd kissed, touched and ended up naked was right in front of her eyes?

Of course she'd forced herself to keep those eyes stoically trained on his face, and the tricky nuances of their dialogue had managed to push everything—including his lack of clothes—to the fringes of her mind.

Until now.

As he moved closer, the edges of her vision and the core of her senses swam with the knowledge of how little he wore and how exposed she felt. Her heartbeat thickened and bumped painfully hard against her ribs. She didn't know what he wanted, why he'd suddenly shoved to his feet, why that narrowed gaze had suddenly focussed so intently on her—

"Why aren't you wearing a ring?"

Susannah stared back at him. She opened her mouth, found no answer and shut it again. In that beat of time, he picked up her left hand.

"Isn't that the usual procedure when you're engaged to be married? A diamond ring on this finger?"

He illustrated by grazing her ring finger with the pad of his thumb. It was a simple touch, but he stood close enough that she breathed the male heat of his skin, and her body acknowledged a myriad of other touches that were not so innocent. Warmth suffused her skin and pooled low in her belly but she fought it gamely. "I don't have an engagement ring."

"Carlisle didn't buy you a diamond? What did he give you then? A share package? Expansion capital? An exclusive agreement to use your service in the Carlisle hotel chain?"

His voice was soft and mocking, but his watchful eyes never left hers. Wasn't this why she'd hiked up here—to dispel the misconceptions and tell him the truth? To explain why the demand he'd made of her was impossible to deliver? Her stomach churned with trepidation, but she had to try.

"He offered a rescue package for my business."

"You're in financial trouble?"

Susannah tugged her hand free, but the warmth of that contact still tingled through her skin along with the shame of admitting her sorry business plight. Both flustered her; she could feel the heat in her face and couldn't stop it leaking into her voice. "I expanded too fast, my ideas were too grand and I wanted to prove I was capable of succeeding on my own. I made a poor borrowing choice and, yes, I've struggled with the debt."

"I'm finding that hard to fathom. You're a Horton. Your parents—"

"I didn't want their help," she cut in. "I didn't want to use my father's money. That was the point. You know why." She'd told him about her father's secret life and why she'd left the family company to start her own business, but there was something in his expression that suggested she should add this to the list of things he'd forgotten from their weekend.

"Accepting your parents' help is different to accepting help from your husband-to-be?" he asked.

"Yes," she said fiercely, "it absolutely is. This is not a one-sided situation."

"What *does* Carlisle get in return for his investment?"

"He gets me."

Their gazes clashed for a long, heated moment. Something flickered in Donovan's eyes, a hint of anger or denial that was quickly doused. He drew back and studied her with undisguised disapproval. "So, he's buying himself a wife. A blue-blooded Horton with all the right credentials and a resort on the side."

That mocking arrow found its target but Susannah didn't flinch. She held no illusions about the marriage contract she'd entered into. She understood the terms; she'd spent a full week dissecting them before reaching her decision. Lifting her chin, she met her adversary's disparaging gaze. "Alex believes he's getting a bargain."

"But then he doesn't know everything about you, does he?"

"I don't know what you're talking about."

"You do," he countered, his voice a silky contrast to the steel of his gaze. "What does your Alex think about his wife sleeping with clients?"

"His *wife* may have made some poor choices in the past, but that was before she made any vows of fidelity. Once she committed to one man, she would never cheat. She knows the hurt that can inflict on everyone involved."

"Have you made many of these poor choices?"

"Just one comes to mind."

"It can't have been all bad," he said, and their gazes tangled for an unnervingly quiet second. She couldn't lie, she couldn't construct a smart retort. She doubted she could even hide the truth that ached in her chest from showing in her eyes.

Memories, she told herself. *It is nothing but false memories.*

"No," she managed finally. "Not all bad. I learned a valuable lesson about making rash choices, about staying true to my naturally cautious nature. About thinking my actions through to the consequences. I learned to ask, why does this man want me? And to be honest with the answers."

Heat flared in his quicksilver eyes. "You don't believe I could have just wanted you?"

"You wanted me," she replied, "and you made sure

you got me. You just didn't disclose your reasons until after you'd had me."

A muscle ticked in his cheek and his mouth tightened in an uncompromising line, but for a fraction of a second, she imagined a softened note of regret in his eyes. Then he turned and started toward the kitchen. He'd only taken a half-dozen strides—she'd barely had time to suck in a deep breath to ease the pounding in her chest—when he swung back around to face her.

Oh, yes, she'd definitely imagined the softening. Now his expression was inscrutable, but the sharp lines of his cheekbones and the straight set of his mouth lent him a hard, dangerous aura. Her instincts shivered back to high alert.

"You didn't mention this place." He indicated his surroundings with a sweep of his hand. "Where does it fit into the Carlisle-Horton merger?"

"It didn't initially, not until after Alex proposed."

"Which was when?"

Susannah pressed her lips together and withheld her none-of-your-business response. He wanted the facts; she would give him the facts. Then, perhaps, he might see the impossibility of his quest. "In late July, just after our weekend. I was feeling a little…burned by that experience."

"And so you were receptive to a cold, business-contract proposal?"

"I was receptive to his honesty," she replied, and was rewarded by the glint of irritation in his eyes. Good. He'd delivered enough backhanded blows, he deserved to take one back. "I weighed up the pros and cons. I talked it over with my mother, and in the process, she found out what had happened between us. To say she wasn't happy would be an understatement."

"Your mother requires approval of your lovers?"

"She wasn't happy that you'd used me to influence your bid. She withdrew her approval."

The spark of irritation she'd lit in his eyes turned cold and hard. "She occupies one seat in that boardroom. Are you saying the rest of the board agreed?"

"Not immediately but as Edward Horton's widow her opinion holds some sway. She argued against your business scruples and they listened but they also had your bid on the table. So my mother asked for a week to come up with an alternate buyer."

"So she found Carlisle and added a clause to the marriage contract. 'You can have my daughter, but only if you better the bid we have for The Palisades.'" He made a short, rough sound, the perfect punctuation for the scathing tone of his delivery. "And that's where you came in, with your intimate knowledge of my bid."

"No," Susannah objected vehemently. "I had no part in that."

"Are you saying this was all concocted between your mother and Carlisle? Without your knowledge?"

"I agreed to the marriage contract. I agreed to all the terms, including The Palisades. I didn't want you to get this place. I didn't want to ever see you again." An objection lit his eyes and she hurried on, not wanting to argue that point. "But I did not divulge anything about your bid. How could I have known what to divulge, for heaven's sake? Do you think I read your mind or that you murmured sweet multimillion-dollar figures in your sleep or that I sneaked a look at your files?"

Susannah stopped, her eyes widening at the stillness in his face. He *did* think that. She shook her head slowly and coughed out a disbelieving laugh.

"How, exactly, do you think I might have managed that? We spent all our time here—" she waved her arm, indicating the rooms around them, but her tone was as cool and disparaging as the subject demanded "—in the villa I had booked. Do you think that after wearing you out in the bedroom, I picked your room key from your pocket and clambered down the cliffside in the dead of night to peek at your laptop?"

Consternation tightened the line of his brows, but Susannah was beyond dissecting what he was thinking or feeling or pretending not to feel. Always she had taken pride in her ability to contain her emotions, to present her side of an argument with logic and clarity. Yet now the bubble of anger tightened her chest and disillusionment burned the back of her throat.

Earlier, he'd claimed that it hadn't been all bad, and she'd allowed herself a fleeting memory of the good. The stimulation she'd felt from conversations that ranged from wicked banter to sharp debate. The simple pleasure of walking beside him, the strength of his hand around hers, smiling when their strides fell into a matching rhythm. The more complex pleasure of his body joined with hers, delivering her to places unknown, to emotions unfelt.

She'd thought the aftermath, the consequences, his failure to respond to her phone calls, had destroyed all the good memories, but she'd been wrong. Some had lingered, enough for him to trample with today's insulting allegations. Enough that she now felt angry and bitter and profoundly disappointed in him and her own judgment.

Drawing a strengthening breath, she forced herself to face him one last time and to say what still needed to be said.

"I was about to tell you why I agreed when Mother suggested adding The Palisades to the marriage contract, but I will save my breath. It's obvious you don't remember anything about my character or my background or what we shared that weekend. I'm beginning to wonder if you remember me at all."

Suddenly she felt cold and drained and tired. She wanted home and the security of the choices she'd made, nice and orderly and safe. With strides that gathered strength and pace as she went, she circled the dining table and headed for the door.

He called her name, but she kept right on moving. When she heard the heavy pad of his footfalls against the timber floor, she moved even faster. Clumsy fingers struggled with the lock before, finally, she yanked the door open. But a large hand flattened against the timber beside her head and pushed it shut.

For a long second, she stared at the broad curve of his thumb, while her heart raced and her body registered the familiar heat and weight of his body at her back. Far too close, all too familiar. Anger welled up inside her, and this time, she welcomed its rescuing strength.

"Let me go," she said through gritted teeth.

"Not yet." His voice was low and conciliatory, his breath warm against the side of her face.

The traitorous response that prickled through Susannah's skin only made her madder. She refused to be taken in by false apologies or belated attempts at placation. She ungritted her teeth, but only so she could speak. "You have three seconds," she said tightly, "before I scream blue murder. If you remember nothing else, then you should remember how far my voice carries across this headland."

Closing her eyes, she started the count but only made it through one before the warmth of his breath distracted her. At two he started to speak; at three his words took hold.

"I don't remember, Susannah. You, your scream, anything."

Three

Stunned, Susannah peeled herself from the door and turned within the wide stance of his body. He didn't back off more than a few inches leaving her little room to manoeuvre. The impact of his words blurred with the shock of contact between his knees and her thighs, her elbow and his chest. Renewed heat bloomed beneath her skin, quick and unquenchable.

Squeezing her eyelids tight, she forced the memories—only memories, she told herself again—back under control so she could concentrate on the present. *His* memory, or lack thereof. But when she opened her eyes, her gaze caught on the broad vee of chest exposed between the gaping sides of his robe. The exposed skin, the sprinkle of dark hair, the line of raised flesh…

She sucked in an audible breath and without conscious thought, reached up to push the towelling aside. To reveal scar tissue that hadn't existed ten weeks ago. "My God, Donovan. What happened?"

When he didn't answer, she raised her stunned gaze and found his attention fixed on where her hand clutched the edge of his robe, the backs of her fingers resting flush against the heat of his skin. She released her grip, reclaimed her hand, and slowly his gaze shifted to her face, silvery eyes narrowed and aware. It was a look she recognised but didn't want to remember.

Without answering her question, he pushed away from the door and strolled back to the table where he'd abandoned the bottle of red wine earlier.

When he held up the bottle and raised an eyebrow in question, she nodded, and the familiarity of that silent exchange brought a confused frown to her face as she watched him pour two glasses.

I don't remember. You, your scream, anything.

"You don't remember… Is that because of what happened to cause the scar?" Her mind churned over his revelation and the possibilities. "Were you in an accident?"

"An accident, no. I was mugged." He gave a shrug, as if it were nothing. Or something he preferred others to see as nothing. "Woke up with a memory block."

Her gaze dropped to his chest, to the now-concealed scar. She had to moisten her dry mouth before she could speak. "And that?"

"One of their weapons, apparently, was a broken bottle."

With every appearance of complacency, he held

out the glass of wine he'd poured for her. Leaving the sanctuary of the door, Susannah managed to walk the dozen or so steps to take the proffered glass, despite the unsteadiness in her legs. Amazingly her voice sounded calm when she asked, "Where did this happen?"

"On my way home."

"You told me you don't have a home."

Surprise stilled the glass he'd been raising to his lips. It echoed briefly in his eyes before he answered. "I have a temporary home in San Francisco."

"When?"

Their eyes met over the rim of his glass and Susannah's racing heart skipped a beat, waiting, anticipating the answer. "In July. The day I returned from here."

"You were in hospital? Is that why—" She had to stop, to shake her head and clear the image of him broken and beaten from her mind's eye. "You didn't return my phone calls."

"Not until I returned to the office."

"How long was that?" she asked, her voice no longer even or steady.

"Two months, all up."

That's why he'd been constantly "unavailable" or "out of the office" over the weeks she'd tried to contact him. She'd assumed his assistant was screening his calls, that he'd chosen to ignore the messages, and she'd given up trying to get through.

Two months to recover from his injuries. My God.

Unable to master the trembling in her hand or legs, she put down the untouched drink and when Donovan pulled a chair from the table, she murmured her thanks and sank to its solid support. "That is a long time to be laid up."

"Tell me about it." He punctuated the wry response with the same hitch of his shoulder as before, a fake casualness that masked the tension etched in his face. For the first time since she'd watched him unobserved from the foyer of the gym, Susannah allowed herself to study him fully from head to foot. He looked so straight, so strong, so healthy. She didn't want to imagine the scale of injuries that would have kept him hospitalised for such an extended time.

"You look fit now," she said, when he caught her thorough inspection. She didn't need details of those injuries, she told herself. She didn't need to ask why his assistant had been so obstructively short with information. It was impossible to change what had happened and too late for regret. She needed to lighten the mood, to lift the crushing weight that had descended on her chest. "The punching bag I found you working over this morning—did that have the face of one of your attackers painted on it?"

A hint of amusement touched his lips as he took the chair next to hers. "Something along those lines."

"Did it help?"

"Not as much as hitting the real guy."

"You went down fighting?" Eyebrows arched in faux surprise, Susannah asked the question even though she knew the answer.

The day in July when he'd walked into her office unannounced, when she'd told him she wasn't available to take him to Stranger's Bay, warned her that he never gave up on anything without a fight. Then he'd set to work negotiating a price she couldn't turn down, talking her into dinner, seducing her with disarmingly direct words and the silvery smile of his eyes. She'd been charmed to the mat before the bell ended round one.

And now he'd returned to pursue the same fight, and a fight meant winners and losers. That foresight settled deep in her bones and when she lifted her gaze to Donovan's, all sign of amusement was gone.

"So I'm told," he said in response to her question about going down fighting. "I don't remember, but apparently I put one of them in hospital with me."

Although she strived, Susannah failed to keep the edge of dismay from her face. It didn't help that the chilling action played through her mind like a scene from a movie. Her gaze drifted up, to the shorter hair. Funny how that little detail hadn't really registered until now. "You were hit over the head?"

"And rendered unconscious," he confirmed, "thus ending the fight."

She nodded, swallowed. Her restless eyes shifted over him, searching out what else she may have missed, before returning to his eyes. "Do you remember *anything* from before the accident?"

"Everything, up until I left America. I remember bits and pieces of the days I spent in Melbourne. Meeting with the CEO at Horton Holdings. The hotel where I stayed. It was the Carlisle Grande," Van said with an unamused smile. Selected before he knew anything about Alex Carlisle and his family-owned group of hotels, other than he liked the beds and the service was impeccable.

"You don't remember coming here to Stranger's Bay that weekend?"

"No."

She shook her head and puffed out a short note of scepticism. "I thought amnesia only happened in books and movies."

Van's eyes narrowed on hers. "You think I'm making this up?"

In the pause, in the hint of a shrug, Van read her doubt. He jackknifed to his feet and stalked away a few paces.

"I believe you, I just find it so difficult to imagine not remembering anything."

That quietly spoken comment turned him back around. She sat straight and tall in the stiff-backed chair, her ivory coat still buttoned to the base of her throat. Against the rain-lashed windows, her hair was a bright splash of colour. Her eyes remained unsettled with a mixture of compassion and doubt.

It struck him like a blast of that rain-fuelled wind that he'd spent a whole weekend with her, here in these rooms. That coat he may well have unbuttoned and tossed aside. He might have stripped those boots from her legs. Kissed her in all the places that had drummed through his mind in those seconds he'd held her pinned against the door.

"I look at you sitting there," he said, his voice low and laced with the frustration of not knowing, "and I find it hard to believe that I don't remember you."

She blinked. A slow-motion movement of dark lashes against pale cheeks. "That must be a little…odd."

Van gave a hollow laugh. "There's one description."

"How have you dealt with it?"

He swirled the wine in his glass, wondering whether to answer. How much to share. But then he recalled the compassion in her eyes and, what the hell, he'd likely shared a whole lot more than this with Susannah Horton. "I talked to the people I was dealing with that week. I retraced my footsteps. I reconstructed. I cursed a lot."

"Cursing sometimes helps."

Van studied her sitting there all prim and proper in her buttoned-up coat, and he thought about her cursing in that crisp private-school voice. The image was intriguing. *She* was intriguing. "I have a business backer, a mentor, who believes curses are the spice of our bland language."

"Mac," she said softly.

Van's hand stilled and tightened around the stem of his wineglass. "I told you about her?"

"Yes, although there's no need to look so worried. You didn't let any family skeletons out of the closet, nor did I sneakily access the information from your possessions."

Although her words were flippant, there was a bite to her tone. He deserved it, and she deserved an apology. "I'm sorry that I insulted you with that insinuation. That wasn't my intention."

"Really? What was your intention?"

"To find out what had happened with the acquisition deal. When I left Melbourne, I had a deal on the table. When I woke up a week later, it was gone."

He saw a flicker of guilt and what could have been regret cross her face. If possible she blanched even more. "Telling me about your amnesia from the start would have made that conversation go a lot more smoothly."

"For you, yes."

"And you?"

Van met her eyes with unflinching directness. "I came here knowing *these* things about you, Susannah. You're Miriam Horton's daughter. I employed you to show me Stranger's Bay. You were engaged to Alex Carlisle."

"I wasn't en—"

"This is what I knew from your mother, and everyone I asked vouched for her integrity. But my point is," he stressed when she looked like interrupting, "I came here thinking the worst of you. If you'd known I remembered nothing, how could I have trusted anything you told me?"

"And now, do you believe anything I told you?"

"Yes."

Surprise widened her eyes and some colour returned to her face. She looked almost pleased, and Van felt a kick of satisfaction low in his gut, the kind that came from a surprise win on the markets or an unexpected victory at the negotiating table.

"Why?" she asked.

"Who could make up a story like that?"

Their eyes met and shared the dry humour of that answer in a rare moment of connection. Then wariness returned to chase away the smile. She stood suddenly, a quick, jerky movement at odds with her normal grace, and in the awkwardness he caught a distracting glimpse of knee, thigh, skirt. It was nothing overt, nothing sexual, but the sight threw him right off balance.

He'd seen that exact shift of motion before. It moved in and out of focus in the darkness that used to house his memory of that weekend.

"It doesn't make any difference, does it?"

Van looked up, the sensation gone in a blink, leaving him unsure if he'd remembered or only imagined remembering. "What doesn't?" he asked, frowning.

She lifted her hands and let them drop in a gesture of defeat. "Your amnesia—me now knowing about your accident—it changes nothing."

"Not even your perception of why I lost this acquisition?"

Her eyes clouded with an emotion Van hated. Pity. Sympathy. Compassion. Whatever label it wore, he'd seen enough these past ten weeks to last ten lifetimes. "I understand why you feel robbed and I'm very sorry, but that doesn't change what has happened since."

"One thing hasn't changed. I still want The Palisades. And after hearing why I lost out, I want it even more."

"I'm sorry," she said again, her voice rasping on the infernal word. "But it is too late. Can't you see that? The agreement has been made with Alex, the contract is drawn."

"But won't be signed until you marry Carlisle." He paused, swirling the last inch of red wine and allowing the idea that circled his brain to take root. "What happens to The Palisades sale if the marriage doesn't go ahead?"

"That is not going to happen," she said resolutely. "Alex is a man of this word. He will not pull out of this deal, no matter what you say or do. The threat you made about exposing our affair won't change his mind."

"And yet you came down here, presumably to stop me doing that."

"I came to find out what was going on, and why you

were back. Alex knows we weren't engaged that weekend, he knows I didn't cheat or lie to him, so he won't change his mind about marrying me."

"And what if *you* change your mind?"

"You're suggesting that *I* break my engagement?"

"We're not talking about a love match, Susannah. This is a business contract. You've been bartered like a high-price commodity."

A shadow crossed her face, but a spark of vehemence lit her eyes and lifted her chin. "Perhaps I wasn't clear earlier, but you're reading this wrong. Yes, this is an unusual alliance and it is bound and tied up like a business deal, but there was no coercion involved. I want to marry Alex. From this union I am getting everything I want. A husband I respect and admire, children, an extended family, as well as all the advantages being a Carlisle will bring to my business.

"I'm sorry, Donovan," she said drawing herself up tall. "I really am, but there is nothing I or you or anyone can do to change what's transpired. I really have to go now or this flight will leave without me, but when I get back to civilisation I will talk to Alex. He's a fair man. Perhaps he will reconsider that part of the contract."

His eyes narrowed. "I thought you said he wouldn't back down."

"I don't believe he will, but I'm offering to try. That's all I can do, other than suggest some other properties that would suit your purposes just as well as The Palisades."

"I'm not interested in another property. I came here to buy this one."

"Then I guess it's up to Alex."

* * *

"Not if I can help it," Van told himself after she'd left. He always steered his own ship. No way was he leaving his destiny in the hands of a competitor. Alex Carlisle might be a fair man, but he was also a businessman with a reputation for smart dealing.

Why would he give up The Palisades?

Sure, sweetheart, I'll tear up the contract so your last lover can have another shot at a prime property.

No, that was not going to happen. Carlisle wanted the property; he wanted Susannah as his wife; why the hell would he give up either?

From his terrace, Van tracked the careful progress of the resort's courtesy pickup as it schlooshed a wet path back to the central resort buildings. It had picked her up from his door, presumably to transport her to the helipad and her four-o'clock departure. Van couldn't see her going anywhere in this weather. In the hour since he'd stepped from the tub, the squalls of wind had grown flukier, the rain heavier.

The fact that she wasn't leaving—that she couldn't scurry back to the fiancé she respected and admired—did nothing to ease Van's darkening discontent. It was a tangle of frustration, of missed opportunity, of all she'd told him and all he didn't yet know.

Hands braced on the balcony railing, he glared out into a landscape tailor-made for his mood. Past the dark jut of the clifftop, he could just make out the churn of whitecaps against the obsidian waters of the bay. Somewhere out there, shielded by the thickening curtain of rain, sat Charlotte Island. The private and exclusive island was the heart of the resort property and the reason no substitute would do.

He would have visited in July, he had no doubt about that despite his lack of memories or photographs. Both were lost to the chance of fate that put him the same place at the same time as that trio of brawny thieves. They'd taken more than his possessions, they'd also stolen a chunk of precious time.

He slapped his hand down against the steel rail as a bead of suppressed fury exploded inside him.

With every week he'd been laid up mending broken bones and bruised organs, Mac had slipped another week closer to the end. Now, more than ever, he wanted this land returned to her ownership. His last and only meaningful gift to the woman who'd shaped him from a cocky young upstart to a respected equity player.

Lifting his face to the icy kiss of the rain, he considered his options. He could tell Susannah why he was set on acquiring this land. Maybe that would stir sufficient sympathy for his cause, maybe she would even talk to Carlisle as she'd promised, but compassion was not recognised currency in the cut-throat world of business. And no matter how many ways she cried family-husband-happiness, this marriage was a business arrangement.

Bottom line, he had one chance—and one night—to buy himself back into this deal.

All he had to do was stop the wedding from going ahead.

Four

"Listen to that rain! I bet you're glad you decided to stay."

The reservations manager came out of the bathroom where she'd been checking to ensure Susannah had all the necessary toiletries. Since she'd left home with nothing but a hastily packed tote bag, she was grateful for whatever the resort could supply for her unexpected overnight stay.

Before she could respond to Gabrielle's comment, the drumming of rain on the villa's iron roof intensified to a deafening din. Susannah closed her mouth. She might not be exactly glad about staying, but the weather had robbed her of any choice.

Gabrielle joined her in the bedroom, her nose creasing into a wince as she gazed out the window. "We made the right decision in talking you out of driving."

By *we* she meant the resort staff. Susannah had been all for leaving by whatever means available. With the helicopter shuttle grounded, she'd asked about hiring a car—heck, she'd even offered to buy a four-wheel drive belonging to Jock, the doorman-cum-resort-chauffeur! But everyone from Jock to the manager had declared her crazy to consider attempting the long drive in such hazardous conditions.

Watercraft had been suggested as an "if you absolutely must leave" option, and Susannah shuddered. There was a line between absolutely-need-to and really-want-to, and that line was the wide expanse of choppy waves between here and Appleton.

"You'll be comfortable here for tonight." Gabrielle finished plumping the massed arrangement of pillows on the bed and straightened. "And if the worst comes to the worst, we will look into the boat option tomorrow."

"Is there a possibility the shuttle won't be flying?" Susannah asked on a rising note of concern.

"I trust it won't come to that." The other woman's cheerful smile was spoiled by a flicker of concern in her eyes. "I am sorry I couldn't put you in your usual accommodation. Unfortunately our other guest had already reserved The Pinnacle."

"There's no need to apologise, Gabrielle. I didn't have a reservation and you've known me long enough to realise that I never expect deferential treatment just because of my name."

"I know, but thank you for the reassurance. It's been quite a day."

"It has," Susannah agreed. *And it wasn't over yet.*

Her heart kicked up a beat, recalling the wording Gabrielle had used. "Did I hear you correctly when you referred to 'the other guest'? Are there just the two of us here tonight?"

"We had a late cancellation due to the weather, from a group who'd booked most of the resort for a corporate team-building exercise."

"Is the forecast that bad?"

"For beach games and bushwalking?" Gabrielle's smile was wry when she tilted her head as if listening to the remorseless rain. "I'd say, yes."

For *anything* outdoors, Susannah conceded as she studied the view—or lack thereof—from the bedroom window. Her thoughts zeroed to the only other guest and his intentions. Why had he come back to Stranger's Bay? Was he really reconstructing that weekend?

Her pulse thudded. Her gaze skimmed over the bed and a vivid memory of how they'd spent much of their weekend flared low in her belly.

She chased it away with a reminder of where she was supposed to be tonight and the heat turned chill.

"Is there anything wrong with your bed?" Gabrielle sounded puzzled. "If you require more pillows, or a specific—"

"No, no," Susannah said quickly. "I was miles away, thinking about something else entirely. I had a...date... for tonight."

"I'm sure he'll understand."

Susannah wasn't so sure, but she followed Gabrielle out to the state-of-the-art kitchen where the other woman continued her check of the pantry and refrigerator. "The basics are all here but I'll order a hamper from catering and send it along once the rain eases. As for dinner—"

"Please, don't go to any more trouble on my behalf," Susannah implored. "I'm sure the hamper will be more than enough without ordering in dinner."

Gabrielle made her way to the door. "You know nothing is ever too much trouble. If you change your mind or if there's anything else you need, I'm a phone call away. And if there's any update on the weather or transport, I will let you know."

"I would appreciate that. Thank you."

After Susannah closed the door, she roamed from room to room, contemplating the ramifications of being stranded here longer than overnight. In an effort at optimism, she told herself this would delay facing the wrath of Alex for another day. Unfortunately that couldn't dispel the ominous downside—she and Donovan Keane were here alone.

Knowing he was ensconced in the luxurious villa where they'd shared that other weekend left her feeling restless and uneasy. It was a sensation she understood far too well. From the moment she first met Donovan Keane, he'd unsettled her senses and her equilibrium.

Even now, with the curtain of rain adding an extra layer of isolation to each of the scattered villas, she felt his presence in every overly responsive female cell.

Paused at the window facing out toward the bay, she lifted her hands to rub the goose bumps that had sprung up on her arms. She needed warm. She needed dry. But first she needed a long, hot shower.

When she exited the steam-shrouded bathroom a half hour later, her hair wrapped turban-style in a towel, she felt toasty warm and as relaxed as possible given the robe was identical to the one Donovan had worn. She hung her clothes on the dining chairs and thought about lighting the fire. The more quickly they dried, the more quickly she could shed this reminder of Donovan.

Unconsciously her hand came up to clutch the lapel, and her stomach tightened again with the shock of that moment of discovery. The scar, his story, her imagining of his injuries.

A knock at the door startled her out of her introspection.

Her first thought—*it's him!*—gave way to a deprecating huff of breath. It would be catering with the promised hamper. Her nerves breathed a sigh of relief and her stomach rumbled in anticipation. She'd missed lunch and the airline breakfast had been insubstantial and too long ago.

"Just a second," she called, unpeeling the towel from her hair. Skirting the makeshift laundry, she hurried to the door. And where she should have seen a uniformed member of the resort's catering staff smiling a greeting, she saw Donovan Keane leaning against the door frame.

Dressed in dark trousers and a white shirt, he looked hauntingly familiar. Just like their first night here at Stranger's Bay when he'd appeared uninvited on her doorstep.

As he straightened, the silver drift of his gaze took her all in, from the tips of her bare toes to the top of her tangled curls. All the blood drained from Susannah's brain into her skin. Annoyance and agitation and dismay warred with those unruly female responses.

Stop it, she warned her hormones. *You do not want to see him. Especially straight from the shower with no underwear, no makeup, no defences.*

"What are you doing here?" she asked curtly.

He inclined his head, indicating a hefty picnic-style hamper at his feet. "Dinner, I hope."

Taking advantage of Susannah's slackjawed surprise, Van picked up the weighty basket and brushed past her.

She recovered enough to catch at his shirtsleeve. "Stop. Wait."

If he'd wanted, Van could have shrugged off that attempt to stop his entry. Instead he paused a step inside the door and half a step from her flushed countenance. For the first time, he noticed the scatter of freckles on her nose, visible because her face was scrubbed clean from the shower.

His gaze dipped to her throat and then to her chest. Barely visible beneath the rosy tint of her skin, more of those freckles spanned the deep V created by the wraparound garment. He would wager his entire portfolio of blue chips that she wore nothing underneath…nothing but a blush and that faint sprinkle of gold-dust freckles.

He noted the rapid beat of pulse at the base of her throat, and her hand released his sleeve to clutch the robe tight across her breasts. Slowly his gaze lifted to her face. He'd placed her at a distinct disadvantage turning up unannounced, and that's exactly what he'd hoped to do.

Catering had delivered his hamper of provisions first

and, in an idle conversation about the weather, the waiter named Rogan revealed that his second and only other port of call was, "A day visitor caught out by the storm. Chopper's grounded so she had to stay the night."

Van's plan had formulated in a fortuitous heartbeat.

To avoid a drenching he'd hitched a ride with Rogan in the catering van, and along the way he'd planned his approach. Patience, finesse, play that compassion he'd glimpsed in her eyes earlier. He hadn't considered that he might enjoy himself in the process.

Looking down at her now, at the tremble in her slender fingers as they held the sides of her robe together, at the nervous swipe of her tongue as she moistened her lips, Van knew he was going to enjoy this far more than he had any right to. He reached past her wet tumble of curls and leaned his weight against the still-open door. Apparently her grip on the doorknob matched her one on the robe. He applied more pressure until her death grip gave and the door closed with a muffled click. Although the wicker hamper provided a safe barrier between their bodies, she flattened herself against the cedar door as if she wanted nothing more than to slink inside it.

Suppressing a smile, Van eased his weight off the door. Earlier, when he'd held her captive against another door, he hadn't indulged himself with anything more than breathing her scent. This time, he selected one tightly spiralled curl and tucked it behind her ear, deliberately brushing her cheek with the knuckle of his middle finger.

Her skin was as silky soft as the sound of her indrawn breath, as warm as the response cutting through his veins.

"What do you think you're doing?" she asked in a pitchy rush. Worry carved a frown into the space between her perfectly shaped eyebrows.

"Don't worry, Susannah." He gave her a wolfish smile, and just for the hell of it touched his fingertips to that frown. "I'm here to eat dinner, not you."

He left her there, all wide-eyed shock and open-mouthed indignation, and strolled to the kitchen portion of the open-plan living space. He hefted the hamper onto the countertop and started unpacking the contents.

"Why?"

Van looked up. He hadn't heard her bare-footed approach, but he noticed how she carefully skirted the island counter, keeping its solid width between them. He noticed that her cheekbones were still tinged with pink.

"Why what?" he asked, inspecting the label on a local Gewürztraminer, before putting the bottle down. He looked into the wary distrust of her eyes. "Why am I eating dinner, or why aren't I eating—"

"Why are you *here.* And why did you bring my supplies instead of catering?"

"Rogan was doing the delivery but I took pity on the poor man, running about in the rain."

"Didn't he have a vehicle?" she asked.

"Yes, but it isn't easy keeping dry." Van's gaze shifted to the room beyond her, to where the articles of her clothing hung on every available piece of furniture. "It would appear you had a similar problem."

"*You* managed."

"Ah, but I'm quick."

"Not al—"

She stopped, her lips compressing into a tight line. Van went still. "Not al-*ways*?" he ventured.

Oh, yeah. That's what she'd been about to let slip. The truth swirled in her eyes even as she shook her head. The notion of a long, lazy exploration of those long legs and freckles ambushed his brain for a sweet second…

"I was going to say that not all the staff would care about getting a bit damp."

Van had to admire her quick improvisation.

"I wouldn't have thought Rogan would mind," she continued. "I believe we're the only two guests, so he hasn't exactly got a lot of running around to do."

"Since we are the only guests, I suggested he go home." He unearthed a corkscrew from the well-stocked utensils drawer and looked up enquiringly. "Which wine shall I open, the red or the white?"

A frown creased her brow as she looked from one bottle to the other, then she drew an audible breath. "Look, Donovan, I really don't think this is a good idea."

"Why not? Don't you trust yourself to share dinner with me?"

"It's *you* I don't trust," she fired back. "You invited yourself here without any forewarning, and I know it has nothing to do with dinner or sparing Rogan from extra work. You always have an agenda."

"And what agenda do you think I'm pursuing here, apart from dinner, company and conversation?"

"The one that brought you to Stranger's Bay in the first place. An eight-figure deal you spent a lot of resources working on, and that you don't appreciate losing."

"There are a lot of things I don't appreciate losing,

Susannah," he said mildly, but there was nothing mild in his gaze. "Especially when the fight isn't fair."

"I understand why you might feel that way, but—"

"Do you? Do you understand what it's like to lose days from your life? To not know what you'd said, what you'd done, what you'd shared?"

Her gaze glittered under his for a moment, before falling away.

"I figure we shared dinner, company and conversation that weekend in a villa just like this one." He applied himself to opening the Gewürztraminer while he selected his words and their casual delivery for maximum effect. "Your fiancé can hardly complain about the circumstances that have been thrust upon you. You said he's a fair man. Would he object to you joining me at the dinner table and helping me recover something of what I've lost?"

"Helping you…how?" she asked after a moment, her voice edged with wariness.

"You asked how I was dealing with this memory blank. I told you I'd worked on backtracking, gathering information, recreating events. I've put everything together…everything except those days here."

"I'm sorry, Donovan. I can't do that. I can't help you recreate that weekend."

"I'm only asking you to talk to me, to share some of where we went, what we did." He poured a splash of the pale golden wine into a glass and slid it across the countertop. "You can tell me where we ate, what we drank."

He could see her vacillating, her gaze uneasy, the infinitesimal slump in her shoulders as her willpower weakened. Reaching forward he touched his index finger to the back of her hand. Just that one touch to bring her uneasy gaze winging back to his.

"You might not be able to help me with anything else I lost, but you can help me with this."

Although she didn't answer straight away, he saw the capitulation in her expressive green eyes. Satisfaction churned rich and strong through his blood, but he waited, his posture deceptively casual while she prepared her answer.

"I can try." She lifted her chin a notch. "But I want to make it clear that all I'm providing are the facts."

"That's all I expect."

"I can't promise to remember everything."

"I'm sure you remember the important things."

Her gaze fell away, and she lifted a hand to rub at her upper arm. Cold...or nervous? "We can talk over dinner, but afterward I have things to do."

"Hair to wash, laundry to do," Van murmured. She'd already swung away to gather up the clothes scattered around the table. A pink skirt and white sweater. Lacy white bra. A wisp of nothing that had to be underwear.

She held them all tight to her chest as she faced him across the table, clearly unamused by his aside. "I have phone calls to make."

To Carlisle, Van guessed. *The man who'd won what he had lost.*

That thought killed the buzz of warm satisfaction he'd had going. The touch of mean left in its place wouldn't let him watch her scurry off with her armful of clothes without one last bite. "You don't have to change on my account. I imagine I've seen you in a robe before…and without."

At the door to her bedroom, she paused to cut him a disparaging look. "That is precisely the reason I suggested this dinner was a bad idea."

"Because I've seen you naked?"

Colour flared in her cheekbones, but her eyes remained cool and steady on his. "Because I can't trust you not to mention that fact."

"And that makes you uncomfortable?"

"I'm engaged to marry another man. Of course it does."

As if Van needed that reminder. Or that extra jab to his prickly mood. "Do you think I would try to seduce another man's bride?" he asked.

"I think you would do whatever it takes to get your hands on the contract to The Palisades."

With the hair dryer on high, Susannah blasted the remaining dampness from her clothes before turning the appliance on her hair. That was a necessity, not a vanity. Plus it ate up some time while she worked on her composure. Perhaps if she remained locked in the bathroom long enough, her "guest" would go away and leave her to regret past mistakes in peace.

Or perhaps not.

She allowed her memory to slide briefly to that weekend, to recall an exchange where she'd described him as a can-do man. With an amused grin he'd shaken his head and said, "No. I'm more *will-do*."

She didn't allow herself to dwell on the memory of how he'd demonstrated that *will-do* quality. Instead she used the knowledge to bolster her defences. She had agreed to help him out because she did sympathise over his lost memory and the circumstances that had led him to lose the deal.

But it was only a deal. He would get over that loss and move on to another deal, another property, another asset. Alex did not have the luxury of that time. He needed a wife now, and The Palisades was part of that marriage contract.

Tonight's dinner was only about helping Donovan fill in some blanks in his memory. She could do that. And she could do it while remaining cool and calm and not letting him get to her with his incendiary taunts.

She was not going to let him forget that she was another man's bride.

Leaning back from the mirror she studied herself in the unforgiving light and crinkled her nose. Not exactly the picture of cool, calm and collected that she was aiming for. Despite her best efforts, her hair had taken on a life of its own. A pulse beat noticeably at the base of her throat. Her skin remained rosy-pink from the blow-drying.

Well, at least the colour matched her skirt.

With a last wry grimace at her reflection, she padded through to the bedroom. Wet boots or bare feet? Stitched-up composure or comfort? Dithering over that choice she heard the low rumble of his voice from beyond her closed door.

Perhaps the storm was easing. Perhaps salvation had arrived.

Discarding the boots, she hurried back to the living

area only to find Donovan as alone as she'd left him. The microwave whirred busily at his back. The table was set. He looked up from slicing what looked and smelled like a homemade sourdough loaf. "Hungry?"

Susannah ignored her stomach's growling response and the unsettling notion of how comfortable he looked in her kitchen. "Did I hear you speaking to someone just then?"

"Phone." He pointed out the instrument across the living room with the wickedly serrated knife. "It was Gabrielle. A courtesy call to check the food had arrived and that everything was to your satisfaction."

She glanced at the dishes he'd set out on the table, and nodded. Of course the food would be better than satisfactory—it was one of The Palisades' premium selling points. "Did she mention the transport situation?"

"Yes, but the news is not what you wanted to hear. The helicopter won't be back until Monday at the earliest."

A sick feeling of dread tightened Susannah's throat. "The weather forecast is that dire?"

"The forecast isn't bad, but the rain was even heavier and more prolonged farther south. There's flooding over a widespread area and the chopper used for this service has been seconded for rescue operations." He looked up from his bread cutting and met her eyes. "Since we're safe and dry here, I suggested that we could wait until after the emergencies."

"Do you mean we're stuck here indefinitely?"

"Gabrielle mentioned a charter service they use for day trips. If the sea settles, it can ferry us across the bay," he said with irritating calm. While he spoke, he carried the bread and whatever he'd nuked in the microwave to the table, depositing both alongside a bowl of salad. He held out a chair, inviting her to sit. "You might as well make yourself comfortable."

Stiff-backed and a long way from comfortable, Susannah slid into the chair. She took extra care to avoid contact with the hands resting casually against its back. "For how long?" she asked, her voice husky with nerves.

"A day or two, at most." He took his place across the table, the glint in his eyes as silvery sharp as the knife he'd wielded before. A shiver tracked her spine like the trickle of raindrops on glass as he slowly smiled. "But who knows? It's in the hands of the Gods. Why don't you relax and enjoy?"

Five

Relax and enjoy? I don't think so.

But when Susannah watched him ladle a generous serving of chowder-style soup into her bowl, her stomach decided that, yes, it could very-much enjoy. The dish was as good as it looked and smelled, and with the edge taken from her hunger she was able to relax enough to see the positive side of her situation.

As long as they couldn't leave, no one could arrive. And the only thing worse than being trapped here alone with Donovan Keane, was being *discovered* trapped here alone with Donovan Keane by, for example, Alex. He hadn't called and her mother hadn't called back, either. She'd expected to hear from someone…unless the phones were out.

"Did Gabrielle mention the phone lines being down?"

He looked up from buttering a slice of bread. "No. Why do you ask?"

"I just wondered, with all the rain, and mine has been so silent." She cast a glance in that direction, then sat up straight as it struck her that— "I didn't hear it ring earlier."

"Above that wailing hair dryer?"

Point taken, but still… "It's strange that Gabrielle didn't mention the flooding when I spoke to her. She seemed quite optimistic about tomorrow."

"Are you suggesting I fabricated her phone call?" he asked after a long beat of consideration. He set down his knife and leaned back in his chair, his hooded gaze inscrutable. "To what end?"

"To keep me here," Susannah replied, mimicking his deliberate intonation.

"Kidnapping? Isn't that a little extreme?"

Despite the lazy amusement in his voice, the weight of his steady gaze made her heart beat a little faster, a little harder. And her earlier words resonated in the thickening silence between them.

You would do whatever it takes to get your hands on the contract to The Palisades.

"What lengths do you think I would go to," he said conversationally, "to keep you here? Would I use restraint, for example?"

"Hypothetically speaking, I would pick blackmail or some other form of verbal coercion as more your speed. You're far too clever with your tongue to need to use physical force or restraint."

For a long moment he studied her in silence, and the warmth of a flush rose unbidden in her face. And she silently berated herself for allowing him to lead her down this path. It was too suggestive, too sensually alluring.

"Now you've gone and aroused my curiosity." Leaning forward, he captured her gaze and held it in place with the silky restraint of his tone. "We never got kinky then? I didn't have to tie you up to have my wicked way with you?"

"I was willing."

"Past tense."

"Absolutely."

His lips tilted at one corner in the sexy half smile that had rendered her willing on so many occasions. He picked up his wine and there was the hint of a salute in the gesture, as if he appreciated her candid responses. But there was a different appreciation in his eyes, one she should not be enjoying, but it was also a challenge from which she couldn't back down.

"Now—present tense—if I wanted to keep you here I might need to tie you up. Toss you on that boat Gabrielle mentioned. Take you out to the island."

Susannah pretended to give that some thought. "How proficient are you with a captive who's prone to brutal seasickness?"

One eyebrow quirked. "I take it that's not a hypothetical?"

"Unfortunately, no."

"Then I'll take that into account, should I ever wish to abduct you."

"I'd appreciate that." With a serene smile, she tilted her face toward his plate. "Are you finished with your first course?"

She removed their plates, and on her way to the kitchen, she could feel him tracking her every step of the way. Her heart continued to beat too fast and the tight heat in her skin was *so* not good, but she liked the intensity of sensation. She'd forgotten how much she liked the word play, the eye play, the play of his smile. She'd forgotten how one simple exchange with this man could turn her self-perception from cool, cautious and composed to smart, sharp and sexy.

And it was wrong. Already she had indulged herself far more than she had any right to.

She shut the dishwasher on their first-course plates with an audible snap and returned to the table, to the safe and sensible second-course salad.

"I'm intrigued by the boat thing," he said.

Susannah's stomach dipped as if she'd stepped from land onto a moving deck, but she didn't look up from her plate. "Why is that?"

"With your job in the travel industry, I thought you'd be an expert on all means of transportation."

"I book them," she told him. "I don't have to do them. Besides, travel is only one part of At Your Service."

"The other parts being?"

"Whatever a client wants, we'll find it. Travel, transport, accommodation, entertainment, shopping, staff."

"Is that how you met Carlisle?" he asked. "Through your business?"

Susannah so did not want to go there, but what could she do? Return to banter about abduction and bondage? She'd promised conversation and it stood to reason that the conversation would circle on back to the common conflict. Alex Carlisle, her marriage contract, his business contract.

She took a sip of her wine and placed the glass carefully on the table. "Yes and no. We'd crossed paths many times at business and social events over the years, and when I started my own business, those connections were vital. My early growth was all word-of-mouth and making myself known to the people who could provide the level of service my clients require. Last year, I entered into an alliance with Carlisle Hotels."

"They scratch your back, you scratch theirs?"

The cool note in his voice stilled the play of Susannah's fingers on her wineglass and steadied her gaze on his. She lifted her chin a fraction. "Only when it best serves a client's needs."

"The Carlisle hotels have their own concierges."

"Yes, but my service is at another level. Sometimes they bring me in to help at a hotel level or they recommend a client contact me directly for a specific or unusual request."

His eyes thinned with an expression she recognised, and she braced herself for another of those disparaging remarks. Possibly about Alex's specific request for a wife. But whatever he'd been thinking, remained unsaid. He took another drink from his wine.

"Why personal concierging?" he asked.

"It plays to my strengths."

"Which are?"

"A known name, a lifetime's knowledge of the lux market and a BlackBerry filled with excellent contacts."

"That would be the flip answer, but you're serious

about your business. Otherwise you wouldn't be working so hard to save it."

Although he lazed back in his chair, his tone as casual as his posture, Susannah sensed real interest. In her, the woman, not the conduit to his own ambition.

Careful, she warned herself as her body warmed to that interest. *Don't be fooled by those silver eyes and tongue.*

"It's important because it's mine," she said simply, although the truth behind that answer was not so simple. "I conceived it, I chased capital to start it, its success or failure is all down to me."

"You believe you can succeed in such a specialist field with a limited pond of possible clients?"

"That's my point of difference," she said, leaning forward as she latched on to her favourite topic. "My target clientele isn't limited to the billionaire market. At Your Service is available to anyone, for any service, not only the big-dollar extravagances that anyone can buy with the right-sized cheque."

"The everyman concierge service?"

He sounded dubious and Susannah smiled as she conceded his point. "Okay, so not quite 'every' man. Most of my clients are either professionals with stacked schedules or visiting executives with the same time challenge. My job isn't only providing specific requests but also accessing what the client *really* wants...even when he or she doesn't know exactly what that might be."

"For example?"

"A place like Stranger's Bay. The experience is the isolation and the wild beauty, it's the escape from civilisation without feeling uncivilised. Every whim is catered but not in an obvious fashion. The staff, the service, everything is first-rate and discreet. That appeals to one client, while another wants staff on tap and constant pampering. My strength is in knowing which experience matches each client."

"Your strength is in looking after other people's needs," he suggested.

She smiled right back at him and said, "Yes. I guess it is."

There was an honesty in that moment, a connection that lasted a long moment before she remembered that this is what she'd warned herself about earlier. Not once, *but twice.* Yet again she'd stumbled into the dangerous trap of sharing too much, feeling too much and responding too easily to the wrong man.

Dinner was over. It was time to return to the real world.

Under the guise of clearing the table, she started to stand, but he stilled her with a hand on her arm. "Leave it. Stay and talk."

"I can't."

Her words were barely audible above the pounding of her heart. He rose to his feet and using that hot encircling grip on her wrist, he drew her around the table. "You can," he said. "You said you would tell me the important things."

"I said I would try," Susannah corrected, as inch by inch, he urged her nearer. With nothing to anchor her, she couldn't resist, could do nothing but hold herself tall and stiff as the steely heat of his hand permeated her skin and raced through her blood.

She came to a halt toe to toe with his black leather

loafers. In bare feet, she barely reached his chin and that put her eyes on a level with the open neck of his shirt. She felt ridiculously weak, even before he slackened his hold and let his palm slide up to her elbow and back to take her hand in his.

"Is this the part you thought you'd have trouble remembering accurately?" His words sloughed against her temple; their meaning swirled with liquid desire low in her belly. "Because when I get this close to you, I can't believe that anything we did together would be forgettable."

Susannah hadn't forgotten. *Anything.* Including the reason she shouldn't be standing here thinking about touching him. Thinking about kissing him.

Lifting her free hand to his chest, she pushed until he had to let her go. "This is the part I won't let myself remember," she said. "Now, I think you should go."

"You have phone calls to make."

Susannah nodded. "I do. If I'm going to be away more than overnight, there are people I need to let know."

"Family?"

"My sister. Half sister," she corrected herself. "And my neighbour. She worries." She folded her fingers into her palm, trapping his heat there. It was a small thing to keep of him, but all she would allow. "Good night, Donovan."

He surprised her by turning to go, then he stopped and turned back. "If you're thinking of calling Gabrielle, she's off duty tonight. She said you're welcome to call anytime, regardless. Front office has the number."

"Thank you, but I won't bother her at home. I know she will call if there are any further developments."

"You don't want to verify my story?"

"I believe you. Who could make up a story like that?"

It was supposed to be tongue-in-cheek, a reference to his comment about believing her convoluted explanation of how the deal on The Palisades had become tied up in her marriage contract. But after the door closed behind him, after she'd packed away the remains of their dinner and tried calling Alex, Zara, Alex's brother Rafe, then the suite at the Melbourne Carlisle Grande where she and Alex should have been staying tonight—the only person who picked up was her mother, and at least she promised to call Alex—she had nothing left to do but think.

And her thoughts were all an eddying whirl of Donovan Keane.

Did she trust him? On the transportation issue, yes. It was a story she could easily check with the resort staff or the company which ran the helicopter shuttle.

Did she trust him in a wider sense? No. Although she had to give him props for not taking advantage of the moment when he'd pulled her close. He could have kissed her. He could have insisted on staying, he could have pushed her for intimate details of their weekend activities. But he'd left almost too easily and without any goodbye, which made her more suspicious and more intrigued.

Was that his intention?

Standing at the scenic window looking out into the night, the dark shiver deep in Susannah's flesh was part chill, part apprehension. She couldn't stop her mind turning over the possibilities of why he'd accepted the end to the evening with such uncharacteristic compliance. Their dinner couldn't have helped his memory a great deal. It couldn't have furthered his need to reconstruct the lost weekend.

Yes, they'd covered some of the same conversational ground as last time but he hadn't pushed for specific details or asked the did-we-do-this, did-we-eat-that questions she'd anticipated. She understood his need to know, and she understood the kind of man he was—the kind who needed all the facts, the kind who controlled his own life, the kind who didn't give up.

Those missing days had to be like a burr digging into his psyche. She'd feared he would be unrelenting; that when he'd taken her hand and pulled her close to the tempting heat of his body, he would keep on in a relentless quest for details of how the seduction went down. So to speak.

Intimate memories whispered through her skin and she leaned closer to the window and pressed her overheated cheek against the cool glass. Why hadn't he pressed for more? Why had he let her go without taking advantage?

Perhaps tonight had been only the start. Perhaps she would wake tomorrow to find him on her doorstep again, this time with breakfast. Perhaps he would use their isolation and her growing restlessness and the compassion she felt for his situation to chip away at her resolve until he'd exposed every secreted emotion from its hiding place.

Looking out into the pitch-black night, she realised that the rain had stopped and the resulting quiet felt almost eerie in its intensity. The aloneness, the isolation, crept out of that quiet like Donovan's thieves, catching her unawares. If he'd arrived at her door right then, he would have found her exposed and vulnerable to anything that eased the choking grip of loneliness.

Dangerous thoughts.

Susannah pushed away from the window to prowl the confines of her villa. She was honest enough to recognise that danger, in herself and in her responses to Donovan. He had a way of making her feel a curious combination of strength and weakness, of safety and insecurity, of knowing what she wanted yet fearing everything that exposed.

She had to get away. She had to get back to Alex and the sanctuary of a future that answered all her needs. Tomorrow if—please, God!—the rain had really stopped.

Do you want to escape badly enough to get on the boat Gabrielle offered?

She paused by the window and thought about all she'd risked by coming here today. She'd let down Alex, her mother, everything that mattered.

Yes, she would brave the boat trip. Heck, if somebody strapped her into a canoe and handed her the oar, she would paddle like a crazy woman all the way home.

It's only a boat, she told herself. Just a short trip across the bay. How bad could that be?

"I've never known a punctual woman who was worth knowing, so I'm willing to wait another five minutes."

"This one's worth knowing," Van assured the owner of

the charter boat, who'd introduced himself as Gilly. "My guess—if she's not here by eleven, then she's not coming."

"Your call," Gilly said affably. "Just holler when you're ready to cast off."

He jumped back on board—nimbly for a man the size of a linebacker—and disappeared inside. The luxury motor cruiser was more boat than Van had expected but Gilly explained that his business was geared more toward fishing and pleasure charters than today's impromptu ferry trip to the nearest town across the bay.

Van assumed Susannah would have a car arranged and waiting to take her to the airport and her flight home to Melbourne.

Arms folded across his chest, he scanned the hillside that rose steeply toward the resort. She'd told the desk staff she would make her own way down to the jetty, but now he wondered if she'd chickened out. The tone of last night's exchange about seasickness might have been teasing, but he sensed she'd not been kidding about her aversion to boats.

But if she wanted to leave here badly enough…

A now-familiar flash of colour bobbing in and out of sight on the hillside path brought his musing up short. Not the bright yellow umbrella but the sheen of red-gold hair. Behind him Van heard the thump of Gilly's feet as he landed on the timber pier. He hmphed in satisfaction. "That looks like our other passenger now."

Van didn't answer. His attention remained fixed on Susannah, his heartbeat thickening as he anticipated the moment when she caught sight of him. He'd imagined his presence would be a surprise, and he wasn't wrong.

Her stride faltered infinitesimally. Her head came up. Her fingers tightened on the tote bag slung over her shoulder.

Then Gilly called out a greeting and she straightened her shoulders and stepped onto the timber planks of the jetty. She wore the same coat as yesterday, the same boots, but there was something different about her, Van mused, studying her approach with narrowed interest. When a sudden snap of breeze grabbed at her hair, she lifted a hand to push it back into order and he was struck by another minibolt of déjà vu.

It was the wind in her hair. Or the sun lighting it in a dozen shades of gold. Or the way she caught the bright mass all together and held it at the side of her throat, bunched in one hand.

Whatever it was, he'd seen it before. The first instances he'd discounted as insignificant, but not anymore. Just being around her tapped into that deep well of forgotten moments, and that made another good case for keeping her close.

Straightening from the mooring he'd been leaning against, he greeted her with a lazy smile. "Good morning, Susannah. Enjoying the sunshine?"

Designer sunglasses obscured half her face but they didn't disguise the pique in her voice. "What are you doing here?"

"Same as you, I expect."

"You're leaving today?"

"Can't see much point in staying," he said, "once you've gone."

Gilly cleared his throat, a reminder of his presence

and a reminder that they needed to get going. "Morning, Miss Horton. If you're ready, I'll help you aboard. Is that all your luggage?"

"Yes. I—"

"I'll help Susannah," Van said smoothly. Then to Gilly, "You have to admire a woman who travels this light."

Her lips tightened ominously but when she didn't fire back the expected salvo, Van took a closer look and realised that she wasn't only surprised at finding him here or angry that he'd hijacked her attempt to escape him. Against the dark frames of her glasses and under the clear September sky, her skin looked even paler than yesterday, that gold-dust sprinkling of freckles more pronounced. And the fingers gripping the leather straps of her bag reflected the same tension he saw in the tight set of her lips.

His smile faded. "You really do have a thing about boats, don't you?"

"Only about getting on them," she muttered. Then her shoulders went back and her nostrils flared as if she'd drawn a swift breath. Deftly, she stepped around him and allowed Gilly to hand her on board.

Van intercepted before she reached the cabin, and steered her toward the flydeck. At the base of the steps she dug in her heels. "I would prefer to sit inside."

"Your stomach won't thank you," he said mildly.

"I've taken something for that."

"You got the Dramamine then?"

"How did you know…?" Beneath his hand, he felt her stiffen. She drew an audible breath. "*You* sent that?"

Van shrugged. "It helps. So does being on deck, in the fresh air. You can fix your gaze on a set point—"

"Like all that water?"

Suppressing a smile, he widened his hand against her lower back. "Trust me on this. You'll feel much better up on top."

Trust him? After he'd pulled this *surprise, I'm coming with you* stunt? After he'd dropped that sly suggestion about her feeling better on top.

Okay, Susannah conceded, perhaps she'd only imagined that double meaning. When she met his eyes, she read nothing beyond mild impatience when he asked, "Upstairs or down?"

Either way she had his company. Downstairs, alone. Upstairs, with the laconic-looking captain, as well. "Up," she decided. If she was going to humiliate herself by upending her breakfast, it might as well be with a full audience.

Five minutes later, she was happy with her decision. Whether it was the medication, the open air in her face or her preoccupation with Donovan close at her side didn't matter. She tipped her head back and the speed of their progress across the water whipped her hair into a dozen wild streamers and lashed colour into her face. If she just concentrated on that swift progress instead of each wave-to-wave bump she might live through this.

"Enjoying yourself?"

"'Enjoy' might be pushing it," she admitted with a rueful grimace. Until her feet were back on solid ground, that was as near to a smile as she could manage.

"Come on. We've got the sun on our skin for the first time in days. Poseidon's blessed us with calm water and a hot yacht and nothing for miles and miles but open water. Look at this place. How could you not get a kick out of this?"

Susannah's hands tightened their grip on the railing. Eyes fixed dead ahead on the distant chunk of land she'd chosen as her point of reference, she refused to surrender to temptation. She would not sneak a sideways look to see if his face reflected the appealing mix of reverence and quiet pleasure that coloured his voice. It was enough that it curled through her, blurring the edges of her senses and melting the grip of her fear another degree.

"I'm going to sit down," she decided.

"Stay." His hand closed over hers on the rail, warm and solid and grounding. "We're almost there."

Sure, they'd been speeding across the bay at a great rate of knots but they couldn't be even a quarter of the way to Appleton. Then, as if to make a liar of her judgment, the cruiser's speed slackened and she realised that she'd lost focus on the anchoring chunk of land.

It rose from the water before them, the white posts of the jetty a stark contrast to the thick green scrub.

Charlotte Island. A beat of alarm pulsed through her as she slowly turned to meet Donovan's cleverly guarded eyes. "Why are we stopping here? What is this about?"

Six

What is this about?

"This," Van said in response to her question. He turned to face the tiny pocket of land sitting in the middle of Stranger's Bay.

Until now, he'd kept his focus on Susannah—no hardship there—but now his narrowed gaze shifted over the island and his chest tightened with a familiar frustration. Despite its significance, despite his previous visit, there was nothing familiar in the rocky shoreline or the gentle lap of waves against a bite of sand or the sharp roofline he could see peering out above the trees.

This time, he didn't even attempt to shuck the vise-like grip of emotion. He let it take hold, let it mould his mood as the yacht cruised in to the pier. A lone figure waited there, hand raised in greeting.

"The caretaker," Van said, turning back to Susannah. "Gilly's giving him a lift into town."

"We're just stopping to pick up another passenger?"

"And to let one off. I'm stopping here," he said. "For a couple of nights."

He watched her take that in, saw the slight easing of tension around her mouth. The infinitesimal slump of her shoulders. But when she pushed her sunglasses to the top of her head, the gaze she turned on his was clouded with confusion. "What did you mean by *this?*" she asked.

"This is why I want The Palisades. This is why that substitute property you offered to find for me was irrelevant."

"You want this island, not the resort?"

Lifting a hand from the rail, she grabbed her hair into that makeshift ponytail just as the yacht came to a rocky halt. She lost her balance for an instant, until Van steadied her with a hand at her elbow. She regained her foothold quickly, but he didn't let her go. "I take it you didn't come out here with me last time?"

"No."

"Because of your aversion to boats?"

"You didn't come by boat last time. You had the helicopter drop you off. And you didn't invite me," she added with a tight shrug that missed casual by at least a nautical mile. "I rather gathered that you wanted a break."

"From you? I rather doubt that."

Their gazes met and the inference of Van's rejoinder hummed between them. Wary heat flared in her eyes and low in Van's belly. He lifted a hand and threaded a loose strand of windswept hair behind her ear, and she shook her head slightly as if to refocus. "Why is the island so important?" she asked.

Van let his hand slide from her elbow to her hand. "Come and steady your legs on solid ground," he said, "and I'll tell you."

Feet fixed firmly on something that didn't rock and roll *and* an answer to the puzzle of why he wouldn't let The Palisades go. How could Susannah resist a double-edged invitation like that?

Once on firm land, she realised just how shaky her sea legs were, so when Donovan suggested they stroll down to the beach, she had no objection. After a short distance her legs started to feel more normal and so did her head. "This is why you came back," she mused.

She felt his glance on her face. "Here?"

"To Stranger's Bay. If you'd only wanted to apply pressure about the deal, you could have landed on my doorstep in Melbourne or gone straight to Alex."

"I needed to come back here. To see if I remembered."

Retracing his footsteps, recreating the past weekend. Last night's anxiety over that endeavour resurfaced in a slither of unease that travelled the length of Susannah's spine and tingled in the palm of her hand. Where he'd held it, she realised, last night and again leaving the boat just now.

It should have seemed small, insignificant, compared to all the intimacies they'd shared already. But it didn't. Perhaps because they'd skipped the preliminaries and landed straight in bed the first night, perhaps because he'd returned as a virtual stranger with no memory of those intimacies, perhaps because beyond the innocent touch she felt every memory in vivid, visceral detail.

She pushed both hands deep into the pockets of her trench coat and forced her focus back to his words. "You needed to come out here, to Charlotte Island, to see if you remembered that first visit?"

He didn't respond immediately, pausing instead to help her down a rocky section of path. They'd come quite a distance from the boat—far enough for her peace of mind. She glanced back to where it sat, rocking peacefully to sleep in the deep-blue water.

"You said I mentioned Mac."

Susannah's attention shifted back to his face, the boat instantly forgotten. "Only in passing, when I asked who the MacCreadie was in the Keane MacCreadie business name."

"Elaine MacCreadie," he supplied now. He started to move as he talked, and she kept pace beside him, her eyes trained on his face. "She was a client when I worked on Wall Street, a businesswoman with a boat-load of investments and a steel-trap brain. She said she appreciated my low BS quotient, and when I was shafted by one of the big bosses, she encouraged me to go it alone. She provided the start-up capital and the smart advice. I provided the man hours." He cut her a look. "Did I tell you she's an Aussie?"

"No, you didn't."

"From here," he said, indicating *right here* with a sweep on his hand. "Born and raised on Charlotte Island."

Susannah stopped dead in her tracks. "You're buying the place on her behalf."

"I'm buying it *for* her," he said, making the distinction with subtle emphasis as his eyes locked on hers. "Is there anyone in your life you would do anything for?"

"There was," she replied without hesitation. "My grandfather. Pappy Horton."

"Then you understand."

"I'm not sure that I do," she said slowly. "There is a wealth of difference between doing something and buying something."

"You think that's what I'm doing? Making an expensive gesture?" He expelled a rough breath and turned to stare fixedly out to sea for a long moment. And when he continued, there was a raw note to his voice she'd never heard before. A note that ripped straight to her heart. "Mac's not well. Hasn't been for a while now. This is probably my last chance to do something for her, and the one thing that would have any damn meaning would be seeing this place back in MacCreadie ownership."

"Does she have family?"

"A grandson."

And this would be her legacy to him, a link to his heritage in Australia.

"So, you understand why I won't give this up without a fight?" he asked.

"Mostly," Susannah said huskily, forcing the words past the thick ache at the back of her throat. "Although I don't understand why you didn't tell me about Mac before."

"It's not something I talk about," he said, and the shutters had come down on his eyes, just as they had done in the past when she'd asked anything too personal.

"Then why now?" she persisted, wanting to batter down the barriers. Wanting, God help her, a piece of the man inside.

"I had to do something. You were leaving."

She was achingly aware of his meaning. She was leaving, she was marrying another man, he would lose this last tenuous toehold on his quest to repay Mac. But her heart imagined another meaning in his words, in the quicksilver flame of his eyes.

"It will make no difference," she said. "I can't change what's been set in motion."

"You can. If you don't marry Carlisle." His gaze dropped to her lips. "Stay, Susannah. Convince me that this marriage is what you really want."

This is what she'd expected last night and she'd armed herself against the assault. Now he'd caught her unprepared. She needed to breathe, to ease the swell of emotion in her chest, to think. "I can't stay, Donovan. I can't."

"I'm afraid you have no choice."

"I don't know…" Her voice and her thoughts trailed off as she detected a new determination in his expression. She turned quickly, eyes drawn to the empty jetty and then to the gleam of white speeding away from the island.

"You brought me here, you talked me into leaving the boat and you'd already arranged for Gilly to leave without me?"

Van knew she wouldn't be happy. He was ready to face the heat of her anger, to answer all accusations, but the disenchantment burning at the back of her eyes caught him low and hard.

"Hey," he said softly. "I had reasons."

Giving in to the temptation to touch her, to soothe her, to hold her, he started forward, but she backed away as far as the water's edge, both hands raised with the same warning that flashed in her eyes.

"Last night I spent half the night worrying over why you'd left so easily. That was so out of character for a man who always pursues what he wants without compromise. Now I see. You were already planning this. You teased me about restraint and force and abduction—"

"Hang on just a second," he cut in.

But she wasn't hanging on for even half that time. She continued down that same path, her eyes growing more disillusioned with each word. "But you didn't have to resort to force, did you? Not when you could manipulate my emotions so easily. Sending me the seasick medication, your solicitous attention on the boat and then you crown it all with Mac. You know what? I would have preferred if you *had* brought me here by force. At least that would have been honest."

"You think I lied to you?"

"I think you manipulated me."

Van's eyes narrowed at that accusation. At the implication that he'd bent the truth, that he'd used Mac's illness in an underhanded way. "After the way you and your mother manipulated Carlisle on this deal, I'd be careful which stones you sling from that glass house, Susannah."

For a beat of time, that softly spoken counterstroke hung between them. Then she lifted her chin and he noted that the earlier swirl of disappointment had turned to cool disdain. "How long are you holding me hostage?" she asked.

"As long as it takes."

"To?"

"Stop you marrying Alex Carlisle."

Van's luggage, her one bag and the fresh food supplies sent over for their stay had all been delivered to the house perched high on the island's highest ridge. The original weatherboard cottage where Mac had spent her childhood was now the caretaker's residence. In recent years, the resort had added the luxurious timber lodge to its private island; the ultimate get-away-from-civilisation retreat with no phones, no television, no Internet.

"Ever been out here before?" Van asked, joining Susannah on the long veranda. The sweeping vista of water added to the sense of sitting in majestic isolation, alone in the middle of the wild and rugged southern ocean.

When she didn't answer his question, he let it slide. He figured she would get over her huff soon enough—possibly when he divulged why he'd sought her out. "I have a small favour to ask."

Her fingers curled around the railing, as if to consolidate her grip. "A favour?" She might as well have said, "A slimy toad?" She employed the same level of distaste.

"I'm heading out to take some photos," he told her.

"Have fun."

At least she was talking, Van decided. He much preferred these snooty comebacks to the frosty silence of their walk up from the beach. "It's not a sightseeing stroll. I want photos for Mac."

"You didn't think of that last time?" She favoured him with an incredulous look. "You had a camera with you the morning you came out here."

"Yeah, I had a camera. I had photos. Past tense."

Realisation flitted across her expression and her gaze snapped to his. "They stole your camera?"

He didn't answer. He just held her gaze a moment longer before asking again, "Will you help me out with the pictures?"

"Why do you need my help?"

"Mac wants a shot of me, at the cottage."

"I'll help," she said. "But just so you know, I'm doing it for Mac, not as a favour to you."

Van stretched the afternoon excursion for photos as far as he could, until the impatience simmering beneath her ice-cool facade snapped. He'd been helping her down a steep path at the time, his destination a stretch of virgin sand he'd glimpsed from the elevated veranda. But instead of giving him her hand, she slapped the digital camera into his outstretched palm.

"I think you have more than enough pictures of yourself," she said. "I'm not a mountain goat. I'm not dressed for hiking. I'm going back to take a shower."

Two hours later, Van knocked on the door of her bedroom—on arrival, he'd offered her the upstairs master, and after a suspicious moment's deliberation, she'd accepted. Now he gave her ample time to make herself decent or to tell him to go to hell, but beyond the door he heard nothing.

With her fear of boats, surely she wouldn't attempt to escape. Still, a tinge of worry clawed at his gut. He'd brought her here and he would keep her safe.

He knocked again, and when she didn't answer this time, he opened the door. Perhaps she was out on the balcony, out of earshot…

She wasn't.

Wrapped in a bath towel, she sat in the middle of the king-size bed, legs long and bare, hair a wet tangle of curls, her face turned toward the stunning view of tree-tops and ocean beyond the wall of louvred windows. Van paid scant attention to the backdrop. There was something in the picture she painted—not her unenhanced beauty, nor the knowledge of all that skin warm and scented from her shower, but the fragility of her expression—that stirred a world of yearning inside Van.

It echoed the moment down at the beach when she'd looked at him with naked disappointment; when he'd reached for her and she'd slapped him down. This time he forced himself not to reach. He sucked up that desire and waited a patient count of five for her to acknowledge his presence.

When she didn't, irritation ate away at his patience. "Still sulking?"

"Thinking, actually."

"About?"

"Our conversation down at the beach." She turned her head a fraction, enough that the angled rays of the sun caught her hair with fire. His breath caught with the same hot burn when he saw the hint of moisture on her lashes, the uneven redness in her cheeks.

She'd been crying.

"When you asked me if there was one person I would do anything for, I answered reflexively. There are others I'd also walk on hot coals for. Zara says I need to cultivate a little healthy selfishness. She thinks I'm a sap."

"Zara is your sister?" he guessed.

She nodded in silent assent. "She is also on my list of people I would do anything for, but Pappy came to mind instantly even though he's been gone ten years. Probably because I didn't have a chance to do any last things for him. He was gone too quickly." Her gaze lifted and locked on his. "She's dying, isn't she?"

The frankness of her question knocked the remaining air from Van's lungs. He couldn't answer. Ultimately he didn't have to because the sudden sheen of understanding in her eyes reflected his answer.

"That's what I thought." Lips pressed hard together, she turned away. "Did you only come up here to enquire about my sulking, or was there something else?"

"I brought you some clothes. I thought you might appreciate something clean to change into for dinner."

He put them down on the dresser beside the door, and prepared to leave before he said any more. Before he revealed the tenuous thread of emotion unravelling inside. He was halfway out the door when she spoke again.

"Mac's your grandmother, isn't she? You're the grandson."

Sucker punched by her perceptiveness, Van didn't answer. He didn't turn around. He kept on walking.

Seven

When the shadows of dusk fell over the house, Van started a fire in the huge open fireplace that dominated the living room. Susannah hadn't made an appearance—he didn't know if she would—and for a while after he'd come downstairs, he'd been glad. He'd needed time and solitude to soothe the raw emotion prodded to life by her perceptive questions.

That was done now, courtesy of the Vivaldi he'd set on rotation and the therapeutic benefit of applying a large knife to raw foodstuffs. The sauce for a simple pasta marinara now simmered on the stovetop. A bottle of light red breathed on the countertop. And he'd reminded himself of what mattered.

Not filling his memory with details of Susannah Horton, not wiping disenchantment or tears from her eyes, not protecting his male pride from further bruising.

If Susannah joined him for dinner, he would use whatever compassion he'd stirred up with today's revelations to pursue his goal. If she didn't come downstairs, then there was always the option of delivering room service. This time he'd be better prepared. He wouldn't let the sight of her naked vulnerability put him on the back foot; he would use it to his own advantage.

As much as he enjoyed the notion of feeding her by the fireside, the image of her stretched out on that bed, dressed in the clothes he'd left…*his* clothes, against *her* skin…lit a different kind of fire. When he caught the first shadow of movement on the stairs, he suffered a minor jab of letdown. The bedroom alternative had been looking so very attractive.

He closed the pantry door, the linguine he'd been searching out in hand, and the sight of her coming down the stairs incinerated the disappointment and redefined his definition of attractive.

He'd wondered how she would take to the intimacy of wearing his clothes…especially the boxer shorts. But, no. There they were, peeping out from beneath the hem of his 49ers sweatshirt. It hung halfway to her knees but still exposed enough of her long, slender legs to turn his mouth dry.

Two stairs from the bottom, she caught him eyeing those legs and stopped dead in her tracks. Palpable tension crackled in the air between them until Van forced his gaze away. If this was going to work—if he was going to build her sympathy into seduction—then he needed to make her comfortable. Keeping his eyes above her collarbone would be a good start.

Depositing the forgotten pasta on the countertop, he nodded at the outfit. "Nice look."

Still looking wary, she descended the last couple of stairs. "I appreciated having something clean to put on. Thank you."

"I have my moments."

"This was a good one," she conceded. Across the width of the living room their eyes met and held, the caution in hers edged with her gratitude. A promising start, Van decided. But then she straightened her shoulders and started toward the kitchen like a woman on a mission. "I'm just going to grab something to eat in my room."

"No need to do that. Dinner's coming along. Why don't you sit by the fire? There's antipasto to tide you over. Wine, beer, soda—take your pick."

She hesitated, her nostrils flaring slightly as if taking in the flavoursome aromas wafting from the kitchen.

"Linguine Marinara. My signature dish."

"You cooked?" she asked on a note of surprise. "From scratch?"

"No need to sound so stupefied."

"In July, you told me you travelled too much to bother keeping a home. You ate out. You ordered in. So, yes, I am surprised that your culinary skills have progressed from microwave reheating to claiming a signature dish."

"There has to be an upside to being off work for weeks on end."

Her wary gaze turned serious as she met his eyes. "It's nice that you could take a positive from that experience."

"Learning my way around the kitchen was one," he supplied with a half-shrug. "Why don't you take a seat? Your waiter will be along shortly."

She hesitated, but only briefly, before crossing to the fireside. In that moment's pause, Van saw the questions in her eyes, and while he watched her sit on a cushion beside the hearth, he staunched his instinctive resistance.

He'd snared her curiosity. She would stay. They would talk. He would soothe the remaining apprehension from her eyes, the same as he'd done last night.

Except this time, he wasn't leaving.

"Wine?"

"Thank you, yes." Twisting at the waist, she looked back at him over her shoulder. The curiosity he'd detected earlier came alive in her face as she watched him pour and then transfer the appetisers to a serving plate. "Is waiting tables another skill you picked up while you were in stasis…or would that have been superfluous?"

"I live alone, if that's what you're asking."

"I thought, given your circumstances…"

"That I might have needed live-in assistance?"

She shuffled her position on the cushion, presumably so she wouldn't crick her waist or neck looking back at him. The new position afforded him an excellent view of her killer legs, but that was a momentary distraction. Her next comment brought all his attention winging back to her face. "Actually, I wondered if you may have moved in with Mac. She is your only family, right?"

Ever since she'd asked the question upstairs, he'd

known she would return to his relationship with Mac. He hadn't expected the edge to her tone, however. Hands planted on the bench, he held her chary gaze. "Why do I sense that you won't believe my answer?"

"In July you said you had no family. I believed that."

"In July I had no family."

"And now you suddenly do?"

"Another of those upsides I mentioned."

She shook her head slowly, her expression a mix of confusion and exasperation. "You acquired a grandmother?"

That pretty much summed it up. And if he concentrated on the upside instead of the hot cauldron of regret and frustration that seethed inside him then he could impart the bare facts. "Mac had an unplanned pregnancy when she was a teenager, a daughter she gave up for adoption. She didn't track her down until ten years ago. By then my mother was long dead."

"But she found you?"

"She sought me out, became my client. She never intended to tell me about our relationship."

"Whyever not?" A wealth of emotion swirled in her eyes as she looked up at him; the kind he'd sworn to avoid. The kind that stirred the hot ache in his gut. "Why did she bother finding you if she didn't want to claim you as her family?"

"She wanted to know me, to help me, but she could see I was doing fine without family."

"Then why tell you now?" she persisted. Half a second later, she made a rough sound of discovery and distress. "I answered that earlier, upstairs, didn't I?"

"Yes, she's dying." He shrugged, a tight gesture that

did nothing to ease the tension in his muscles. "But that wasn't the only motivation. When I woke up in hospital with this amnesia, she talked to help me work out what I remembered and what I didn't. Then when I was recovering, we just talked, a lot. Not only about business or politics or the state of the economy. She told me about her past. Her regrets. When she started talking about my mother, the rest came out."

"That must have been quite a shock."

He brought her glass of wine and hunkered down to put it in her hand. Then he took his own seat on the floor, close enough that their knees brushed with a frisson of heat. It was a response he welcomed, the physical that he understood and could deal with, that didn't burn like twisted metal in his gut. "Don't feel sorry for me, Susannah. As you so accurately put it, I acquired myself a grandmother."

"A grandmother you're going to lose," she said, and the emotion in her eyes—and his body's response—blew away the remnant heat of the physical contact. When he would have pulled away from that confronting emotion, she leaned forward and captured him with the quiet intensity of her gaze. "I know you said I couldn't understand what you've been through but some of this I do know."

"Your grandfather?"

She nodded. "He loved to fish. That was his escape from the pressure of corporate life and the pretensions of society. He hated the functions he was forced to attend...he despised small talk. One weekend he went out chasing the big fish and he didn't come home."

"Hence your aversion to boats?" he guessed.

"No, that's all about the seasickness. Although I suspect psychologists would have a field day with the connection." A whisper of a smile touched her lips. "Pappy Horton was…he was so much more than the tycoon robber-baron the media depicted."

"I'm sorry."

"So was I. He left me his cabin in the high country where we stayed when he took me trout fishing."

Her wistful expression stirred an unfamiliar emotion in Van's gut. Part was the dull ache of empathy, part the sharper need to stop her hurt, to turn the storm clouds gathering in her eyes to smiles. "You fish? If you think I'll buy that—" he shook his head, exaggerating his surprise "—how big was the one that got away?"

"My grandfather taught me how to fly cast when I was knee-high to a grasshopper."

Eyebrows raised, Van studied her in this new light. Even dressed as she was in his oversize clothes, Susannah exuded class and city style. He couldn't for the life of him picture her in the guise of fisherwoman. "I am impressed."

"Not half as much as when I caught the first bream from the rocks!"

A reference to their last weekend—to a happening Van didn't remember. He could have pursued that angle; he could have sought more detail; he could have teased her about the relative merits of their catches.

But as he watched the play of firelight in her hair and the play of shadows in her eyes, the past held no interest. He wanted to know her, not to engage his memory, not to kill the sale contract on The Palisades, but for himself, for this moment of time.

"This cabin," he began. "Do you go there often?"

"I always seem to be too busy." She shook her head and made a rueful sound. "And that's no excuse. I did take Zara once. I taught her the grand tradition of the Pappy Horton fly cast. She was a natural."

"Your grandfather didn't teach her?"

"He never met Zara. She's my half sister, you see." The smile brimming in her eyes clouded with regret. "We only found out about each other a few years back when she came searching for her father."

"And she found you?"

"Fortunately, yes."

Her gaze fell away, lost in silent introspection of her untouched wine. Forgotten along with the plate of appetisers. Van wanted to continue feeding a different appetite, reconstructing his image of the woman inside the polished facade. The woman who looked more comfortable in a sweatshirt and bare feet than in a buttoned-up designer coat.

"Is your sister like you?" he asked.

She took a slow sip from her wine, her eyes meeting his over the rim of her glass before she lowered it. Something had shifted in the mood, he realised, in the last minute or two. The earlier conflict and mistrust soothed by a new understanding and empathy. "You asked that same question the first time I told you about my family."

"And how did you answer?"

"I said, not at all. Zara is a knockout. Tall, blond,

beautiful. She's studying medicine, so she's super smart and dedicated to a future in medical research. And as if that's not enough, she's also athletic and works part-time as a personal trainer. If I didn't love her, I might possibly hate her for all that amazingness!"

Van smiled at her deprecating tone. "I imagine you're more alike than you credit."

"And *that's* also the same response as last time."

"Are you suggesting I'm predictable? Unoriginal? Boring?"

She laughed, a soft, husky chuckle that drew his gaze back to her lips. To the pinkened sheen left by the wine. To the satisfaction of knowing that the vibe arcing between them was here and now and only about them. "Oh, no," she said softly. "You are many things and not one of them boring."

In the aftermath of that admission their gazes tangled in a ripple of sensual energy, as delicate and multifaceted and intoxicating as the pinot noir she lifted to her lips. He could have asked about those many nonboring things, but only one held his focus.

"Was it like this before?" He gestured between them, illustrating the subtle tension that he couldn't label with words.

"Yes. Always."

The honesty in her answer was real. No question, no hesitation, no artifice. And whether she realised that she'd been too candid or whether she saw the intent in his eyes—whatever the reason, her expression grew cautious as Van removed the glass from her hand and, eyes locked on hers, set it down on the hearth tiles.

The wary widening of her eyes sparked a surge of satisfaction deep in his chest. The heat of contact as he rested his hand on her knee sparked something more primitive lower in his body.

He leaned closer and she drew a swift breath. "No. Don't."

But that was all the objection he allowed her. He didn't want the spectre of her arranged marriage hovering between them, didn't want the name of her sainted fiancé on her tongue.

He took her chin in his hand and silenced any complaint with his lips on hers. Beneath his touch she stiffened in surprise or in denial, and his objective instantly changed shape. No longer intent on simply tasting, he wanted her response, her acceptance, her participation.

Her kiss.

Cradling her face between his hands, he gentled the initial pressure of his mouth on hers. He traced the shape of her lips, kissed the corners and the dip in her chin, held her captive in the snare of his gaze before he reclaimed her mouth in a long, slow seduction. For a while he lost himself and the passage of time as he learned her taste and the silky texture of her skin beneath his hands.

Her hands, lifted initially to push him away, clutched in his shirtfront and the sound against his lips was a throaty mix of satisfaction and surrender. That evocative sound and the first stroke of her tongue against his fired something in Van's synapses. A burst of vivid memory of her giving mouth under his, his hands twined in her hair as he rolled her beneath him, the sun streaming through glass to set fire to her red-gold hair and to the passion drumming through his blood. And the echo of his voice deep in his mind.

Now I have you right where I want you.

He ended the kiss abruptly, shocking Susannah up from the sensual depths with the lash of an earthy curse. She stared up at him, clueless as to its motivation. One second he'd been immersed in the kiss, in her mouth, in sliding his free hand from knee to thigh; the next, abandonment.

"What's going on?" she asked slowly. "What just happened there?"

"I thought I—" He broke off, raked a hand through his hair, let go his breath in a sharp exhalation. And when he started to turn away, Susannah grabbed at his sleeve and forced his attention back to her. "For a moment—not even a second—I had this…flash."

"You remembered?"

"I don't know. I don't even know that it was an accurate memory or a…" He lifted a shoulder and let it drop, but the enormity of his frustration resonated in the deepened rasp of his voice. "I don't know what I recognised. It was just an impression of you and a line of dialogue."

"I didn't say anything. I couldn't." Apart from the fact of her tongue being elseways occupied, the overwhelming impact of his kiss had stolen her ability to think in whole words. "Was it something you remembered me saying?"

"No, not you, *me.* And I don't know if it's something

I said to you. It was there in my mind, as clear as if a light had switched on, and then gone—" he clicked thumb against finger "—like that. I'm left with one pinpoint of illumination in a big, dark void and I don't know if it's a memory or a figment of fantasy."

A reflection of that fantasy flared in his eyes for a moment, alerting Susannah to its erotic nature. She relinquished her grip on his sleeve. She didn't want to pursue this. She wanted to spring to her feet and run, hard and fast, from everything this man aroused in her—the physical, the emotional, the then and the now.

The knowledge that she could never have him; that she could never tell him what they had shared for such a fleetingly fragile piece of time.

But the storm of frustration raging in his eyes—not sexual frustration, but the exasperation of not remembering—plumbed the depths of her heart. How could she turn her back? How could she not try to help?

"It may well have been a memory," she commenced cautiously. Nervous fingers, the same ones that had gripped his shirt and held his mouth hard against hers, curled into the cushion beneath her backside. She tightened her thighs, tucking her knees closer beneath her in a vain attempt to quash the heat he'd ignited in her body. "Do you want to tell me about that line of dialogue?"

He stared back at her for a long second, the frustration honed to razor's-edge sharpness. "Just tell me one thing. Did I make any promises to you?"

Susannah's heart thumped heavily against her ribs. She couldn't tell him. Opening up that wound in her heart would serve no purpose.

Mustering every ounce of bravado, she met his eyes and for the first time in her life, she straight-out lied to him. "There were no promises, Donovan. None whatsoever."

Van didn't believe her but he curbed the desire to call her on the lie. Pushing to establish the truth about past promises would put her on the defensive again. Right now he needed—and wanted—to concentrate on the present and keeping her in the same room, in his company, was tantamount to his plans.

Putting a stop to her marriage, he realised, had become more than a means to securing a deal. Through dinner he watched her eat, drink, talk, and all he could think about was that mouth beneath his. Not as a conduit to the past, but because he wanted. For him, for now.

The craving coiled more tightly with each passing minute, every awkward pause, each time her gaze slipped away from his. And with each passing minute the certainty grew that she, too, was steeped in the same sweet agony of wanting. It was in the heightened colour that traced her cheekbones, the unsettled play of her fingers against glass and tableware, the falsely cheerful bursts of small talk that grew less frequent and more desultory as the meal stretched on.

Van could have picked up the conversational reins, but some perverse part of him enjoyed the crackle of tension in the lengthening silences. He let it play out as long as he could, until she set down her napkin and started packing up the plates. "Leave them," he said. And when she looked like protesting, "The dishes aren't going anywhere and neither are we. They'll still be there in the morning."

"And so will we," she said, and the spark in her voice was reflected in her eyes as they met his. This time they didn't drift away. "For how many more mornings?"

"Why don't we take this conversation to the fireside," Van suggested smoothly. "I'll make coffee."

"No, thank you."

"Okay, so no coffee."

"And no fireside conversation," she added. "Please, Donovan, just answer my question. When is Gilly returning to pick us up?"

"When our business here is finished."

"Our business?" She leaned forward in her chair, her fingers tight on the plates she'd yet to relinquish. "How can we even start to sort out this mess when we're stuck here?"

"That's not the only business. *We* have unfinished business."

For a moment his words hung between them, and Van felt a kick of anticipation when their meaning registered in her expressive eyes. They darkened to a turbulent sea-green as she shook her head.

"You're denying there's something between us? After that kiss?" Van's voice deepened with the memory, with the impact, with the certainty that he would have that mouth under his again. "I can still feel it, Susannah. I can still taste you in my blood."

"That doesn't change anything."

"Doesn't it? What if I hadn't stopped? What if that kiss had continued the way it started? What if you'd ended up naked with me inside you?"

"Then I would know that you'd succeeded," she replied. "You brought me here for one reason. You want to end my marriage plans—what better way than by seducing me?"

"It's not only about the deal, Susannah. You're discounting this burn between us."

"I'm not discounting it. How can I?" she asked simply, but the heat of passion was in her eyes, in her cheeks, in the throaty ache of her voice. "But as much as I want you, Donovan Keane, there is one thing I'm determined not to do. My father cheated, with Zara's mother and Lord knows how many other women, and he hurt a lot of people in the process.

"I would never do that to Alex," she continued in the same softly impassioned tone. "I would never do that to anyone I respected, and I don't believe you would want me to. Not even to win this deal for Mac."

Eight

Van had no argument and no countermeasure. If he forced the issue, he would lose her respect and sometime during the past twenty-four hours that had assumed a vital importance.

Yet everything inside him rebelled against standing aside. For close to two months he'd been forced to do nothing. Impatience, impotence, thwarted desire—hell, there must have been a dozen other equally abhorrent ingredients curdling in his gut. A long night where his insomnia kicked in—and where he'd heard Susannah moving restlessly upstairs into the early hours—had done nothing to improve his outlook.

Neither did the storm clouds darkening the southern sky.

They'd come up quickly in the late morning, as if

summoned by his own turbulent mood. He'd tried to run that from his blood in a controlled set of sprints up and down the sandy curve of beach. It had worked for the time he'd taken climbing the steep incline back to the house.

Lost in contemplation of the lunch he aimed to prepare after a long, relaxing shower, he started shucking his sweat-dampened shirt as he came in the door. Susannah sat curled up on a sofa. A book lay open on her lap but her gaze was fixed on those billowing clouds until his arrival startled it back toward the door.

Then she focussed on his bare chest and Van's post-exercise relaxation evaporated under her silent scrutiny.

When her sea-green concern shifted to his face, she must have read the warning signs in his hardened expression. Smart woman; she didn't say a word about the scars, but as he crossed to his bedroom he felt the incendiary touch of those eyes track his every step.

"Is Gilly coming today?" she asked.

"No." And he felt mean and moody enough to pause with his hand on the door to add, "If you're concerned about this weather coming in, there's a small runabout in the boatshed. We can leave now."

"How small?"

He turned back. Her fingers had quite a grip on the book; but she still held her chin high and proud. Despite her fear, she was actually considering this option, and while he showered, he recalled a snatch of conversation from the previous evening. When she'd told him about her grandfather who'd gone out fishing and never come back.

* * *

He came out of his room fifteen minutes later with an apology ready, but she was gone. From the veranda he caught sight of her down by the boathouse—checking the size of the runabout?—and he cursed himself for mentioning it.

Two hours later, she still hadn't returned. The concern gnawing away inside took a stronger bite. Surely she wouldn't do something so stupid. She didn't only dislike boats, they straight-out petrified her.

Then he saw movement on the track just above the pier. The white of his shirt—this morning he'd left it and a pair of his trackpants outside her door—as she loped into view. Not dawdling, but not exactly making haste.

His chest tightened with a contradictory mix of intense relief and annoyance.

If she didn't get a wriggle on, she'd be caught out in the storm. Right on cue, the clouds growled ominously and the first fat drops fell from the darkening sky. Van hit the steps at a run.

He found her a couple of minutes down the track, just as the heavens opened. By the time they made it back to the house they were both drenched and Van itched for a confrontation. The island's terrain was barely friendly at the best of times. In the rain she could have lost her way, slipped, fell.

Beneath the shelter of the porch, he rounded on her. "Have you no sense of self-preservation?"

Gathering her wet hair in hand, she paused. Her eyes met his and held. "I thought I did. I didn't take the boat."

Hell. She had considered it.

Fear, cold and fierce, held him in its talons for several rough heartbeats. And when he caught up with her at the door he saw that she wasn't only wet, she was shivering cold. He pushed the door open and, when she didn't move, urged her forward with a firm hand at her back.

"You're freezing." Shouldering the door shut behind her, he indicated the unused bedroom with a curt nod. "That shower's closest. Go warm yourself under it. I'll get you dry clothes."

"I'll use—"

"Don't argue, or I'll pick you up and carry you in there myself."

When her mouth tightened mulishly, Van took an advancing step. She took several backward, her hands held up in a stay-right-there gesture. They were trembling with cold.

"I'm going. I can manage."

Van wasn't so sure. Eyes narrowed, he watched her retreat. Despite the trembling hands she started to unbutton the shirt as she walked. "Are you able to manage the buttons?"

In the doorway she half turned, and he noticed what he'd been too fractious to notice before. The rain had soaked right through, and the shirt clung to her skin revealing the lines of her lacy bra and the lush shape of her breasts. His thighs tightened with a jolt of desire so strong it riveted him to the spot.

An image flashed through his brain and his blood, his hands unthreading buttons, the shadow of aureole through sheer lace, the kiss of her silken skin beneath his tongue.

Slowly, finally, he lifted his gaze. Their eyes clashed with heated knowledge but she didn't bolt or berate him. She faced him with pride and poise and answered the question he'd long since forgotten asking. "I can manage."

Susannah spent only enough time in the shower to warm herself through. She couldn't afford to loiter, to allow her mind to linger over the way he'd looked at her and the way she'd looked back. She wouldn't think about him soaked to the skin, the fine white fabric plastered against hard muscles…or peeled off.

No. She would not think about Donovan Keane undressing. She. Would. Not.

She wrenched the shower controls off but the muted sound of running water continued, filling her senses with a crystal clear image of tall, dark and naked. Right next door. The knowledge that he was warming his chilled body the other side of this thin wall stripped her of all discipline for several steamy seconds.

Then she grabbed a towel, intent on racing upstairs and locking her unruly self away until the storm had passed—or at least the tumult in her body—but in the bedroom she pulled up short. Laid out on the bed was another set of clean clothes, chosen by him, for her use. There was no other explanation for their presence in this unused room.

Quickly she gathered them up and with an ear to the next room—shower still running, time to make good her escape—she made a dash for the stairs and didn't stop until she was leaning her back against the closed and secured door. Her breath was coming hard, and not only from the mad sprint. The soft cotton fabric of the undershirt and snug white boxers clutched to her breast seemed incredibly intimate.

Yes, they were clean but he'd worn them at some point. Against his bare skin. If she had any sense of self-preservation, she would discard them in favour of her own underwear, washed and drying over the towel rail in her bathroom.

If she had any sense of self-preservation, she would drop all the damn clothes and kick them to kingdom come. She would remind herself how he'd trapped her here against her will, a virtual prisoner, and that he had no right to redress her for being caught out in the rain. She should be a dozen kinds of riled with him, but how could she when she understood his motivation?

Is there a person in your life you would do anything for?

Last night he'd vacillated over her appeal for respect, but in the end, he'd let her go.

Today he'd come out in the rain looking for her, making sure she made it back to the house safely.

Then he left the clothes.

Every one of those factors, she realised with a gloomy sense of fatalism, spelled more danger to her self-resolve than a hundred imaginings of wet, well-toned muscles.

A renewed squall of rain-heavy wind blasted her windows and shuddered through the house, a timely reminder of the storm's growing ferocity. She pushed off the door and dressed quickly. In her own clothes. And despite her earlier vows to seclude herself up here, she knew the howling insistence of that wind would drive her down to the security and the warmth of the lower level.

Why delay the inevitable?

Downstairs she could find something to occupy her mind…or at least redirect her thoughts. Although the resort promoted a get-away-from-the-modern-world ethos, they supplied indoor entertainment in the form of an extensive library of books and music and old-fashioned board games.

Who are you kidding? Downstairs there is Donovan, the only entertainment needed to fully occupy your mind.

Her stomach tightened with nervous apprehension as she descended the stairs. She hadn't wasted a lot of time dressing; she'd given up on pretending to tame her hair days ago, securing it in a loose braid. And, okay, she still had enough vanity remaining to apply tinted moisturiser but that was it.

Yet, he'd beaten her to the living room. Squatting down at the fireplace, he applied match to kindling and the fire caught in a crackle and hiss of sparks. The same sensation roared through Susannah's senses when the flames limned his profile in golden light.

What was it about this man, his particular masculine beauty? Why him, why this connection, this depth of knowing and wanting?

Then he turned, saw her and unwound his sinuously muscled frame to its full six and a bit feet of familiar impact. Outside the storm howled a warning to bunker down, take cover, stay safe; inside her mind a voice cried the same warning. It went unheeded, drubbed out by the thundering of her heart.

"You're back to your own clothes," he said, taking in

her skirt and sweater. Stockings. Boots. “I hope you’re comfortable.”

“Not really,” she admitted. After last night, that kiss, her response, there seemed little point in denying what simmered between them. “But your things—thank you, again. If this keeps up, I may need them tomorrow.”

Reflexively, she lifted her hands to hug her upper arms.

Donovan’s expression narrowed. “Are you cold? Come and sit by the—”

“No, not cold,” she reassured him quickly. “It’s the storm. The wind. I’m not a big fan of the rattling of glass.”

“Bad experience?”

She nodded. “One of those trips to my grandfather’s mountain cabin. And it is only a cabin, one room and outside bathroom. A real rustic retreat with no mod cons. It was Pappy’s way of staying attuned to his roots.”

“A self-made man?”

“Yes.” Abandoning her sanctuary at the foot of the stairs, she came farther into the room. “Property, development, investments. Anyway, we were at the cabin one weekend and a storm came up and the whole place groaned and shook and this great big mountain gum came crashing down right at the edge of the porch. I didn’t think I would live to see my ninth birthday.”

“That would have been a pity,” he said gravely. “I imagine birthdays in the Horton household would have been quite something.”

“Oh, yes. Big showy somethings.” She’d aimed for blithe, but somehow it came out sounding too cynical. Too revealing, under his silent regard. She expelled a deprecating laugh. "As you can see, I survived unscathed. I suspect the storm wasn't as bad in reality as in my imagination. Probably a tepid sea breeze compared to this. Upstairs, with the wall of windows—I thought half the island might end up in my room."

As if to illustrate her point, the wind and rain buffeted the eastern wall in a muscle-flexing show of strength. *I am nature, hear me roar.* Susannah flinched, but Donovan stood tall and unmoved. "This not-so-rustic retreat has been built to withstand worse than this, Susannah."

"If you say so."

"I know so. I might not remember coming here, but I had all the reports and appraisals. I knew exactly what I was buying." His gaze, steady, strong, reassuring, locked on hers. "You're safe here."

"Am I?"

There was a beat of pause, while the barely audible syllables hummed between them. Last night, she'd asked the question, he'd responded by walking away. Tonight, before she settled, before she trusted, she needed his word.

"I brought you here, Susannah. I will keep you safe."

Susannah trusted him. The notion, surprising, pleasing, terrifying, shifted the mood between them as the afternoon wore on. She refused to sit idly by the fire and be waited on; he was no good at sitting and passing the time.

He hadn't needed to tell her that; it was part of his will-do nature and part of the restless spirit that kept him moving and seeking new challenges in business. Another reason why he had no need of a home.

She slotted another piece into the jigsaw puzzle

she'd been working on for the past half hour, before turning to track his progress into the kitchen. "Nuh-uh," she said with mild rebuke. "My turn to make dinner tonight."

"You cook?"

"Quite well, as it happens."

He leaned his hips against the island counter, folded his arms across his chest and a small grin tilted his mouth. "You don't say."

"What is the smile for?" she asked, suspicious.

"You."

Their eyes met in the wake of that simple response, but there was nothing simple about it. Asking for more was pure masochism but she couldn't stop herself. "Me…in what way?"

"You're a constant surprise. When I first saw you—even before I saw you—I pegged you as a princess."

"In wading boots and a tiara?"

The smile widened on his lips; deepened in her heart. "Now, there's a picture."

"I've always been more comfortable in the wading boots," she admitted, exaggerating a tony accent. "The tiara tends to get tangled in the hair."

"There is a lot to tangle in." His gaze tracked the braid and its many escaped strands, before returning to her face. "Is the colour natural?"

He'd asked that before. Their first night. Before he'd chosen to discover the truth in his own will-do fashion.

Her skin prickled with remembered heat, with the sensation of his fingers sliding beneath her skirt and stroking her inner thigh. And, damn her redhead's complexion, that memory suffused her skin with warmth and she swore he saw right through her discomfort to the very, very bad images playing in her mind.

"Yes," she said in a husky breath. "All natural."

The focus of his heavy-lidded eyes grew hazy as he considered her comment. "And the curls?"

"What you see is all me."

"Unaided and unabetted," he murmured, and the appreciation in his silky, low voice and the hooded heat of his gaze turned every nerve alive in Susannah's body. "Very unprincessy."

"That isn't entirely by choice. This—" she flipped the plait back over her shoulder "—would normally be blow-dried and straightened. There would be makeup. Zara maintains that I could groom and primp for Australia."

"You don't need to."

"Oh, yes. A princess who grows up with frizzy red hair and gangly legs and freckles, learns how to primp!"

He chuckled, a low, smoky sound that hummed through her heightened senses. It struck her that for all the time she'd spent with him that previous weekend and in the past few days, this was the first time she'd heard that devilish laugh. She'd barely had time to savour the new knowledge, to stow it away with all the other memories, before he said, "You grew up just fine, Princess."

They ended up preparing dinner together, a long and leisurely process drawn out by the mood of teasing truce they'd established. She told him she preferred Princess to Goldilocks. He chipped a place even deeper in her heart by asking what her Pappy had called her.

"Princess," she admitted. Then, to ease the sudden choking tension, she added with faux gravity, "Or by my full title, Princess Susannah of Horton Ponds."

"That works with the wading boots and fishing pole image."

"Exactly."

They returned to the business of dinner, working alongside each other in a delicious combination of accord and teasing dispute. They debated the optimum combination of herbs for the oven-baked schnapper, swapped tastes of fresh salad ingredients as they chopped and sliced, fought for control of the garlic press but not for the job of dicing onions.

But beneath the surface lurked the sleeping beast of their attraction, just waiting for the chance to pull them under.

Like when Susannah refused his offer of wine—"After last night…no, I'll refrain." And the memory of their kiss burned bright in his eyes.

Or when her hair came free of the braid while she was whisking the makings of a crème brûlée, and he stepped in and said, "Let me fix it for you." His voice, low and gruff, stroked her like roughened velvet and then his hands were in her hair rethreading the sections and filling her with a yearning for more. Then he stopped and she looked up and caught the flare of his nostrils and felt the glancing touch of his gaze on her erect nipples.

She could feel her body listing toward him, the pull so intense, so necessary, that she couldn't right herself.

Until a piercing crack of breaking timber shattered

the moment. Susannah yelped. The bowl clattered to the countertop. And Donovan was already halfway to the door, gone a second later.

A branch had come down on the front path. No damage to the house and a saving grace as far as Van was concerned. If Susannah had continued to look at him in that touch-me, take-me way, if she'd put that outstretched hand on him—anywhere—he would not have been accountable for his actions. It had taken a good ten minutes pacing around in the sleety wind to cool his body's raging need before he could trust himself to return indoors.

Two hours later, they had eaten, the storm had abated, but not before a second severed branch crashed noisily against the side of the house.

"I see what you meant by the scream," Van said, recalling the night at The Palisades when she'd threatened to scream the place down. Not a smart move, remembering, because with that recollection came the scent of her skin in his nostrils, the heat of her temper bubbling so close to the surface, the rising urge to get that close again.

"*That* wasn't a scream," she said now. "It was more of a…loud gasp."

Van leaned back in his chair and regarded her with a simmering mix of amusement and desire. Princess Susannah really was something. With every hour in her company there was something else. "Out of curiosity—what led to your hair-raising scream that other weekend?"

She, God help him, finished licking the caramelised sugar from her dessert spoon before answering. "A frog."

"Like Kermit?"

"An ugly frog. It may have been a toad," she added defensively. "We were in the hot tub and I turned to get something and it was sitting on the edge of the tub. Right. There."

"Don't princesses kiss frogs?"

"Princesses kiss princes."

He should have laughed. Or continued teasing her about the frog/toad. But somewhere in the midst of that exchange he got lost in the remembered taste of her kiss and the frustration he'd kept at bay bubbled to the surface. "Like Carlisle?" he asked.

The spoon went still in her fingers for a beat before she answered. "I've never kissed Alex."

Van's heartbeat seemed to slow and deepen with the magnitude of that admission. She'd never slept with Carlisle.

"Are you still going to marry him?"

"I don't know," she said. "I may have no alternative."

His eyes narrowed to silver-sharp slits. "Is that what you're looking for, Susannah. An alternative? In what form—another proposal?"

"No!" Chin up, she stared him down with what looked like genuine outrage. "I know that you don't want marriage. That you value your independence too much to be looking for permanent ties."

"Then what do you want? Would you like me to take the choice out of your hands? To get out of my chair and come around the table, pick you up and carry you into my bed and do—"

"No!"

"No, you don't want me?" His voice dropped, low and rough as his mood. "Liar."

"You know I want you," she fired back, an agony of that wanting in the vibrato edge to her voice. "And you know why I won't let myself have you."

"Your father, the cheat?"

"Yes. My father, the cheating bastard. I won't be him. And I won't go back on my word to Alex."

Heart in mouth, Susannah watched him rise to his feet. Would he come around the table? Would he force this issue, now, after ceding to her appeal last night? But all he said was, "I'm going to check if there's any damage outside."

"Can I help?"

Something like grim amusement ghosted over his face. "You can help by taking yourself to bed. Use the spare bedroom downstairs, if that makes you feel safer."

Her gaze flickered from the spare room to his, next door.

"Yeah." There was a wealth of meaning in that soft sound and the speculation that flared in his eyes caused her nipples to tighten into hard buds. "You might consider locking the door."

After he was gone she did consider the downstairs room, but then she recalled the adjoining showers and how vulnerable—and how tempted—she'd felt with only that one thin wall between them. All night, too near, too dangerous.

She could sleep upstairs. It was only wind. Yesterday she'd conquered a boat ride without humiliation. If she embraced this tumultuous night, who knew, tomorrow she might face down a frog.

She attacked the stairs and started undressing as soon as she closed the door. If she kept moving, without thinking, she could dive under the covers and stay there covered and secure. In the privacy of the bathroom she stripped out of her underwear and pulled on her make-shift nightdress.

Donovan's shirt.

The fabric shimmered against her oversensitised skin, as fine and cool as silk. Fitting for Princess Susannah. A small smile teased her lips as she folded back the cuffs and started buttoning.

Two buttons down a huge wrenching crash of wood against glass halted her fingers, and in the space of a heartbeat her smile turned to a scream.

Nine

The storm had passed, the night turned quiet but for the creaking of wet timber and the trickle of overflow from rooftop to ground. Van circled the house with a restless frustration. He should have rejoiced in the aftermath and the lack of damage to what could soon be his property, but the storm was still building to a thunderhead in his body.

He'd sent Susannah to bed, but a perverse part of him hoped she'd thumbed her nose at that edict. That he'd walk inside and find her curled up on the sofa, the firelight painting golden shadows over her all-natural body. If that happened, then damn the trust she'd placed in him.

He paused beneath the window of the spare bedroom, dark, silent. Perhaps she had stayed up. His heartbeat quickened as he moved on, his steps surer and growing with purpose.

From the east side of the house he heard the wrenching crack of a limb breaking from a tree. The shuddering impact as it struck. But it was her scream, loud enough to split the night and his inflamed body asunder, that sent him careening into the house…only to find the spare bedroom empty. All of downstairs rooms were empty.

Wild with dread, he tackled the stairs three at a time, the pull of fear more powerful than the pull of pain in his tight hamstrings. He tore the door open and came to a brickwall halt when he saw the branch protruding through the shattered wall of windows. Sharp-ended timber and glass fragments littered the floor and bed, which was blessedly empty.

"Susannah!"

Her name rasped raw in his throat. Maybe he'd missed her downstairs. Maybe she'd been in his room, in his—

The bathroom door opened, the light illuminating the scene of destruction. Van heard her gasp, saw the shock on her blanched face as he barked an order to, "Stay put. Don't move."

She was in the bathroom, out of harm's way.

Van's brain deciphered the information but the fierce tension in his gut did not relent. The brittle crunch of glass beneath his feet twisted it tighter still as he crossed the room.

Without hesitation, he slid one arm under her thighs and the other around her back and picked her up. Her shocked exhalation blew warm against his cheek, but he didn't hang around enjoying the sensation. He strode back the way he'd come, and the arms wrapped around his neck tightened their purchase.

It was enough, that one gesture of trust, to ease the chokehold of fear. Enough that he could notice how she wore his shirt and snug white boxers. Enough to register the tickle of a stray curl against his throat, the silken texture of her bare legs against his arm, the soft press of her breasts against his chest.

"I can walk," she said huskily, when he reached the bottom of the stairs. "You don't have to carry me."

"There was glass everywhere."

"Not down here," she pointed out, but her voice shook enough that he held her more tightly to his chest as he made a beeline for his bedroom.

"I'm all right," she said with more force. Then she sucked in a breath. "Where are you taking me?"

About to shoulder open the door to his bathroom, he paused and looked down into her face. "I need to make sure you're all right."

"I am. Really." Except her face was still too pale, her eyes pools of darkness, her voice tremulous. And a deep shudder rolled through her body when she added, "It's just the shock of…of seeing my bed. And all that glass."

Cursing silently, he carried her through the doorway and slid her onto the marble-topped vanity that spanned the width of the room. Briefly he caught his reflection in the mirror at her back. His face looked gaunt, tight, fearsome in its intensity.

Little wonder she'd wanted to be put down. Or that her pulse beat wildly in that vulnerable spot at the base of her throat. In addition to the shock of the branch falling on the bed she'd been about to get into, he'd managed to scare her half to death with his reaction.

"I'm sorry," he murmured gruffly. "Just let me check your feet for splinters—"

"I was in the bathroom. The whole time."

"Show me," he rasped, unwilling and unable to take her word.

He didn't wait for her permission. Setting her hand on his shoulder for balance, he swivelled her on her backside until her legs and bare feet were illuminated by the bright downlights. He heard the shuddery little breath she drew when he took her foot in his hands. Felt the reflexive clutch of her fingers on his shoulder.

And when he looked down at the slender arch of her foot, the delicate bones of her ankle, the pearly colour painted on her nails, he felt a surge of possessiveness so strong it threatened to bring him to his knees. It was partly aftershock of his fear and the panicked rush upstairs, partly the adrenaline surge of acknowledging that she was unharmed. But the other part was raw, primitive desire.

Finally she was here, her skin silky smooth beneath his hands, her legs bare and warm all the way up to *his* boxers.

Bare and warm and shivering, he realised belatedly, and when he put her foot down and swung her back around, he realised that she wore nothing beneath his shirt. Largely unbuttoned, the garment had rucked up and twisted to reveal the rose pink tip of her breast.

She was either very, very cold or very, very turned on.

Van was struck by a wave of yearning. To rip his shirt from her body, to take that breast into his mouth, to feast eyes and mouth and hands on the body he'd once known and could not remember. He forced his hands to pull the shirt back together and set it right, but beneath his fingers the sweet warmth of her body beckoned. He trembled, she trembled—through the roaring in his blood he could not tell which, and when he drew a breath to centre himself, he looked up and caught her eyes on him, intent, unguarded and lambent with the same desire that swamped his senses.

She was trembling. He could feel the delicate tremor in the fingertips still resting on his shoulder. Shock, he told himself.

He picked her up and carried her through to his bed.

He could hold her, just hold and warm and soothe her until she felt safe again. He figured that wouldn't take long. She would realise that this was his bed, his arms around her, that she was burrowing close against him, her nose pressed into the hollow of his throat, his face buried in the fragrant spread of her hair.

She would soon realise that the tight heat of his body was not all about comfort, that he rode a delicate line between restraint and desire.

Then she would know she wasn't safe at all.

But for now…

He lifted a hand and combed the tangle of hair back from her face and she sighed, a soft relenting sound that soothed the jagged edges of his arousal. He pressed his lips to the crown of her head and stroked her back and crooned the words that she needed to hear and the message that he needed to remember.

"It's okay, Susannah. You're safe now. Go to sleep."

Safe, yes, but she was not okay.

When she closed her eyes, her heartbeat scurried like

a frightened rabbit and her only solace was the strong, sure beat of Donovan's heart. One of her hands still clutched at his shirt and she unfurled her fingers to smooth the fabric aside, so she could rest her palm closer to that reassuring pulse.

For a second or two it worked. The other fear faded under the sweet pressure of his lips against her crown, the heat radiating from his body, the stroke of his hands over her back and the thick heartbeat anchoring her in the moment. Then her fingers shifted infinitesimally and she felt the raised scar tissue and everything went completely still.

Him, her, the moment.

No wonder he'd looked so shell-shocked in the bathroom. No wonder he'd needed reassurance of her safety. It wasn't only because he'd brought her here and felt responsible for her safety.

The big hands at her back had stilled and Susannah eased herself up onto her elbow. Enough light bled through the half-open bathroom door for her to see his profile and guarded expression. "Are *you* okay?" she asked.

His jaw tightened. "You're in my bed. I'm very okay."

"You know why I'm asking."

Yes, he knew. That's why he'd made that incendiary comment—to distract her. To stop her asking about something he would see as a vulnerability.

In the shadowy light she caught the glint of dangerous purpose in his eyes. Felt the shift of pressure in the hand at the base of her spine, felt it like an electric surge of awareness in every female cell.

"I have scars, Susannah," he said, low and dark. "I

had cuts, stitches, multiple surgeries. We can play show-and-tell, if that's what you want, but if you put your hand on my body—anywhere—I'll take that as a sign of different intent."

Susannah looked into his eyes and became lost in an agony of wanting. She ached for those lost weeks, for thinking the worst of him, for not trusting how her heart had first judged him. She knew it was wrong, she knew she would regret it, but she couldn't turn away. She looked at him lying there—white shirt, dark trousers, quicksilver eyes—and her whole being yearned.

She lifted a hand to touch his face and he intercepted its path, held her fingers tight and trembling in his.

"Be very sure, Susannah."

Throat tight with emotion, she nodded. She wanted to say the words, to let him know she'd made this choice, but the affirmation got lost in the flash of his eyes as he took her hand to his mouth and kissed her palm.

Her eyelids drifted closed for that intensely erotic second and then came open again as his hands shifted to her shoulders and turned her onto her back. As he covered her with his body and his kiss.

The completeness of that contact—eyes, lips, bodies—engulfed her in a sweet gulp of heat. She became acutely aware of everywhere they touched. The slow seeking pressure of his lips, the penetrating heat of his hands through the thin fabric of her shirt, the texture of his trousers against her bare thighs.

The slow sweep of his tongue elicited a shudder of response deep in her flesh and she opened her mouth in silent invitation, welcoming him to fill the hollow of her mouth, to drive the last cold fragments of shock from her heart, to reaffirm that he was here and she was safe, that neither of them lay broken and bleeding amid a mountain of splintered glass.

Oh, yes, he was here.

Trailing his mouth along her jawline, nuzzling her neck, gently nipping her earlobe and sucking the pearl stud between his teeth. Her back arched from the mattress, and he whispered something in her ear, a teasing erotic promise that was lost in the elevated rasp of her breath and the swift race of her pulse.

It didn't matter—the words did not matter. It was enough that this was Donovan. The skim of his breath on her sensitive skin, the rough edge to his whisper, the knowing that he—and only he—could bring her body to life and fill the lonely ache of her heart.

And then he was kissing her again, kissing her and sliding his hands down to her hips, melding their bodies as closely as possible without removing the barrier of clothing. For a long moment, she savoured the sensation. Then, with mouths still fused, he rolled to his back and pulled her on top.

This kiss was new again, a wild explosion that fed their greedy passion. His hands on her thighs, on her buttocks, pushing her hard against him—her hands at his shirt, frantic in their haste to bare his chest to the sweet heat of her touch. He relinquished her mouth to nuzzle the fragrant warmth of her throat, to bite the tender skin at the juncture between shoulder and neck.

To absorb the deep-seated quiver of response that wracked her body from fingertips to toes.

"My special spot," she whispered, palming his face. "How did you know? Did you remember?"

Van had acted on raw instinct. He couldn't have known this intensity, this driving need to please her, to spend the rest of his life inside her.

It was completely, terrifyingly new.

To rescue himself from the unknown, he applied himself to what he recognised. Hot swamping desire. He undid the one remaining button on her shirt, exposing her breasts to his eyes. With a long, slow sweep of his tongue he lathed each nipple and then tugged with gentle teeth until she cried out his name.

"Donovan."

He loved his name on her lips, and when she repeated it, her down-under accent penetrated the wall in his mind and echoed through his memory, again and again and again, the breathless cry of a woman's climax.

Driven by a desperate need to hear that same sound now, he flipped her to her back and slid down to stroke the silken skin of her inner thigh. His fingers slipped inside her pants and found her wet and indescribably hot. Beside her hips her fingers clutched at the sheet as if she needed to anchor herself and that sight was powerfully erotic.

Beneath his fingers her body vibrated with the same need that smouldered in her eyes. He didn't need any further explanation or invitation. With quick efficiency he stripped the underwear from her body and then he sat back on his heels to drink in the sight.

Everything from the curve of her elbow to the dip of her waist was a picture of feminine beauty.

His earlier frustration returned with a vicious streak that made him want to howl at the moon. Because for all the glimpses, the flashes, the snaps of sound and image and scent, he couldn't remember this most alluring, transfixing, knock-back-on-his-heels sight.

How could he not remember?

One last time his eyes moved over her, learning that sight, committing every detail to memory, before he rose to his feet and strode to the bathroom to turn out the light.

Susannah had forgotten just how dark it could be in this isolated part of the world, without the constant illumination of a million city lights, without the digital radiance from a score of household electronics.

It was very, very dark.

Last July, they had made love in the dark and in the full light of day. There'd been no cause for modesty at Stranger's Bay and there was definitely no cause here on Charlotte Island. Lying in bed, listening to the sounds of him undressing, Susannah's heart constricted.

Did he really think she would be turned off by his scars?

Did he think her that shallow?

Then she realised that the scars themselves were not the problem, but her reaction to them. With her emotions teetering grimly on the edge of this day's overload, she couldn't guarantee her response. She might go over the top imagining the initial injuries, his pain, his mortality.

She shivered slightly and perhaps she inhaled a gust of air because she sensed his sudden stillness beside the bed. "Does the dark bother you?"

"Only if you can't find me," she said softly.

The mattress dipped under his weight and he was there, causing her heart to skip and her temperature to spike. With one hot hand on her hip, he turned her onto her side, facing him on the big bed.

"I found you."

The simple statement deserved a teasing answer, but Susannah had nothing to offer. He was here, naked, *hers,* and the enormity of that knowledge seeped into every part of her body until she quavered with the intensity of wanting. All she could do was show him, touch him. She skimmed her hands slowly up his arms, over his shoulders, down the long contours of his back.

When she slipped lower, he trapped one of her legs between his and held her firmly in place. Their eyes sought and held despite the darkness, their bodies so close she felt the surge of his response against her belly. Their thighs slid together in a restless dance, and in the beat of a second, the mood had changed, sliced by the edgy hunger in his eyes, in her body, by the growl of his voice.

"I need to be inside you."

Darkness and desire had robbed Susannah of any shyness, and she watched him take care of protection with steady eyes and very unsteady emotions. Then his hand was on her face, touching her lips, asking for her guidance as he settled between her thighs. Their gazes linked as he nudged the entrance to her body, as he started to slide inside, and Susannah forgot everything as longing and loving overlapped in a wave of yearning that claimed her body, mind and her soul.

She welcomed him, hard and strong and vital. There

had only been this man; there could be no other who fit her body, who matched her desire.

His nostrils flared, his gaze gleamed with satisfaction as he filled her to the hilt. He went still and a long, low, pleasured groan escaped his lips and suffused her with the purest bliss. *This is what I lost,* she thought, as they kissed with their eyes open and their bodies joined. They kissed in a rhythm that mimicked the rolling give-and-take of their lower bodies, they kissed until their lungs required sustenance and the sounds of their choppy breathing filled the air.

And just when she thought the exquisite pleasure of his touch could take her no higher, he caught her lower lip between his teeth and stilled. Held rigid over her body, poised on the brink of release, he looked into her eyes and she knew he recognised something in the moment.

She lifted a trembling hand and touched his face, stroked his jaw, and he began to move again, thrusting deep and strong. Susannah hovered, not wanting this over, greedily wanting him there in her body, soaring in this perfect moment forever.

After there would be words, guilt, confessions, and everything would change again.

She wrapped her legs more tightly around him, and that new angle broke both their control. The climax came quickly, catching her in its sweet, savage grip and flinging her high and wild. As she spun out, she chanted his name, a low breathless ache that resounded in her blood and her mind and her heart.

He drove deep one last time and held himself rigid,

straining with the intensity of his own release. With arms and legs and thundering heart, she clung to him, stroking the slick heat of his back and nuzzling her face into his neck, dragging the masculine scent of his body into her lungs and her senses.

Afterward, too, their sated bodies fit together in a perfect melding of hard lines and giving curves. Donovon's arm held her close to his side. His elevated breath on her temple lifted a fine frizz of hair into her vision.

If she had the energy Susannah would have brushed it aside. But she was happily spent, unable to move anything beyond the fingers that traced an indolent pattern across his chest. "Did that trigger your memory?" she asked softly, remembering what she'd seen in his face, what she'd felt in his intensity.

"No."

He sounded relaxed, completely unperturbed, and Susannah's hand stilled. "Doesn't that bug you?"

"Not anymore."

She didn't know what to make of that. Back at Stranger's Bay the frustration of not knowing had reverberated around him like a force field. Beneath her hand she felt the ridged edge of one of the scars that crisscrossed his abdomen. Earlier he'd warned her off asking, but now he was at ease. Now she could ask. "And the attack…does it bother you not remembering how that happened?"

"It bugs me that I was caught out and the bastards got the better of me." The arm at her waist tightened momentarily and Susannah held her breath until he relaxed again. "At least now I see why I might have been distracted."

"By me?"

"By a whole weekend of you. Yeah."

The low rumble of his answer rippled through her, a sweet antithesis to her chilling thoughts about his injuries. "I like the idea that you were thinking of me in your hometown, but I hate what happened because of it."

"The scars?"

"The wounds that caused the scars," she corrected. "What you went through because of them, and everything that happened afterward."

"We can fix that," he said after a moment.

"Can we?"

"Tomorrow."

"And now?"

She felt a change in the mood. The hand at her waist applied a different pressure, a renewed heat, as his fingers splayed wide over her belly. The weight of his legs shifted, pinning her to the bed. "Now—" his voice deepened to a thick growl as he nuzzled her hair from her throat "—I have more memories to replace."

Ten

Van had never been a big sleeper, but for once he welcomed his insomnia. In the pale light of dawn he watched Susannah sleep with a deep-seated satisfaction he'd never felt before…or that he didn't recall feeling before.

And he didn't remember being with her. He hadn't lied about that. All he'd suffered these past days were fleeting impressions, and if anything was capable of blowing those glimpses of the past into fully realised memories then those explosive hours in his bed should have been it.

For once the lack of memory didn't bother him. Now that he'd had her, all he cared about was making sure she stayed. In his bed, in his home, in his life. The permanency of that thought should have scared the hell out of him, but it didn't.

Impatient to move on from the past to a shared future, he left her sleeping and dressed quickly. In the wake of last night's storm, The Palisades' management would send a craft for them. Their seclusion would soon be at an end and he might not get another chance to seek the answers he needed.

He'd walked the island assessing the damage. Seeing the size of the branch that had crashed through the upstairs windows, his gut churned sickly with what might have been. He came in through the back door, and immediately noted the open doors to his bedroom and onto the veranda. She was up. Good.

He crossed the room, finally catching sight of her on the deck. Morning light traced the lines of her body through her shirt and when she lifted a hand to hold her hair back from her face, her striking beauty hit him anew.

His gut tightened with more than morning lust, with more than appreciation of the picture she made. There was something in her body language, in the taut stretch of her neck and the way her hand gripped the balcony rail that spoke of her inner tension and hot-wired straight into his.

In the clear light of morning she wouldn't like what they'd done in the dark of night. He figured she would lay the blame at his feet, but he had no intention of dwelling on culpability. What was done, was done.

He'd brought her here to seduce her, to give her cause to end her marriage plans. That goal had been the farthest thing from his mind last night, but he couldn't pretend to be sorry.

He wondered if Carlisle would be at the resort, awaiting their return. He couldn't believe the man wouldn't be. Or that he wouldn't fight tooth and nail to keep Susannah.

She looked around then, as if the surge of his possessiveness had growled her name. When he approached, she smiled, but the gesture looked as strained and fragile as the shadows of regret in her eyes.

"I saw you out walking," she said, her gaze skating away over the storm-ravaged vista. "There looks to be a lot of trees down. Is there much damage down at the cottage?"

It was a tossup which Van hated more—the recrimination in her eyes, the false cheerfulness in her voice or the fact she'd resorted to small talk. "Are you going to pretend last night didn't happen?" he asked.

She let go of her hair, let the breeze pick it up and screen her face, but that didn't hide the stiffening of her spine. Or the ache of a plea in her response. "For now, yes. I'm not—"

"It has to be now."

She scooped back her hair to reveal wide and wary eyes. "Why?"

"There are boats out on the bay. I imagine one of them is heading our way."

"Oh." Her gaze flickered over him—fully dressed—and then down at her revealing attire. "Then I had better shower and dress."

"After we've talked, Susannah."

He blocked her attempted exit, forced his attention away from the distraction of her nakedness beneath the shirt and waited for her to meet his eyes. The annoyance he saw there was aimed internally, not at him, and the knowledge caused a subtle relenting in his stance.

"Hey," he said softly, "don't beat yourself up." With a gentle hand he threaded her hair behind one ear and held it there, his thumb tracing the tense line of her jaw before touching the pearl in her earlobe. A hot memory of his mouth, right there, rocketed through him and coloured his voice when he added, "It was inevitable."

"No." Shaking her head, she stepped back from his touch and his hand fell away. "You gave me the choice last night. I didn't take it."

"You're here on this island because of me."

"I'm here because I chose to be," she said, her voice choked with the same emotion that darkened her eyes. "I shouldn't have been anywhere near you. I should have stayed in Melbourne. I should have been on my honeymoon."

For several seconds, Van stared at her, unsure if he'd heard correctly. When he realised that the steadily escalating thrum wasn't his heartbeat, he turned and looked out over the bay and saw a helicopter zeroing in on the island. His attention zapped back to Susannah's face. "You're not marrying Carlisle."

"After last night?" Her soft words was barely audible above the *thwap-thwap-thwap* of the helicopter's rotors as it circled overhead, and her eyes swam with the same self-castigation as earlier. "No, I guess I'm probably not."

* * *

Donovan had intimated on the deck at Charlotte Island that they wouldn't be able to talk once the rescue craft arrived. He'd been right. Once back at the resort, solicitous staff hovered over them. A shuttle whisked them to the airport to catch a late-morning flight to Melbourne. It was all so quick and efficient, there'd been little chance for talk until they were seated on the plane. Then his focussed gaze settled on her face and she knew the question of what-now couldn't be avoided any longer.

Tilting her face, she turned to meet his eyes. "What happens when we get back to Melbourne?"

"We sort out the contract on The Palisades. Then we talk—" he leaned closer, tapped the back of her hand with his finger "—about us."

Susannah's heart kicked up a beat and she had to caution herself not to leap into the promise of those words. First she needed to sort out her agreement with Alex. Then there was her business, which could choke and die without an urgent injection of funds.

"I'm meeting with Armitage this afternoon," he said.

Wow. He hadn't wasted any time getting back to business. She didn't even know when he'd found time to make the phone call to Horton's CEO. The pleasurable ripple he'd started in her veins with his talk of *us* braked to a sudden halt. "So soon?" she asked. "Shouldn't you at least wait until I've spoken to Alex?"

"I need to set things in motion before I leave."

She straightened, her gaze springing up to meet his. "You're leaving? *When?*"

"That depends on this meeting, but as soon as possible?"

"Because of Mac?" she guessed.

The attendant interrupted with a polite admonishment, drawing their attention to the pre-flight safety instruction. Staring blindly at the video screen, Susannah digested this news. She hadn't considered that he might be leaving so swiftly. She hadn't allowed herself to think beyond—

"Come with me."

His voice, low and intense, was close to her ear. Had she heard him correctly? Startled, she looked around and found those eyes—silver, sharp, determined—focussed on hers. Her heart gave an excited bump. "I can't. I have to talk to Alex, and there's my business. I can't just drop everything and leave."

"You weren't going to do that for this honeymoon you mentioned?"

"Yes, but..." Her voice trailed off as her gaze slid back to the screen. A honeymoon was two weeks. He was asking her to... She didn't know what *come with me* implied. "Can we talk about this after I've talked to Alex?"

"When?"

"I don't know. As soon as I can."

He fell silent, leaving her to spend the rest of the flight worrying over that upcoming conversation. Donovan had told her not to beat herself up, but how could she not? She'd acted dishonourably, without willpower, and she took ownership of that choice. She refused to blame it on fear or adrenaline or the need to affirm life.

Now she had to tell Alex that the temporary delay on their wedding plans was permanent.

She couldn't marry him, not when another man lay claim to her heart.

Her mother met the flight, her reception for Donovan a chilling contrast to her effusive embrace of Susannah. Out of politeness Miriam offered him a lift to the city, which he declined with a pointed, "I prefer to make my own plans."

"Call me," he told Susannah, and she read the unsaid rest in his eyes. *After you've talked to Carlisle.* Watching him walk away without once looking back, his stride long and purposeful, she felt a panicky sense of loss. That fear—that emotion—must have been written all over her face because her mother tsked her disapproval. "Oh, Susannah, didn't you learn the last time?"

"I don't know what you're talking about."

"You can try to fool me, darling, but please don't fool yourself." Her mother spoke briskly, but the look she turned on Susannah brimmed in castigation. "He used you the first time and he's used you again."

Susannah's stride faltered. "What do you mean by that?" she asked, hurrying to catch up.

"Do you know he's meeting with Horton's this afternoon? He called the minute he got off the island, wanting to talk deals. According to Judd, he's very confident that Carlisles won't go ahead with the purchase of The Palisades. Does that mean you've changed your mind about marrying Alex?"

Susannah nodded and although her mother frowned, she didn't break stride until they reached her Mercedes. "Aren't you going to try and talk me out of this rash and foolish decision?" Susannah asked across the roof of the car.

"Unfortunately I agree with you. You can't marry him."

Susannah blinked in surprise. "I thought you were set on having a Carlisle for a son-in-law."

"I was, but…" She made a dismissive gesture, her expression tight. "Never mind."

But Susannah did mind, and once they were cruising south on the freeway, she turned toward her mother. "What aren't you telling me? What shouldn't I mind?"

"Some things are better left unknown."

"I am twenty-eight years old. Please, don't keep anything from me for my own good."

"Very well," Miriam said stiffly after a moment's consideration. "I wasn't going to tell you, but I suppose it may come out anyway. Lord knows why this hasn't been splashed around the gossip sheets already."

"Do you mean Donovan and me? I don't think—"

"No, not you. Alex Carlisle. He spent the weekend with another woman."

Susannah's mouth opened but no sound came out. She shut it. Shook her head. Tried again. "No. Not Alex. He wouldn't."

"I saw them, outside the Carlisle Grande on Sunday afternoon. The woman was blond, tall, very distinctive in a common sort of way. She was riding a motorcycle." Miriam all but sniffed with disdain. "He kissed her, right there under the hotel *porte cochere.* In broad daylight, for anyone to see, and I am not talking a sisterly peck. This was a long and indiscreet embrace. I'm sorry, darling, but can you see why I wasn't going to tell you?"

Struggling to digest the information, Susannah didn't answer. Alex and Zara? No, not possible. Although she had sent her sister to deliver her message to the hotel. And it would explain why Alex hadn't called or tried to track her down. If this were true, then backing out of her marriage agreement might not be as difficult as she'd imagined.

"Are you sure it was Alex?" she asked slowly.

"It was Alex. Now," Miriam continued briskly, "about this Donovan Keane. Do you love him?"

What was the point in prevaricating? Her mother had read the truth in her face at the airport, when she'd watched him walk away. "I wouldn't have gone to Tasmania if I didn't."

"That's what I feared."

Susannah sat up straight. "Don't pass judgment, Mother. You don't know him. You don't know what he's been through or how badly he wants The Palisades."

"Oh, I think I do." There was something in her mother's frown, in the dark look she slid Susannah's way, that stopped Susannah's heart for a second. "The question is, how badly do *you* want him?"

Coming to Donovan's hotel was not the smartest thing Susannah had ever done. She should have taken time to think, to let the dust settle, to gain a better perspective than her gut reaction to what her mother had revealed.

So here she was, sitting in the foyer of the Lindrum, waiting for Donovan to pick up his room phone. When it switched to voice mail, she closed her eyes in dismay. Was this to be the story of her life?

Susannah Horton lived to a grand old age of ninety-eight. Lamentably, half those years were spent narrating messages and waiting for the calls to be returned.

Where was he? During the taxi ride from her South Yarra duplex, she'd calmed her nerves by setting the scene in her imagination.

She would call his room, he would answer, she would say, "I need to see you," he would say, "Come on up," and—

"Susannah?"

She came to her feet in a rush, her heart doing a joyous dance of welcome even though she cautioned it to behave. "I was just calling your room."

"I'm not there."

No, he was here.

Looking altogether too gorgeous, damn him, in a dark suit and tie. His gaze drifted over her, taking in the shoes, the stockings, the dress. The hair she'd groomed to within an inch of its natural life.

Nerves fluttered in her belly, but she felt immensely pleased that he was noticing. She might have been miffed with him, but that hadn't prevented her spending significant time deciding on the little black dress and even longer primping.

"When I saw you sitting here, I hoped to see luggage at your side. This—" his gaze skimmed the dress before returning to her face "—looks more like a dinner date than travelling."

"Sorry to disappoint."

"I'm not too disappointed, except if I'd known you were here waiting, I wouldn't have let the meeting drag so long."

Exactly the reminder she'd needed of why she was here. She drew a quick breath and fixed him a cool glare. "I'm surprised the meeting dragged, given how you went in there with such a set idea of what you wanted."

The lazy drift of his eyes steadied on hers. "News travels fast at Horton's."

"When you talk to Judd Armitage about anything that concerns a Horton, my mother will hear."

"Do I take it you have a problem with the deal I'm brokering?"

"You don't think you should have run your *deal* by me first?" she asked, unable to keep the indignation from her voice. "Perhaps you might even have waited until I was un-engaged."

"I don't have time to sit around cooling my heels. I needed to get started," he said evenly. "Today was to open negotiations."

"By requesting the same deal, the same terms, as Alex?"

He regarded her narrowly for a moment. "As I said, a starting point."

Susannah choked out a laugh and shook her head. "Why would I agree to another contract marriage?" she asked, holding out her hands in mock appeal. "Why would you even contemplate something like that?"

"Why," he countered after a heartbeat of silence, "are you so opposed to the concept?"

Although his expression was fixed, his voice even, there was something in his stillness that caused her heart to kick in, hard.

"You intended marrying Carlisle," he continued. "If I hadn't reappeared, you would have married him last Saturday. I can only surmise that your objection is to marrying me."

Marry Donovan? Her heart beat hard and fast with the possibility, until she needed to draw a deep breath to settle the giddiness. "With Alex, I knew exactly what was going on."

"And you wanted to marry him."

"Yes, I did. I wanted everything the marriage offered."

"Which begs the question, what part of *everything* can't I offer? It's not the money or the business rescue package. I know it's not the sex." He paused long enough for their gazes to catch and cling in a shimmer of remembered heat, before continuing in the same deceptively level tone. "Is it the Carlisle name? Or the big, happy family?" When she didn't answer right away, he leaned closer, and anger flashed brief and hot in his eyes. "Why him, Susannah, and not me?"

"Because he asked," she replied, her voice thick with the same heat. "It was that easy, Donovan. He didn't take a deal to Horton's because he was impatient. Yes, he was in a hurry, too, but he didn't pick the easiest course to expedite matters. He asked me and he gave me time to consider the offer."

"And yet you didn't go ahead with it…."

"Right now," she fired back, "I'm wondering why I didn't!"

For a long moment, they faced off. The intensity of her angry words still buzzed through Susannah's veins and clouded her vision. So much so that she didn't notice the approach of the front-desk manager until he cleared his throat.

"Excuse me, Mr. Keane."

Intent on their exchange, she'd forgotten all about their surroundings, but now she glanced around. Thankfully the public lobby was deserted apart from the manager, now engaged in conversation with Donovan.

"A phone call," he was saying, sotto voce. "A Ms. O'Hara. She said to find you if at all possible. An emergency. You can use my office—it's over here."

Donovan turned back to Susannah. A distracted frown drew his brows together as he checked his watch. "I need to take this."

"I'll wait."

She sensed he might suggest otherwise, but then he simply nodded. As she watched him stride away, Susannah did the time translation. It was very early in the morning in California, surely too early for his assistant—she recognized the name, after all those stonewalled calls she'd made back in July—to be calling on business.

By the time Donovan came out of the manager's office, she'd circled the foyer on anxious feet a dozen times. One look at his tightly drawn features confirmed her worse fears. "Is it Mac?" she asked, intercepting his long-striding path.

"She's been taken to hospital," he told her, not easing

his pace until he reached the lifts. He punched the up button with controlled aggression. "I'm leaving as soon as possible."

Susannah didn't need to ask for details. The answer hummed in the tightly leashed tendons of his neck, in the jump of a muscle in his jaw. "What can I do to help?" she asked. "I can call the airlines, book you flights."

"That isn't necessary."

"It's what I do," she pointed out. "I can ensure you're on the earliest flight to San Francisco, whether that's from Melbourne or Sydney or Auckland or—"

"Thank you, but Erin is on that." His tone clipped and final, was punctuated by the electronic ping that signaled the lift's arrival. The doors slid open. "This is why I needed to get things moving," he said tightly. "Before it's too late."

"I'll talk to Alex and to Judd. I'll make sure you get the same deal as your initial bid."

Inside the car, he turned and their eyes met—one second where the shutters slid aside to reveal a storm of emotion. One second for Susannah to realise, with a blinding flash of belated clarity, that she'd said the worst possible thing. She'd confirmed his belief that she didn't want to marry him.

Eleven

The rain came with the night, a downpour that blocked Van's view of the bay and trapped him inside with only the bleakness of his thoughts for company.

This afternoon he'd said his last goodbye to Mac in a short, private funeral service. Afterward he'd returned to the Sausalito apartment he'd rented after his hospital stay.

He would have been happy with a hotel suite close to to Keane MacCreadie's offices, but Mac had found and organised the rental. She'd spouted the benefits of relaxing water views, the bayside walks and a nearby health club. Van relented because Mac lived close by and those visits made the inconvenience worthwhile.

Except there'd not been nearly enough visits. A handful of weeks where he'd pushed himself harder than his physio advised in order to recover his physical strength. The rest researching the deal gone wrong in preparation for his second trip down under.

A trip rendered meaningless by Mac's death. She'd passed peacefully—for that, he thanked God—and without regaining consciousness. Van had been too late to say goodbye, his grief at the loss weighed down with the knowledge that he'd failed her.

He'd spent too many precious days in Australia. Day one he could have tied up the deal if he'd not bent his initial plan of swift vengeance. All because he'd wanted Susannah Horton warm and willing in his bed.

He should have been home; he should have been here for Mac; he was the only family she'd had.

The opera playing while he cooked ended in a blistering crescendo of angst, the perfect accompaniment to an untouched dinner and his dark mood. As he crossed to select a more soothing sound track the doorbell rang. He stopped, frowning at the prolonged strident sound. It crossed his mind that someone was leaning on the thing, and could have been doing so for some time. Lord knows, he wouldn't have heard.

It also crossed his mind to ignore it. He wasn't expecting visitors—since he didn't share this address, he never did. But curiosity got the better of him, and he started for the door.

At first he thought there was no one there. Kids pranking, although it was a helluva night for it. Searching for any sign of mischief he glared out through the rain, and on the very edge of the glow cast by his porch light he caught a sign of movement.

The sheen of an ivory raincoat, a yellow umbrella halted and then spun in the light.

Van's heart jerked, his pulse rate rocketing even while his brain rejected the notion. She couldn't be here. Not after their acrimonious parting in Melbourne a week ago.

But she was very much here, scurrying down his path in those familiar skinny-heeled boots.

The bottom of the coat blew open, flashing stockinged knee and thigh and the heat of memory raced through Van's blood. Unwanted but not unwelcome. Suddenly the prospect of her company wasn't so bad. He was in the perfect mood for a confrontation.

She came to a stop under the shelter of the porch, and when she lowered the umbrella the light turned her hair into a fiery nimbus. A tentative smile curved her lips and Van's need of that warmth, that quiet fire, slammed into him like a freight train.

"We seem to have some sort of cosmic connection with the rain," she said, shaking a spray of raindrops from her sleeve. Then she saw his face and the smile in her eyes clouded over. "I'm sorry. I didn't mean to sound so…blithe."

She huffed out a breath and shook her head, and Van let the uncomfortable moment stretch. He hated that a part of him yearned to ease the moment, to bring the smile back to her face. Another part of him wanted to walk back inside, to slam the door in her face, to shut out this fierce raft of emotions she elicited simply by being here. Simply by being *her*.

A larger part ached to pull her inside with him, to turn

her against the door, to unbutton her coat and appease the cold torment of this day in the heat of her body.

"I knew this would be awkward, just arriving on your doorstep—"

"Then why didn't you call?" he asked.

"I tried, several times. You're either not answering your private phone or screening my calls. Erin was kind enough to give me your address."

Erin, kind? Van's brows rose at that oxymoron. "Are you sure you had the right Erin?"

Their eyes met for a second, hers ridiculously pleased by this small sign of relenting. "Yay tall—" she demonstrated with her free hand "—dark hair, pretty eyes. Unfriendly, until I let her know why I wanted your address."

"Did it cross your mind that I might not be home?"

"I saw your lights and heard the music before I let the cab leave."

"And if I hadn't opened the door?"

"That did cross my mind," she admitted. "I went out to see if the cab was still lurking and then your outside light came on." And despite his unwelcoming stance—or perhaps because of it—she drew herself up tall and added, "But I would have called back tomorrow."

"Why would you do that?"

She looked away, her lips pressed together as if she was gathering her composure. And, damn, when she looked back up the green gleam of moisture turned her eyes luminous in the porch light. "You know why."

Yeah, he knew why, but the pull of those tears and the husky edge to her voice twisted him inside out.

"I'm so sorry to hear about Mac."

She took a step toward him, but Van kept her at bay with the cool bite of his words. "I gathered you heard. Unfortunate timing, wasn't it?"

Her head came up, her eyes widening with a combination of hurt and confusion. "I came as soon as I could."

"Really?" The raw remains of the past five days, the guilt, the recrimination, the futility—the wanting her quiet strength beside him—burned like acid. "You've wasted your time. Now Mac's gone, I have no reason to go ahead with the purchase of The Palisades. I don't need anything from you."

Susannah knew she'd taken a big risk. She'd made another of those snap decisions that had gotten her into trouble before, another decision driven by her heart. Despite the coldness of his greeting, she still believed it was the right choice.

Today he'd buried his mentor, business partner, grandmother—the one person he would do anything for—and that grief was etched in every harsh line of his face. If he was trying to shut everyone out as Erin had intimated, if that was his way of dealing with the wretchedness of his loss, then he would have to work a darn sight harder.

Chin high and eyes steady on his, she stood her ground. "I'm not leaving, Donovan. I'm not here about the contract; I'm here for you. Tonight I thought you could use a friend."

"Friends?" He exhaled on a humourless laugh. "Is that how you see us?"

"I thought we were more." Outside in the street a car

horn blared, a distraction that lifted his narrow-eyed gaze from her face and a reminder that they hadn't progressed past his doorstep. "I thought we'd passed the stage of conversing on the porch, at any rate. Aren't you going to invite me inside?"

For a moment she thought he might deny her even that, but then he opened the door and held out his arm in a go-right-ahead gesture. The steely glint in his eyes was not so welcoming. A chill that had nothing to do with the rainy night shivered up Susannah's spine as she took her first tentative steps across the threshold and into his home.

"Can I take your coat?"

The door closed with a thud and Susannah's nerves jumped. Her fingers stuttered over the belt and buttons. Then she felt him close behind her, hands at her shoulders, helping off her coat.

"Thank you," she murmured, looking around.

This was his home—temporary home, she reminded herself, but still she wanted to see. Outside she'd been consumed by nerves and by the angst of the music that soared from inside. Her only impression was of stucco and terra cotta and now she noticed that the Mediterranean theme continued inside. White textured walls, arched openings between the rooms, woven mats and potted palms and bold splashes of red, gold and black in the furnishings.

She was drawn irresistibly toward the kitchen and the redolent scent of cooking. Nerves stirred to life by the dangerous look in his eyes when she came through the door calmed under the memory of their last night at

Charlotte Island, the camaraderie they'd shared working shoulder to shoulder.

"Whatever you are cooking smells delicious."

Hoping to identify the dish, she inhaled deeply and realised that the meaty richness was underlaid with sweetness. Then she caught sight of a sheath of flowers on the low table. White lilies. All the calm and comfort punched from her body.

She turned on her heel, found Donovan still by the door, watching her with a darkly hooded gaze. "I'm so sorry," she said quickly. "I didn't realise when you left Melbourne that she had so little time left."

"No one did."

"Not even you?"

"Do you think I'd have taken the trip to Australia and wasted days at the island if I'd known."

The low, harsh pronouncement echoed in Susannah's heart. On top of everything else, he was lamenting those days they'd spent together. "Those days weren't wasted," she said.

"Days spent chasing a meaningless deal?"

"No, not meaningless. How can you think that? You took the trip because of Mac, to return the place she held so dearly to her ownership. Do you think she would have wanted you to abandon that? Wouldn't she have wanted to see Charlotte Island back in MacCreadie hands?"

"I'm not a MacCreadie," he said harshly.

"Is that what Mac thought? You told me the lengths she went to in finding you. She admitted the truth after years of maintaining her silence about your blood relationship. Of course she saw you as family. Tell me, if the acquisition had gone through after July, if you'd been successful in your bid that time, what would have happened now? Who would she have left the place to?"

"I'm her sole heir." Said as though that was unwanted, unwarranted, unwelcome.

Susannah understood. She ached with his hurt and his anger at being robbed all over again. He didn't want Mac's estate, he wanted time to give back something of what she'd given him. "I understand how much Mac meant to you and how you must be feeling—"

"Do you, do you have any notion what it's like to have no one who believes in you but this one woman who was prepared to back me with everything she owned? Do you know what it's like to spend thirty years not knowing where you came from, to find the answers and the family and then to lose it all weeks later?

"Hell, Susannah, I wasn't even here for her. The one time she needed me, I wasn't here."

The low fervour of his words resonated between them in the quiet. Susannah had no words, no response. His wretchedness pierced her. She wanted nothing more than to cross the space that separated them, to wrap her arms around him, to comfort him with the knowledge that he wasn't alone. That he hadn't lost the only person who loved him. But he kept her at bay with the barrier of his stance and the hostility in his eyes.

"Have you looked at this from Mac's perspective?" she asked, "Or only from your own?"

His features tightened. "Mac died alone," he said bluntly. "That's the perspective I'm seeing."

Oh, Donovan. She hadn't realised. When he didn't answer his phone, she'd imagined him at Mac's bedside. She'd hoped he'd had some time, that he'd at least arrived in time to say goodbye. "I didn't know. I'm so sorry."

He didn't respond, but she could see the muscle working in his jaw. He abandoned the position he'd maintained just inside the room—close to the door, as if he'd not yet decided whether to let her stay or to open that door and order her out—and stalked across to arched windows overlooking the bay.

"From another perspective," she continued carefully, "I imagine Mac was inordinately proud of your success. She wouldn't have invested everything in you, back in those early years, if she hadn't believed in you. And she wouldn't have trusted you with her secrets or with her inheritance if she hadn't trusted and loved you."

"She still died alone."

"No, Donovan. She was alone before she found you. She died knowing she had a grandson who loved her, who I imagine was here for her in all manner of ways these past years."

For a long moment, he stared blindly out into the darkness before he could answer. "Never enough," he said gruffly. "Business, travel, I was never here enough."

In the glass Van saw her approach, the reflected movement of her hair and the blue-green dress that skimmed the lines of her body. He wanted to focus on those curves, the legs, the physical memory of her skin bare and sleek and giving beneath his. But that gave way to a hammering need for her arms, her comfort, the steady strength of her gaze on his as she told him she was here for him.

It was too much, too intense, and Van took a mental step back. Again he'd revealed too much, exposed himself too readily. With this woman it was too easy, and she'd done nothing to earn such trust.

She paused at his side. He could sense her composing herself, preparing her next pretty—and futile—attempt to console him. When she placed her hand on his shoulder, he felt the hot jolt of response and the more powerful underlying need for more.

"If you really want to make me feel better," he said, "the bedroom's right through that archway over there."

"Will that make you feel better?"

"I sure as hell won't feel any worse."

"Okay," she said after a beat of pause, surprising the hell out of him. "If that's what it takes."

Van turned his narrowed gaze on her. "Takes to what?"

"To accept that I'm here for you."

He knew what he should have done. He should have stopped this conversation with his mouth on hers. He should have taken the soft hand that dropped away and put it back on his body. Somewhere infinitely more volatile than his shoulder.

He should have been unzipping the prim and proper dress and pulling aside her lacy underthings to get to the improper. Right here, against that glass.

But, damn her, with that one simple statement, she'd refired his earlier distrust about her reason for coming here and he couldn't let that go. "You say you're here for me—" he turned to meet her eyes more fully "—but what about your own interests?"

Confusion clouded her expression and the tone of her reply. "My…interests?"

"You and your mother and the Horton company stand to lose significantly if you can't talk me into reevaluating The Palisades deal. You've lost Alex Carlisle as a buyer and as a husband. It can't be easy to find buyers who are willing to be screwed around over contract clauses."

"That isn't fair," she countered, eyes sparking green in the low light. "You asked for the extra clauses. That wasn't our doing."

"I only asked for the same as Carlisle. Nothing more, nothing less."

"You didn't ask *me*."

When she started to turn away, he stopped her. With a hand on each arm, he swung her back to the window and blocked her exit path with his body. There were too many questions still unanswered to let her escape. "Why Carlisle? What was the real attraction, Susannah?" When she didn't answer right away, he leaned in closer, his gaze on the curve of her lips. "You hadn't even kissed him, and you were going to—"

"I told you last week. He offered everything I wanted. Everything *and* a baby."

Even as the words left her tongue, Susannah wished them back. She saw their impact, felt the tensing of his hands on her shoulders for a half second before he asked, "You were marrying him to have a baby?"

"He was marrying *me* to have a baby," she corrected. Then, when he continued to study her in unnerving silence, she added, "That may sound like semantics, but it's a significant difference. Alex needed a baby for his family to inherit from his father's will."

"A fine reason to plan a baby."

"He was motivated as you were—by a person he would do anything for. In Alex's case, his mother."

"I was pursuing a piece of land," he said tightly, "not a child."

How could she have not realised what a hot-button issue this would be?

She had to explain, to make him understand…. "This baby was not just a pawn, Donovan. We both wanted a family—not just one child but siblings who would grow up together and fight and love and be there for each other. A family like the Carlisles, who would do anything for each other. It wasn't about the money or the name. It was about family and me turning twenty-nine and the assumption I made when you didn't return my calls."

His gaze narrowed sharply. "What does this have to do with me?"

Susannah's heart thudded hard and high in her throat. She could see no other option but to tell him everything. Including the most wrenching regret of all.

Twelve

"Have you ever wondered why I was calling you? Why I kept calling? Why I was so desperate to reach you even though I thought you were skiving me off?"

Donovan went still. Very still. "You were pregnant?"

She nodded, then had to swallow a choking knot of emotion before she could speak. "For a very short time. Yes."

"I didn't use protection?"

"We used condoms, but the last time…there was a possibility."

He studied her for a long second before swinging away. In stunned silence he stared out into the darkness, his profile harsh and forbidding. Susannah could only imagine what he must be feeling. Shock, disbelief, the impotence of realising what might have been.

"Did I know? Did I promise to call you?"

"Yes."

"Except I didn't and I couldn't take your calls." Finally he turned, and the impact of his next words struck as cold and hard as hailstones. "And Carlisle arrived at the perfect time with the perfect arrangement, for you and my baby."

"No!" Susannah shook her head vehemently. "I'd been trying to contact you, trying to work out what to do if you didn't want to know, and then I miscarried and I realised just how much I'd wanted that baby. That's when Alex asked. That's why I was so open to his suggestion."

"To his suggestion that you conceive another baby? Tell me, is that like hopping back on a bike after you've fallen off? Better done straight away before you forget how?"

"No," she choked out, appalled by that callous analogy. "I wouldn't marry him straight away. I asked for more time. I didn't sleep with him."

"You wanted a wedding ring on your finger this time?"

"I wanted time to reconsider, to think everything through when I wasn't feeling so hollow and hopeless. I wanted to be sure my reasoning was valid and not just an emotional backlash to my loss. I needed to be sure."

"Sure of what?" For the first time his icy control cracked, revealing the fierce churn of anger in his eyes. "That you wanted a baby? It didn't matter if it was his or mine, if your relationship was based on love or greed or a wad of contract pages. You wanted for *you*. You didn't give a flying thought about the baby or how he'd come to view his parents' relationship."

"That's not true. We had solid reasons—"

"So solid you ran away from your wedding day. So solid you spent your honeymoon in my bed."

Reeling from the sustained force of his words, Susannah struggled to hold her head high. To keep the gathering tears at bay. "You know why I came to Tasmania."

"Because I threatened your sham of a wedding…or because you wanted a ready excuse not to see it through?"

"Because you called, because I heard your voice on the phone, because I couldn't help myself," she countered, her voice resonant with the force of her denial. "Damn you, Donovan, I didn't just fall into your bed. You were there. You know that."

"Why did you sleep with me?"

"For the same reason I came here today, the same reason I didn't take the hint on the porch when you tried to freeze me out. The same reason I'm standing here arguing the point about something you're not willing to hear. Because I love you."

"You love me?" He expelled a gust of pure cynicism. "Yet you won't have a bar of a contract that ties you to me?"

"I don't want to be tied to you by business," she stormed back. "With Alex it didn't matter, with you everything has mattered. Everything is amplified. The brief elation when I thought I was having your baby. Not being able to contact you and realising you'd used me that weekend, that you weren't going to be quite so overjoyed by my news. I had the perfect marriage—the perfect future—planned until you came back."

Resistance screamed from every taut line of his body,

and she wondered if anything she'd said had infiltrated that shuttered barrier. Anything that had, he didn't believe…or he didn't want to believe. To Susannah, suddenly it didn't matter which.

She'd tried to explain why she'd found Alex's offer of marriage so hard to refuse. If he didn't accept any of that, how could she convince him of something as inexplicable as her love?

"I know this wasn't the best time to bare my soul," she told him. "That's not why I came here. This wasn't supposed to be about me or my feelings, but now you know everything and I'm not sorry it's been said."

"Why didn't you tell me before?"

"Maybe I knew it would lead to this."

For a moment the antagonism of *this* arced between them, and it was too much. Before he could say any more, she shook her head in warning. "I think we've both said enough for now. I'll call a cab."

"You drop that series of bombshells and that's it?"

"Until we've both cooled down and reflected, yes."

"You need to think some more? To change your mind again? To decide whether this really is true love?"

Susannah had no answer to the cruel slice of those questions. She'd had enough. She couldn't stand here while he ripped apart her avowal of love, while he mocked the heartfelt decisions she'd made these past months. She was walking away while she still had some dignity. Before the tears commenced.

With trembling fingers she pulled her phone from her bag. She'd saved the number, if only she could stop her hands shaking enough to punch the right keys…

"There's no need to call a cab. Where are you staying?"

"The Carlisle."

His mouth tightened into a grim line. "I'll drive you."

She wanted to tell him where to put that offer—but she refused to gift him the pleasure of another argument. Ever since she arrived, he'd been pushing for a confrontation. Perhaps, like a wounded animal, he'd needed to latch out at the pain caused by Mac's loss. Naively, she'd obliged, thinking she could absorb some of that hurt with her love. Now she'd had enough.

In the car, she closed her eyes and shut him out—gathering the silence around her like a cloak as his powerful car sliced through the wet night. At the hotel, he came around to open her door, and she was forced to meet his eyes for the first time since he'd ushered her from his home...and to face the fact that this might be goodbye.

In that moment all her bravado turned to water. She couldn't look him in the eye and brazen it out. Nor could she turn and walk away with nothing.

It was easier—so much easier—to lean into his body and kiss his cheek. She felt his stillness, the tension in his jaw and the whisker-rough texture of his skin beneath her lips. Her fingers curled briefly around his lapel, a last touch, a last deep breath of his scent. "Take care," she said quickly. There was no point in saying keep in touch or call me. She'd done that twice, to no avail. "I'm sorry for your loss."

And as she went to pull away, his hand came up and grabbed her arm. Their eyes met for a quicksilver moment. "I'm sorry for yours, Susannah. I wish you hadn't had to go through that on your own."

The rush of tears at the back of her eyes was instant, overwhelming, but if she let one free she feared they would never stop. With a brief nod of acknowledgment, she pulled free and somehow managed to walk away with her head held high.

"Will you just take the damn call?" Erin's voice came through the speakerphone in measured bites of aggravation. "This is your business, your deal, she can't put you in any worse a mood then we've suffered these past weeks!"

Van figured the call had to be from Horton's about The Palisades. *She* had to be Miriam Horton. And his assistant made a valid point—he was in the perfect mood for this call. "Put it through," he said shortly, his gaze still fixed on the opening charts for today's trading.

"Hello, Donovan? It's Susannah."

Van jerked upright in his chair, his jaw flexed and tight at the unexpected greeting. All the air left his lungs as if he'd been punched. He'd not expected to hear from her, not after the finality of their parting. So many times he'd thought about calling, but what the hell would he say? He didn't know how to make things right. If he couldn't give her *everything* she wanted, what could he offer?

"Donovan? Are you there?"

With a rough note of disgust, he picked up the receiver. Since the memory of her voice was constantly in his head, he might as well enjoy the real thing in his ear. "Susannah, yeah, I'm here." He checked his watch and felt a jab of alarm. "It's the middle of the night in Melbourne. Is everything all right?"

"I'm…not home."

Van sat up straighter. It had been almost two weeks but… "Are you still here, in San Francisco?"

"No," she said quickly. Too quickly. "I'm in the mountains. Since I'd arranged time away from the office, I thought I might as well take a holiday."

What the hell was he supposed to say to that? *Hope you're having a nice time on what was supposed to be your honeymoon. Wish I was there.* "To do some thinking?" he bit out.

There was a beat of silence, long enough for him to call himself an ass for pressing that hot button. "Yes, as a matter of fact. Walking up here is very good for clearing the mind and thinking."

"On the island you told me you weren't a fan of exercise."

"I'm not but I do need to work on my core strength," she said with an irony that suggested she was talking about more than physical strength. "But I didn't call to talk about me."

"No?"

"I spoke to my mother about the contract for The Palisades. I wanted you to know that Judd will be calling about new terms, in line with your original bid."

"Can't find another buyer?" he asked.

"I don't believe that will be a problem, but you deserve first offer."

"I told you I was no longer interested."

"And I hope you've reconsidered." She drew an audible breath, the gesture so familiar he could picture the exact look on her face. The way her chin came up a fraction. The cool green flash of her eyes. "I don't think you're foolish enough to allow your opinion of me to influence your decision, but be assured I have no personal agenda."

"You just wanted to be sure I didn't sign the old version?"

"Exactly."

"What about your business?" he found himself asking. "Do you still need equity capital?"

"I've just come to terms with my mother. She now owns a managing share in At Your Service."

"I'm sorry to hear that."

"Why should you be?" she replied tersely. "She has some excellent ideas for diversifying and making the business more profitable."

Van wanted to ask about *her* vision, about the pride she'd taken in her own direction without her parents' controlling hand, but he bit down on the urge. Satisfied another urge by asking, "And what about the other clause in the old contract?"

"I'm sorry?"

"What if I want you as my wife?"

One swift inhalation in his ear. One second of pure what-the-hell-are-you-asking fear, before his heartbeat settled into a slow and certain rhythm.

"You don't," she rasped out.

"I asked for the same terms as Carlisle."

"Because you wanted to expedite matters. You never wanted anything but that contract."

"No, Susannah, I wanted you." With the phone clutched to his ear, he shoved to his feet and paced to the window. A magnificent view of city and bay stretched before him, unseen, unacknowledged. All he could see was her face, her smile, her wild hair and sea-green eyes. "You said you love me."

"I do," she said sadly, "but that's not enough."

"Because I can't give you that perfect future you had all mapped out?"

"I thought you could, but maybe I was wrong. Maybe I deserve better." Her voice lifted on that last statement and he pictured her chin rising with it. "Goodbye, Donovan, and good luck with Judd. I hope that works out for you. Charlotte Island was meant to be yours."

There was nothing he could do to stop her disconnecting, but the conversation played through his mind, the words exactly as they'd sounded in his ear. The honey-dipped tone of her voice. The distinctive down-under accent. The snotty edge when she told him that maybe she deserved better.

For several seconds, he entertained the notion that she did deserve better. She'd walked away from a marriage she believed could give her everything. She'd flown halfway around the world to offer her support. She'd told him she loved him and he'd fobbed that off, too intent on licking his wounds and protecting himself from another round of love and loss to accept the honesty of that gift.

He couldn't blame her for thinking she deserved better. He wouldn't blame her if she refused to listen to what he had to say. But he would say it—everything that needed to be said, everything that he'd gotten so wrong the first time.

Then she could decide what *he* deserved.

* * *

Damn weather. Susannah swung at the moving target and missed. *Damn punching bag.* She hit out again, this time connecting with an audible thud that jarred through her gloved fist all the way to her shoulder. *Damn man.*

She unleashed a wild series of punches. Some of them actually found purchase on the hunk of leather. More didn't. But there was enough satisfaction in the occasional thud to keep her swinging for several more minutes, until her breath grew short and ragged and her muscles ached from exertion.

Dodging the wildly undulating bag, she pulled off her gloves and reached for her towel and water. A quick cooldown on the treadmill and then she would treat her well-used muscles to a long, soothing bath. The prospect almost brought a smile to her mouth as she turned toward the door.

And then she saw him. Leaning against the wall just inside the door of the Tahoe resort's fitness center. Dark suit, white shirt, silver-grey eyes riveting her to the spot as he straightened.

Everything inside her went still as he closed the space between them with slow, sure footsteps. As he approached, she could feel him taking in the yoga pants and crop top, which made her look the part, and the new haircut. The shortened curls were still unruly, despite the sweatband that was supposed to keep them secured.

"Hello, Susannah." He stopped in front of her, close enough that she could see the softening mix of amusement and appreciation in his eyes. "I like the new look. It suits you."

"I think so." Their gazes met and held in a moment's assessment, but that was all Susannah allowed herself. He'd tracked her down less than a day after that phone conversation, but she hardened her heart against its foolish leap of hope. "You're a long way from home," she said coolly.

"I have unfinished business."

"How did you know where to find me?" A frown creased her brow as she considered the possibilities. "My mother is the only person—" Seeing the answer in his eyes, she stopped. "*Miriam* told you where I was staying?"

He shrugged, that familiar lift of one shoulder that was both eloquent and efficient. And ridiculously attractive. "That was the easy part. Finding you here—" he tilted his head to indicate the gym "—was more difficult."

"It's raining too hard to go walking, and I needed to expend some energy. This punching bag seemed an ideal way to work off some aggravation."

"Did you picture my face on the bag?" he asked. The tiniest hint of a smile lurked in his eyes, and Susannah gritted her teeth. It was bad enough that he'd snuck up on her, that he'd watched her for Lord knows how long, without the amusement. To think that her mother had given up her location, that she hadn't called to deliver fair warning....

"I should have included my mother in the target range," she said darkly. "You must have made a mighty fine offer on The Palisades to win her over."

The smile disappeared and his expression tightened, but not only with the impact of the cynical shot. The determined set of his jawline caused her heart rate to jump about like the assaulted punching bag. "This has nothing to do with business," he said, low and even. "Your mother knows that. She's a romantic at heart."

"My mother? No. She was married to a man who cheated and lied to her for thirty years, but she never let on that she knew. She was afraid of the consequences. She liked being married to Edward Horton. She liked the position and the prestige, she put up with the negatives. My mother is a pragmatist, you see. I doubt she was ever a romantic."

"She wants you to be happy."

"And so she sent you?"

"She says you love me."

"And you believe her?" For a long moment their eyes met and held, and for the first time, she saw the tension, the flicker of vulnerability, behind the set facade. Her pulse started to race, set alight with a new flare of hope. "Why would you take her word, Donovan, when you wouldn't believe me?"

"I was afraid to believe."

"Afraid of letting someone else close?" she guessed.

"There was that," he admitted. "And I was afraid that I could never give you anything close to the everything you talked about having with Carlisle." Serious eyes settled and steadied on hers. "After talking to you yesterday, I realised the truth. I knew the night I dropped you at your hotel. I watched you walk away and—"

His voice broke off as if he couldn't find the necessary words to describe how he'd felt, but words were unnecessary. Susannah saw all she needed in his face, in his eyes, in the fact that, finally, he was revealing himself to her.

"I didn't want you to leave," he continued, "but I didn't know what to say to make you stay."

"It would have taken only a few words."

"You say that as if it's easy." One corner of his mouth lifted ruefully, but his eyes remained intensely serious. "I've never said those words."

"Not even to Mac?"

Anguish flitted across his face and her heart rolled over. "I can't lose you, too."

Heart brimming with desperate optimism, she watched him take her hand in his, and for the first time, she saw a muscle jump in his jaw. He was nervous. Afraid. Patently terrified. A part of her ached to ease his misery, while another cautioned her to hold back and wait for everything she'd yearned to hear from this man's beautiful mouth.

"Someone suggested recently that you deserve better than me. Same person also said Charlotte Island was meant to be mine. I happen to believe that you're meant to be mine, as well." His eyes on hers quickened with a sincerity that stole her breath. "I'm not Carlisle—I don't have the ready-made family. I don't even have a home, but that's what I want with you. I don't care where we live. I can work from anywhere. I'm adaptable."

"You're independent," she cautioned. "You told me the weekend we met that you don't need a home."

"Back then I probably believed it, but that was before Mac revealed herself, before I was forced to slow down and take stock of what mattered. Before you made me reconsider the meaning of *everything*." His clasp on her fingers tightened. The expression in his eyes held her transfixed, wanting, hoping, wishing. "When I came back to Stranger's Bay, my only thought was finding a way to get The Palisades. Then I met you. I wanted you. I made excuses. I told myself it was only about ending the wedding so I could get the contract. But I couldn't stand the thought of you with another man."

Susannah's heart dipped. "You couldn't stand losing out."

"You stood up for yourself, for your principles, and that only made me love you more."

"Wanting me isn't love, Donovan."

"I love you," he said again, this time slowly and clearly, with conviction strong in his eyes. "You told me on the phone yesterday that you need to improve your core strength, but your strength is one of the things I love in you."

She started to shake her head, but he stayed her with a look.

"You're strong when it matters. You left your father's business when you no longer respected him. You didn't take the easy path, accepting his money. You walked away from a perfect marriage arrangement because you love me."

Reading the question in his eyes, she touched a hand to his face. "I do, but—"

"No buts," he said softly. "You deserve a man who loves you with everything he is, who wants to make a home and a family with you." And there, with the soldierly rows of treadmills and StairMasters and weight stations for witnesses, he went down on one knee. "I love you, Susannah, and I'm asking you to be my wife."

"Are there any clauses attached?" she asked solemnly, despite the wild racing of her heart.

"There is one about wearing my ring." Like a conjurer, he dipped into his pocket and produced a perfect white solitaire. "On your finger, a sign of commitment."

He slid the ring onto her finger, and she lifted a tremulous hand so the diamond caught the light and dazzled through her sudden tears. "It's perfect."

"It's forever," he said.

"Yes," she managed around the tearful jubilation that threatened to overwhelm her. "I know that."

"Is that a yes, you will marry me? Yes, you will be my wife?"

"Yes. Yes. I love you, Donovan. I have always loved you."

Finally, as those words took hold, the tension around his eyes eased into a smile. "I love you, too, Susannah. That's the answer, isn't it?"

"To every question."

Slowly he came to his feet and engulfed her in an embrace for a long moment before lifting her into his arms. "Where are you taking me?" she asked on a shriek when he swung her around in a wide arc. The smile on his face and in her heart turned her giddier still.

"To your room."

"To pack?" she asked, and her arms were around his neck, her face nuzzled close to his.

"Eventually."

"Hmm," she mused. "Are you thinking of an exercise I might enjoy more than the gym?"

He laughed, a wicked, smoky chuckle mirrored in his eyes as they looked down into hers. "I'm thinking that now I have you right where I want you. And I am never letting you go."

* * * * *

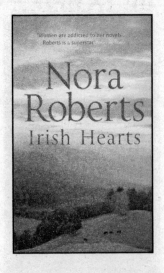

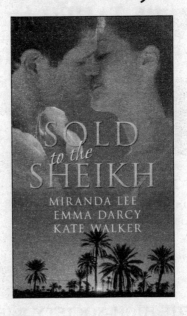